68

31
''

PRAISE

"This is absolutely terrific—thoroughly steeped in Dickens's own idioms and ideas while also taking a step back and coolly assessing them from a distance. It's ... reminiscent (in a good way) of the rich period atmospheres generated by those two neo-Victorian Peters, Ackroyd and Carey."
ROBERT DOUGLAS-FAIRHURST, AUTHOR OF *BECOMING DICKENS*

"A remarkable Dickens-fi debut."
PHILIP HOARE, AUTHOR OF *ALBERT AND THE WHALE*

"A work of sublime psychogeography, a dark hymn to Victorian London in all its grotty glory. Humm follows the ambitious young novelist Charles Dickens into the city's rookeries in search of edgy stories and characters. As he finds himself drawn into a vortex of crime, sexual intrigue and deceit, he realises that he won't be able to remain a detached observer in this seductive, dangerous underworld."
NICK PERRY, AUTHOR OF *NOVEMBER DEAD LIST* AND *THE LOOP*

ABOUT THE AUTHOR

Alan Humm edits the arts journal *One Hand Clapping*. *The Sparkler* is his first novel but he has also written two collections of poetry: *A Brief and Biased History of Love* (Culture Matters) and *My Father is Calling the Neighbours Names*. His second novel, *Rough Music*, follows a journalist and a Labour politician from 1945 to the early noughties and he is currently writing a book about an '80s pop band.

alanhummswriting.com

The SPARKLER

alan humm

Cover design by Jessica Bell
Interior design by Amie McCracken

For Alice

CHAPTER ONE

HE'D MADE A life: a marriage and a nest of rooms. But happiness? What could he possibly make of that?

They were just back from honeymoon, and he watched her with the smugness of a connoisseur. Her hair was parted in the centre and arranged crosswise from ear to ear. There was a slight blurring of her expressions; she was tender, but cautiously so. You could see her watching his mouth.

It was an April night, unusually cold. He smiled and scratched his stomach, stretching his legs in front of the open fire. He admired the soft swell of her breasts, the crown of her head, like a blown egg, and the neatness of her hands.

"Impossible man," she said.

She was arranging her dress around her as she sat beside him on the floor next to his chair. He touched her cheek.

"Is Titmouse coss?"

She shook her head. It was a way, he could feel, of disobliging his hand while keeping it there.

"But I fail to see the attraction ..."

She negligently waved a wrist.

"... of all of that."

Outside, the rain was busy on the window. Inside there was a bell of light and a penumbra that was almost cozy: chairs and books and desk arranged so neatly that they looked like they were ready for inspection. He had created all of this; his will, like the fire in the grate, had conjured it up out of the darkness. He felt as much tenderness for it as he did for her.

"I've folded and starched five of my shirts," he said. "I have found a thoroughly respectable place for the carpet beater, and for the sugar tongs. I've used blacking on a good half a dozen boots and I have filled the range with wood. I am an *intolerably* domestic creature."

She was looking at him with what might, in an unguarded moment, have seemed to be a sad understanding.

"No, Charley, you're not. You are exact. It isn't the same thing at all."

He touched her ear. He had been marvelling at it.

"Kate," he said. "Consider. It behooves me—"

"'Behooves.'"

"To see. To *really* see. I have a public."

"You have readers. They have placed you under no obligation, as far as I can tell. Unlike ..."

But she said nothing more; just dipped her head towards her stomach. It was in these moments of deliberate self-abnegation that he found himself most attracted to her. Was she? Pregnant? Charles touched her other cheek. But, still, he intended to walk all night. He could already see how gaslight amplified the streets. He stood up, half in exasperation, and watched somebody swim in the darkness that spilled into the courtyard beneath their flat. He appeared to be carrying a bundle, but it was really just his stomach in the uneven light.

"I get up a head of steam," he said.

There was still the ghost of tenderness in his face, but it was evident, from the set of his chin, that he had made up his mind. His face could hold expressions in the same way that a glass of water can reflect the light scattered around a room. His eyes had taken fire from the half-hour they had spent in bed. But he was also scratching at his nose too rapidly and pacing up and down.

"Or else I *have* to. It amounts to the same thing. I have to walk it off, or up."

She smiled and shook her head.

"Impossible man."

She seemed to pity him. It was this, more than anything, that enabled him to put on his coat and scarf and jump the stairs, two at a time.

He made straight for the rookeries. He loved them—loved walking through them, rather. The road was dustier here but greasier too, as were the houses, which all seemed to sweat. He walked past girls who stood as though they were lying down. Old ladies were like withered apples; windfall, shaken from the moon. Smoking clay pipes, they failed to notice him, although, in a swallow-tail coat, a waistcoat in full flush and a high velvet collar, he was obvious enough. He would stop for a moment and produce a comb; would comb his hair and lift his head again and aim himself between the houses. Gas beckoned him on. The fog had stage properties: the lantern of the "beer," the boy who had been sent around the streets at supper time, looked like it had been suspended in it. He was never lost, although he allowed himself to feel it. It was a liberation. Gin palaces, like lighthouses, announced themselves at regular intervals. He'd written about them recently: how a "disease" had spread so that all of the old public houses had been knocked down, "depositing splendid mansions, stone balustrades, rose-wood fittings, immense lamps, and illuminated clocks at the corner of the street." This one, near Drury Lane, was one of the handsomest in London and he recognised in himself, again, the attraction of repulsion; how you can love the things you hate: the glibness of the harsh illumination and the little cakes and buns, so out of place, and all the names of drinks; their sleight of hand: "The Cream of the Valley," "The Out and Out," "The No Mistake," "The Real Knock-me-down" and "The Regular Flare-up." How the poor are kept down by the things they're taught to need. How one derives a certain comfort from the fact that one can have that thought, while striding seriously away.

He was remaking the streets he walked along, shifting them slightly so that they showed to their best advantage. Best; worst. It didn't matter. He could afford to feel sympathetic. He had a pretty wife, a set of apartments and a burgeoning reputation. If he was a little too anxious about his trousers, lifting his legs, slightly, above the streets, then it was to be expected: he was in the rig of a gentleman. If he was escaping a feeling of constriction, then it was really only himself that he was running from. Or towards. He could never tell.

It was pay-time on Saturday night and, in the market in Somers Town, people were buying their Sunday dinner. The lights were white and red and gold, the glare of the gas lamps mingling with the flames of the grease lamps and the dull romanticism of the candles. The naked flames and ground-glass globes and open gaslights vied for your attention so that, from a distance, it looked like the street was on fire. All of those voices, too, the street vendors crying "chestnuts all 'ot" and "three a penny Yarmouth bloaters" and "here's toasters!" and "penny a lot, fine russets" and the men and women shouting above them to be heard; they made him feel a little drunk. He wanted a pen and paper, not just to write it down but to make it more orderly. He was an odd figure: a little man, cocked like an angry rooster,

with hair in billowing folds and a face halfway between determination and amusement. He had *always* been out of place; it
was his fondest hope and greatest fear. He leaned over a couple
who were arguing over a halibut, prodding and pulling at it
until the vendor leaned across and slapped the woman's hand.
Charles said "Lor!'" then realised that he'd said it and that all
three of them were staring at him. He said, "Now vat is a fish."

It was a slight touch on the lower lip more than a "v." The
vendor's head looked boiled. His teeth were the colour of sand.

"And what are you? A cocker spaniel?"

Charles did a little bow.

"A boots."

"In that clobber?"

This was the wife. Or not the wife, perhaps. Charles made
a rapid assessment. She was middle-aged but undefeated. Her
breasts were huge: assertive and forgiving. The man was as
round as a dumpling. He wished for a pen. Instead, he impro-
vised. The lights and the woman's credulous face encouraged it.
He felt released into someone else.

"My father's wedding ma'am."

"Your father?"

"Yes. Best bib and tucker, as you can see."

He had slipped into a thick Cockney accent. It wasn't a
stretch; his voice was muddy in any case. Something had always
impeded his r's.

"Never..."

He could see the way he'd write it: "nivir."

"... go to Doctor's Commons. They puts things into old
gen'l'm'n's heads as they never dreamed of. My father, ma'am,
was a coachman. A widower he was, and fat enough for
anything—uncommon fat, to be sure. His missus dies and leaves
him four hundred pound."

He leaned a little forwards.

"Down he goes to the Commons, to see the lawyer and draw the blunt. Very smart, with his top boots on and a nosegay in his button-hole and a broad-brimmed tile. He goes through the archvay, thinking how he should invest the money and up comes the touter. He touches his hat and says:

"'Marriage license. I think you wants one, Sir.'"

Charles made the touter's voice strain upwards, like a fly.

"'No,' says my father, "much too old. Too wide, too.'"

"And the touter says, 'We married a gen'l'm'n twice your size, last Monday.'"

"So my father walks arter him, like a tame monkey."

He made a parenthesis with his arms.

"He goes into a little back office, vere a teller sits among dirty papers and tin boxes making believe he's busy."

"'What's your name, Sir?,' says the lawyer."

"'Tony Weller,' says my father."

"'And the lady's name?'"

"My father was struck all of a heap."

"'Blessed if I know,' says he."

"'Not know!' says the lawyer."

"'No more do you,' says my father. 'Can't I put that in arterwards?'"

The couple were laughing now. Charles, too. He saw them: the father, like a cannonball, and the touter with his squashed mug and flapping ears. The woman wiped her eyes. People had been trying to get around him but he had held his ground. The vendor jerked his thumb sideways.

"''op it."

The woman smiled.

"I would if I was you."

And so he did. Or Weller did. There was a touch-me-not-ishness to his walk, but that was Charles, too. He was still listing sideways in appreciation of himself, but part of him kept hearing the word "spaniel." He kept feeling it in his chest. He should go home. His wife was there; perhaps his child. He had the same renewal of affection that he always felt when he was far away from her. The home; the hearth. It was the thing he told himself that he would fight for. But even as he was reminding himself that it existed, conjuring it so successfully that it was, once again, like being warmed right through, he found himself walking away from it. The rain had stopped, but there was a brisk wind now and he pulled his collar up around his neck. He had wandered to Pentonville, past barbers' shops where mannequins seemed to want a touch of something—the swiftness of a simile—to give them life. This inn, for example: the way that its blinds gave it a sleepy look. Its wagons, each with a pile of goods like eiderdowns. And here: this public house. Its knuckled forehead. He became aware of what looked, through the refraction of the leaded panes, like the female form. The female form unadorned; not squeezed into an inverted trumpet. When he pushed the door open, it was like his impersonation: a wilful jump into the unknown.

But, still, he was thinking, who's the voice? This Weller. What does he wear? It was a way, partly, of reminding himself of who he was: the soon-to-be-famous writer. Swiftly, he took in a room set out like someone's sitting room but with the cheapest of wooden tables. There was a fire and, on either side of it, a group of unsteady old boys. Directly in front of him was the bar. The parlour behind it looked inviting; it was dimly lit, like a forge, and furnished, he could tell, in roughly the same style as his own flat. The raffishness of being on display gave everything an air of knowing invitation. A man nearby was saying something very definite. Was he in earnest? You couldn't tell. The left side of his mouth was halfway up to his ear and, briefly, Charles felt this as a memory: his face; that mouth; the something in his eyes that looked like a building that was on fire.

The girl was behind the bar, ignoring this. There was, he saw immediately, nothing to constrict the figure in the way his wife and all her sisters (and his friends' wives and all *their* sisters) deemed so necessary. She looked denuded, but defiant too. Her beauty was a beauty that had had to flourish in straitened circumstances. Her face was redder than it ought to be. Her mouth ...

But then he heard the voice.

"Coo. Fucking Hell. *Bastard.*"

The man's voice was new but it forced you to look at the face, and the face was not. The face was beautiful, but not because of anything it did or was; it was because of what Charles had once felt for it. The girl was murmuring something in a voice like a rusty hasp. He had a terrible urge to run away, or else to throw something, he wasn't sure what at. He thought: a thieves' kitchen. He saw his wife's translucent pearliness. Her diffidence. The girl was arguing over the freshness of the porter in somebody's glass. Meanwhile, the man's voice was saying,

"'alf a knicker. 'ass all I want. It's not like I'm not good for it. Look at me."

He was in the remnants of what would once have been considered a decent suit, with a stock and collar and a serious jacket. Charles was fascinated by the man's leer. Because he wasn't, obviously, good for it. One side of his mouth was deadly serious while the other was grinning broadly. His eyebrows danced. Charles remembered.

"Grimaldi!" he said.

He found himself stepping forward.

"You're ... I'm sorry. I do beg your pardon. But you're Joseph Grimaldi, surely."

The man's upper body turned slowly round while his legs remained under the table. His face communicated several things at once: gratification and suspicion and a faint hint of enthusiasm and disdain.

"And you're a creditor, I presume," he said.

"No, no." Charles shook his head. "I saw you. Years and years ago. You were—"

"Funny. I was funny."

"*Yes*. You were. You did a duck."

And Charles did the duck's pompous walk. Grimaldi looked on, half in appreciation.

"That's true. I did."

"You punched somebody."

"In the codlins, and I 'ope it hurt."

"And I applauded. I was tiny. I was very proud of myself."

Charles was, momentarily, all tenderness. Grimaldi watched him, shrewdly. He looked him slowly up and down. He smiled.

"Sit down, sir."

He patted the chair beside him.

"I would get up but, as you see, I am rheumatised."

He waved, indolently, at his lower half.

"Goutised and puffised. No more for poor Joey the larks and games, the sausage and baggy breeks."

He had said this before. His face was suffused with something. Drink? No: frank enjoyment. Again, he patted the chair. His veins were like knotted ropes.

"Sit down," he said. "Davey will buy us both a drink."

Davey was something like a dog. He gave the same impression of being wary of your hands and feet. He ascended, slowly, against his will, and rubbed at his nose with the back of his hand. Charles found them both irresistible. The whole pub was like one of his own illustrations. He knew that there was danger here: he saw it in the men beside the fire and in the look that passed, swiftly, between Davey and the girl behind the bar. He saw it, too, in the way that Grimaldi's gestures attempted, like the fire, to fill the room. But it was, all of it, irresistible. He was repelled, yes, but encouraged. He glanced at the girl, who was being careful to pull a proper pint. Her dress went plunging, like a waterfall, over her breasts. Davey was murmuring something behind his hand and Grimaldi was teetering over, laughing at something that he was about to say. Charles put his hand out and said, "Sam Weller." He looked around the pub and wondered what he was going to make of it.

CHAPTER TWO

THE STREETS WERE fizzing with rain. The wind threw gusts of it, like pellets, into his face. There was no gas here, just oil lamps in the windows. They made everything else seem doubly dark. Once, a link-boy appeared from out of a side street. It was difficult to see the men he led in the light of the faggot that seemed to lift and plummet like a lion in a pantomime. He saw how their boots had a life of their own and he felt lonelier when they were gone. He drew his coat around him and then shrank from the inside of his clothes.

He was following the barmaid.

"Sarah," Grimaldi had said. "Her name is Sarah."

Although he hadn't asked. Grimaldi had been watching him. He was a shrewd old man beneath the appearance of bonhomie but now he seemed to be leering out towards an audience. His face was as incongruously expressive as a monkey's. Charles had laughed; he had thrown his head back and then taken out his handkerchief to wipe the porter from his chin. He was aware that Grimaldi's eyes didn't partake of the riot that was going on in Grimaldi's face. They were assessing him, noting the gusto and the finicky self-regard.

But Charles didn't care. Grimaldi! He carried with him all the glamour of the theatre. Of Charles's childhood, too, when what went on between the circles of stage fire had seemed like a bolder and more legible reality. It still did. Grimaldi's back wouldn't shift from one side to the other. His eyes went furtively around the pub. But there was another Grimaldi, the Grimaldi of Charles's memory, that adhered to this one like ectoplasm. Charles still saw the bright white face and the tall ruff of hair. When Grimaldi said "Here we are again" it was so calculated that Charles felt sorry for him. But he was also thrilled. This old man was a lecher; a pander, possibly. But it was his ghost who had spoken to Charles, and who had made everything into a game.

"A boots, my hairy arse," he'd said.

But that was all he'd said. Now he encouraged Charles to buy a drink. While he waited, he watched Sarah perform a sleight of hand. Her hands were tough and leathery and there were places where they had hardened into yellow callouses. This was, on the whole, attractive. They were self-sufficient in a way his wife's hands rarely were. They had purpose and definition. There were four glasses behind the bar and he saw Sarah's hands dip purposefully amongst them. It was a form of prestidigitation. Her back was to the customer and, when she turned, she had the same glass and, ostensibly, the same liquid that she had just taken from the bottle. Only it wasn't. It was duller and less viscous. It moved more adroitly around the glass and it didn't wink back at you like it should. The customer seemed perfectly satisfied. He was drunk, Charles supposed, although he stood there stolidly and made a point of raising his hat. Sarah turned and circumspectly sipped the shot that she had poured.

"Impressive," he said.

But she ignored him.

"Wery."

But still she wouldn't acknowledge him. The customer looked at him then looked at her and, finally, at his glass. There was a long moment in which his face appeared to gather itself together. Mysteriously, he gave his hat a ferocious cock, and swaggered off. The swagger was enough, it seemed, to reassert his place in the universe. Sarah stared at Charles. Her upper lip pushed firmly downwards on her lower and she raised her chin towards him. She served him silently. Her face was a coarse, unhealthy red. Her arms were like a sailor's arms. But she was beautiful. The more the night wore on, the more beautiful she became.

He had tried to be conscious of what he was drinking but he hadn't wanted to appear to be so. In the end, he wasn't drunk so much as appreciably relaxed. He knew that, for as long as he was with Grimaldi, he wouldn't have his pocket picked. Or not exactly. Grimaldi had asked him for two coins; a half crown and a penny. He had placed them back in Charles's hand and then removed one. Ostentatiously, he had waved it in his face. Charles was fascinated, not by the coin but by the dream-like dexterity of the gnarled and knotted hands. Grimaldi placed the coin in his pocket but it was like watching a bird, or a cloud. The hand seemed not to be doing something so much as being it. When he opened Charles's own hand again both coins were resting in his palm. Grimaldi did this twice. Then, after blowing on his fingers, he prised them open. There was nothing there. When he shrugged, Charles knew he wasn't getting them back. He was delighted. The trick itself was adequate, something he knew that he could teach himself in an easy afternoon. No, what delighted him was Grimaldi's face. It was a London face, boiled-looking, with thick chops and gristly ears and eyes that strove, unsuccessfully, to look innocent. It seemed, just for a moment, to be bursting at the seams. Grimaldi took so much delight in his own ingenuity that it was impossible not to share it with him.

Later, he put the bite on him. It was, he was meant to infer, his safe passage out. Grimaldi was wringing his hands and wheedling but Charles barely listened to him. Smiling in understanding, he slid a note under his palm and across the table. Grimaldi was surprised. It was more than he had been expecting.

"Coo," he said. "Fuck."

He pushed the note into his trouser pocket. Then he slapped one hand over his mouth.

"Pardonnez-vous."

Charles's own act of generosity had hardened him a little.

"I am quite capable of saying 'fuck', Mr. Grimaldi."

He had chosen to give him the money; that was the thing he wanted to convey. He could, had he wished, have attempted to talk his way out of the door. He could, like Grimaldi, have been a character; he would have made sundry humorous promises. It might have worked or it might not, but it was important that it was understood that he wasn't frightened. Grimaldi eyed him for a moment. Then he jerked his head backwards, towards the empty bar.

"If you go now you might catch her."

He nodded rapidly and patted Charles's arm. This was a new role: the friendly, fatherly cove. He was one thing and then another. It was in his nature to provide a discernible outline. Charles saw how he would have written him but he also found himself responding frankly to this show of generosity. He leapt up, grabbed his coat and gave a kind of wave, all in one gesture. He *was* drunk, he realised, but he also didn't want to let Grimaldi down. He wanted to show that he was game. It was an act of bravado, partly, but it was also true that he had an unmanageable erection. He was, to all intents and purposes, a marionette.

He tried to keep his distance. Sarah's walk declared itself more frankly than another woman's would. The women's clothes that he was used to emphasised their helplessness. Each movement was exaggerated and circumscribed at the same time. He had barely seen his wife naked; had caught glimpses, as of a mouse edging its way along a skirting board. Sarah was in her dress and a jacket that barely covered it. It was hemp or hessian and it rode up so that you saw her rear. It moved frankly from side to side and Charles was troubled by it. He realised that he was following it; that, in his imagination, he was shaping it with his hands. He never did this. Or almost never. There was mud everywhere and horse dung and he found that he hardly cared. He looked down at his shoes with something like satisfaction. The mud was an emblem; almost a simile.

He kept as far behind her as he could. He was being circumspect but he was aware of a form of excitement that was similar to the excitement that he always felt when in the process of creation. Most likely, he would just see where she lived, he told himself. Then he could write her too. Wasn't that so? His penis nodded assent. They were heading down towards High Holborn. You could see a rind of light, like you would on a dead kipper. London lay stinking in the declivity and it emboldened him. He was so much a part of it that he still felt at home, despite the strangeness of the houses and the way that they all seemed to be shouldering him aside. Sarah had a slight roll to her walk, just like a sailor, but it was really only her reaction to the wind and the rain and the mud. She pulled her coat more tightly around her and Charles was surprised by a burst of fellow feeling. He nearly let her go. What was he doing? He was barely married. His wife was waiting patiently at home. She was, he told himself this deliberately, almost certainly with child. He saw her arranging her skirt around the chair; *bestowing* it, as though it hid the egg that she was trying to hatch. Meanwhile, his hair was like wet wool. His trousers hung like flax. They were in Exmouth Street. They had turned right by Sadlers Wells and now there were hansom cabs rattling past and big trees with empty branches. Shops seemed to breathe a faint blue light. He paused and attempted to take stock. But it was then that Sarah veered off. She had suddenly turned a corner and this, too, was like something in a narrative. A plot device. He felt himself follow her almost despite himself.

He nearly called her name. He was glad that he knew it, although he wasn't going to use it yet. It was like a calling card; something that he would flourish at the right moment. She had led him into an alley and then another that opened out into what he realised was another rookery. Later, when he described it, he wrote that it was "very narrow and muddy, and the air was impregnated with filthy odours. There were a good many small shops, but the only stock in trade appeared to be heaps of children, who, even at that time of night, were crawling in and out of the doors, or screaming from the inside." A light touch; a *comic* touch. There were only, in reality, three or four of them at a time but, in his imagination, they were as promiscuously squeezed together as a nest of rats. When he was a boy, when he was working in the factory, he had kept himself aloof from streets like these. He had done this almost physically; it accounted, partly, for the military way in which he pulled his shoulders back. But he was also intimate with them. He felt complicit with them; they were a part of his own secret.

They had turned another corner. Later, too, he would describe the "ill-looking fellows," the ones who were "cautiously emerging, bound, to all appearance, upon no very well-disposed or harmless errands." But he wasn't scared of them. A labourer was in his way. He was as burly as a horse, but Charles danced around him. He all-but-danced *with* him. He was tempted to kick a child, like a football, out of his way. He had lost her. No. Wait. He hadn't. A door was closing on the left. It was quieter here, and narrower. He was standing on a cinder path with a long line of weeds that seemed to be curdling around its edges. It was so narrow that the air here had a different texture; it felt like you could roll it around your tongue. He did: he felt compassion. But also frustration. Here? She lived here? He was interested in himself. What was he going to do? He knew that he wouldn't knock. Knocking would make it a whole other kind of adventure; one that he wasn't prepared to face. His frustration also had something writerly about it. It was a feeble ending. He wanted to improve it.

As he watched, a light went on in a first-floor window and a female form passed behind the blind. He was as inflamed by this as he had been by anything else so far. The house was sliding into dereliction. It seemed to be shrugging one shoulder downwards, and its roof had more growths of moss than tiles. But the shadow was mysterious. There was no more hessian; no more of the bullish, long-suffering determination that had bent her forward like a man with a pickaxe or a shovel. He watched her in the same way that he watched the candle's flame, between the slats of scaffolding that seemed to be holding the building up. The window was like a stage, something exotically removed from his experience, and the scaffolding was like a balcony. He stood and breathed and watched and thought that, actually, he was drunker than he'd thought he was. He found that he was climbing his way up.

The scaffolding was shaking. There was a pot of paint and a nest of rags and he had to catch them before they danced their way over the edge. He stood with his legs apart and slowed his breathing. The room was radiant with the light of the candle but when he sneaked a look between the curtains it was initially a disappointment: an unlit fire; two chairs of such little distinction that his eyes refused to register them; and Sarah. Sarah naked, he realised, her breasts tolling as slowly as church bells. He was transfixed. Had he ever seen Catherine's breasts? Once, he remembered, but she had been so embarrassed that he had had to cover them up. As he watched, Sarah stood before a mirror that was resting on the mantelpiece. It was a shard, really; something more akin to the scrap of light that you might see in a puddle. She gestured upwards with one arm, and then the other. He heard her voice. It was toneless and awkward. She moved her arms again, and her breasts leapt up and down. Her head was immobile; she was staring determinedly into the middle distance. She was reciting something. A prayer? A spell? Her brow was furrowed and she was leaning earnestly forward. He saw that she was trying to be something other than the person that she was. It was clear in the way she stood and in her dogged intonation. She was acting. Then, suddenly, she wheeled around, she threw her hands into the air, and it was too much for Charles. He jumped backwards and his whole body went backwards too. Landing, he heard the pot of paint fall inches from his head. He waited for the pain in his body to catch up with him. He hardly saw the window opening or Sarah sticking her head out. He heard her, though, and then he was able to see her face: the muted anger and bewilderment and then, after a pause, the humorous resignation.

"You," she said, "are a fucking nuisance."

CHAPTER THREE

WHAT DISTURBED CATHERINE most was the rain. She was knitting or, to be more precise, it was her hands that were knitting while she tried not to look at the sky. She could feel that her face had tightened slightly and that Mary was going to assail it. What Charles was never able to appreciate was how pert Mary could be; how satisfied she could become when discommoding her older sister. They both had the same high forehead; the same large eyes and cupid's bows. But Mary's eyes were steadier. Her lips were often poised. She held her head as though it was proof of something. Now she was riddling the grate. She did it with so much vigour that Charles said that she went at it like a barrel organ. Sometimes, when in good spirits, he would sing along. She had soot on the tip of her nose. It was adorable, and Catherine found that she was frowning. Meanwhile, the rain danced heedlessly on the window pane.

"Thank you," she said.

Mary was rubbing her hands together. She had placed her legs, side-saddle, on the rug. But her cheeks were flushed. Her face would often glow like this—would seem to provide its own source of light. Catherine could hear how her own voice came straining through her throat. She would so much rather be able to prove herself to be an example. Instead, there was a fluttering in her chest. Her eyebrows felt strange to her. Mary was four years younger and yet her look appeared to encompass her. It seemed to understand Catherine and her marriage in their entirety. It was vexing, and Mary knew that too.

Catherine said, "I can appreciate that it is only rain."

"I know."

"I don't think that you do."

Mary was smiling and tidying her hair. Her fingers were busy and clever and quick. Men were not indifferent to them. They saw how briskly they shaped what appeared to be the nest at the back of her head and how little this seemed to affect the serenity of her face. She was what men thought they wanted when they wanted an angel, one who could make their mutton tender if it was required. Meanwhile, it was difficult to explain to Charles how irritating her intuitions could be. They were like horseflies, biting away.

"Rain," she said, "is only 'only' rain if one's inside. Charles ..."

She seemed to push something away from her.

"... plunges through it. He runs gleefully into it."

"Away from you, you think."

"I—"

"Yes, Kate. You do."

"Sometimes I do." This is what Mary did. She made you say the things you didn't want to say, and then you found that you wanted to say them after all. "The weather outdoes itself," she said. "It's like something that he would write."

"And is it the weather that you object to or its relation to Charles's prose?"

"Its relationship to *him*. He cannot be still."

"That isn't true."

"He is—"

"He is your Charles. He is all fire. But when the occasion demands he is perfectly capable of being something else."

"He is a dear, kind man. I know. And I know he loves me."

Gently, she touched her belly. Was it? Swelling? Her hands were attempting to listen to it.

"And yet?"

"And yet he never seems able to enjoy the fruit of his own predilections. He arranges the house with such grace and such dexterity."

Her fingers danced tenderly in her lap.

"He goes at it like he goes at everything. But then he cannot stay. He—"

But she stopped. She shook her head like she was shaking it free of something.

"He?"

"Nothing. No. Nothing."

She had been about to say: he kisses me like he is elsewhere. Sometimes. Sometimes he doesn't. But there are times when I wish that he would savour me. When it wouldn't feel like he was keen to be on his way to somewhere else. That he might know me in the same way that he knows a market or a suit of clothes. She said, "It's late."

"In other words: 'Mary, go to bed.'"

Catherine smiled.

"You forget. I'm *in loco parentis*."

"No, my darling, I am."

Mary brushed her dress with heedless vigour, shook it almost, then used her knuckles to push herself up from the floor. It struck Catherine that Charles had never seen her do this and that, quite rightly, Mary would not have wanted him to.

She was like a monkey. Catherine found that she was smiling properly. But she also wanted to stop her. It was unseemly or almost unseemly or, perhaps, it was simply that it might be construed as being unseemly. But it was also endearing. One didn't necessarily want her to know better. As Mary leant down to kiss her, Catherine felt an urge to hold onto her as tightly as she could.

Outside, handfuls of rain were being thrown against the window. The gas in the streetlamps fluttered uncertainly. The trees flicked backwards and forwards, their leaves like daubs of ink. When the door banged downstairs, they both jumped, guiltily, and Mary sat back down; arranged herself, not in a seductive way but in the same way that a child might try to underline its innocence. Catherine found that she had bent her head towards her knitting. One found oneself, sometimes, being careful in Charles's presence. One approached him in the same way that one might tiptoe towards a sudden noise or unexpected light. He was bounding up the stairs. Each thump seemed to be mirrored in the way that her heart was beating. He was already shouting.

"Hallo!"

And there he was. His hair was matted across his forehead and his face was flushed. Dirt had flung itself over his shoes and trousers and even, she saw, his upper body; his shoulders and neck. But he didn't seem to mind. He was laughing, but there was also the something illegible in his face that she had had to negotiate the first time she met him. His voice had had an over-determined quality. It still did: he did his best to pitch it upwards but his Cockney intonation acted like weights. And there, she saw, was that something indeterminate about the mouth that he was wont to try to hide. He was perfectly conscious of it:

would hold it to attention or fix it into something frisky and
devil-may-care, but still, when it was at ease, it seemed to loll
there. Time was when she had had to look away. Of course, he
had improved. That was what Charles did, always: he improved.
Nevertheless, what *was* the matter with him? Mary was smiling.
Her eyes were glittering mischievously.

"Charley Dickens," she said. "Are you in drink?"

"Tush. It's nothing. I met a costermonger. A coalheaver,
rather. A capital man: all soot. He did the hornpipe. We did, I
mean. I showed him how to do it properly."

He took a couple of steps. He was like a man on a tightrope:
preternaturally graceful but careful, too. He placed each leg in
the same way that he might dot an "i." Mary was giggling, and
Catherine had to look away. There was part of her that was
indignant and a part that desperately didn't want to be. She
felt trapped in her own temperament. This, meanwhile, was
his temperament; he could no more escape it than she could
fling herself into the hornpipe, and she must make allowances.
She attempted to step sideways from herself. She was aware
that she was smiling; indeed, was doing this with such delib-
eration that she could feel how her stomach was implicated in
the effort. But she was aware, too, of the something, like suet,
that seemed to stick to her. Mary was delighted, but Mary was
doing the equivalent of sitting in the gallery; she was able to
appreciate his comic turn. He was saying, "I have met *such* a
potato man."

He did the walk. His legs had formed the letter O. He fluttered his hands at his sides. She didn't know what he was doing.
Was it a form of palsy?

"He was like a bun," he said, "rolling towards me down the
road. I'd left a penny and he came trundling after me and there
was this one boy."

Charles's tongue came flapping out of his mouth. He didn't quite cross his eyes. It was more that he was looking at what he was looking at so avidly that his eyes were ready to bolt it down. He looked like this, sometimes, when they were alone. She was something that he wanted to display to himself. But she was not willing to be displayed. She wanted a soft touch; no more. She would ask him to snuff out the candle and, of course, one had to take pains in the way one asked him. This, she knew, this mumming in front of the fireplace, could easily teeter into something else. She did her best and smiled with a show of ease. But she continued to knit. It was, itself, a form of dismissal.

Charles had snatched an invisible potato. He was devouring it with all the relish of an ogre in a fairy story. His face disturbed her at such times. She couldn't always locate him. Where was he? In the eyes? In the slight tilt of his head? Still. There was nothing phlegmatic about Charles; nothing sedentary or defeated. It was one of the things that she loved most. She was telling herself this, she noticed, like a schoolmistress reprimanding a wilful child. She was thinking it even as she was saying, "Charles. It is one o'clock."

He ran his fingers through his hair. He was both smiling and not smiling. He was, at moments like this, a pantomime in little. He didn't just stop; he wanted you to know how very much he had stopped. He looked at her tenderly—he performed this tenderness assiduously, nodding his head and smiling gently at her—at the same time that his hand went fidgeting through his hair. She knew that what she had done was the equivalent of shouting at a performer. When Charles seemed at his most spontaneous, he was often at his most concentrated. It was like throwing water at a somnambulist. But she saw no alternative.

It was one o'clock. He was drunk and covered in mud. Mary was tired. *She* was tired. She went to speak but he was saying, "Pope Joan? A rubber?"

"Oh Charles. Not cards."

Mary was clapping her hands. Charles had flung himself towards the little table and was dragging it into the middle of the floor.

"One rubber," he said. "I cannot sleep. I *will not* sleep."

And she saw several things. That he was telling the truth, but that he was also prepared to will himself into wakefulness. That, in his own way, he was also making allowances. That this cost him some effort, and a diminution of animal spirits. That it was partly Mary's presence that had encouraged him to be so very lively. That he was using Mary, and Mary's enjoyment, as one might use a nutmeg grater: to wear away at his wife's indifference. And that this was what marriage meant. Or, rather, that this was what marriage to a Somebody must mean. Amelioration. Subterfuge. The sensation of flight, or of falling, even when one was sitting calmly in one's chair. She shook her head. She put down her knitting and picked up her cards. And she smiled, which she knew very well how to do, like this was not a concession so much as a pleasure.

"Charley," she said.

She gently touched his fingertips.

"One hour."

He gave, in his turn, a smile whose gorgeousness was like the unfurling of a flag. The hand that touched her cheek appeared to do it of its own accord.

"Of course," he said.

CHAPTER FOUR

THE SOUND OF the London streets was like the sound you heard when you were in a barrel being pushed downhill. Hooves; footsteps; tradesmen, all rolled into one. Street traders; violins. Of course, that was where the simile collapsed. Charles abandoned it. He began to watch a mote of light that was shivering halfway up the window. Even the light in London was unevenly distributed. In the rookeries, you got next to nothing. Up on Park Lane it was laid out for you, like a banquet. Here, in Fleet Street, it came and went. Sometimes it was sullen. Sometimes it rushed to meet you. And sometimes it did this: it slyly acknowledged you. But then, for Charles, a lot of London was like that. He looked at Beard.

"I do," he said. "Of course I do."

"I'm glad. And I must say I'm not surprised. You're an affectionate man, Charles. You were very much the bridegroom even before your wedding day."

Beard paused. He was looking over Charles's shoulder.

"And things ... ah ... I presume ... are ..." He was stroking his chin. Now he had looked down at his knees. His bald patch was glittering like a coin. "Satisfactory?"

Charles peered at him until his whole face seemed to take it in at once. He pulled himself backwards, but only slightly. Even here he could master a look of almost military rigour.

"Good Lord, man."

Staring at Beard, he made it seem like there was a much greater distance between them than the table and two plates of oysters.

"There are things that one can't possibly discuss."

"No. Quite. I'm sorry."

Charles ran his hand briskly through his hair. His sense of himself was such that he must constantly define it as you watched. He seemed to settle back into his clothes.

"But yes. They are. At least, I think they are. How does one tell? It's not as though you can *ask*."

"No. Heaven forbid."

"I am ..."

He made a vague, embarrassed gesture.

"... not inexperienced. Not *excessively* experienced. But."

Beard smiled.

"You have had an adequate education."

"Yes. Thank you, dear fellow. I have."

Beard was looking furtively at his oyster.

"You're looking at it like it might attack you."

"I never feel as though they're entirely edible. I feel like there's something I should be doing but I don't know what."

"You have to attack them first. Immediately, before your brain realises what it's up against."

Beard looked at him doubtfully, but then Beard did this often. He had a face whose lack of definition made it easy to impress yourself upon it. He wasn't entirely pacified. He was scratching in a desultory fashion at his nose. The oyster room was nearly full, but Charles was known here. His card was on the wall. He had breezed in and grabbed a table and had made a point of choosing for them both. He felt he knew exactly what Beard was about to ask him. He could see him make the decision to look steadily at him. His hat was hung on a hook behind him. It looked like it was waiting for him to speak.

"Then *why*, Charles?"

He was leaning forward, although he never quite managed to appear as though he was.

"No, really, Charles. Why go to all that bother? The mud. The wet. The slum. Although, I understand. You're very fond of a slum. But still. It's only been, what?"

"Two months."

"Two months."

Beard said this gently. Charles saw that he wanted to lay his hand on his arm, but he didn't quite dare. Instead, he appeared to pat air, or a ball. An invisible ball; Charles made a mental note of it. He leaned back, slowly, and carefully stroked his chin. He all-but-drawled.

"You know, I was asking myself exactly the same question. I followed her for a good two miles and all the time I was asking: 'CD, what *are* you doing?'"

"And you do that?" Beard could not entirely repress a smile. "You refer to yourself in the third person?"

"Oh yes. I'm a subject, Beard. I'm endlessly fascinating to myself. How I eat; how I fail to sleep. Why should I not be? It's my bread and butter. And that's what I think I was doing."

"By entering the room of a *cocotte*."

"Hardly."

"At twelve o'clock at night."

"When else?"

"And then what happened?"

"Nothing, I assure you. I stood there like ... like a *bream*. My mouth was opening and closing of its own accord. I looked around so passively that I really rather impressed myself. I neither leapt on her nor asked her an excessive amount of questions. Then I left. When I got home I simply omitted it."

He was shaking his head and laughing.

"Oh Lor. I did an impression of a potato man."

"And that sufficed?"

"It shouldn't have, should it? I pretended to be drunker than I was."

"You are a very lucky man."

"I am. I know I am."

A confession, Charles was thinking, but not a confession. A feint: a circuitous route that led back exactly to where he had started. What was it he thought he was confessing to? Or not confessing to?

"I'll admit that I found her fascinating," he said. "I shall almost certainly write about her. But no: there was no earthly reason for me to follow her. I had her entire, from the moment that I saw her."

"I want to see her too. You should try describing her to Cruikshank."

Charles shook his head.

"She'd look like every woman he'd ever drawn. I am insufficiently, um, *eminent* to discipline him."

He looked unhappy for a moment. Beard, he could see, was trying not to smile.

"And Browne?"

"Browne is a lovely man."

Beard laughed.

"You know," Charles said, "sometimes I wish I could find someone between the two. Between Cruikshank's fire and Browne's—"

"Extraordinary eagerness to please."

"Quite right. You know what I think?"

Charles shrugged. He grinned. It was something like an advertisement.

"It was Grimaldi."

"I see."

"You don't. And in the bold light of day, I'm not sure that I do, either. But it's true. It was Grimaldi. I wanted to live up to him."

Beard studied him. That was the thing about Beard. He was diffident—light seemed, sometimes, to pour right through him—but he was shrewd. "So," he said. "A romantic through and through. And now?"

"Oh. Parliament." Charles shrugged again, but in dismissal. "The same," he said. "Always the same. 'I put it to our honourable friend that he knows, and did from the first know, both what he did then and what he does now; and when he says he didn't mean it then, does he mean it now? And if he means to say that he did not then, and does not now, know what he did mean then and does mean now what *does* he mean? Eh?'"

Beard laughed. Charles rubbed his hands.

"And tomorrow we are hot-footing it to Yarmouth."

"Dear God. Yarmouth."

"A shipwreck!"

"You say that with altogether too much relish."

"I say everything with relish. It's part of my—"

"Trousseau."

Charles roared. The whole establishment, it seemed, turned as one man. Charles wiped his eyes and touched Beard's arm.

"It takes a quiet man," he said, "to bring that off properly."

But, all the time, he had been watching. Or something was watching for him. His napkin had a dark bulge, like a bruise, along one side. The opened door appeared to gather steam; to beckon it. The man who sat beside it sat so awkwardly that he seemed to have given birth to his own foot. Out on the street, the sunlight whitewashed everything. The wheels of the carriages mixed it up and flung it everywhere. Walking into the middle of it, he felt like he was leaping into an element that he would have to learn, all over again, to keep his balance in. Bravely, he squinted up and down the Strand.

"I'll walk," he said, and went off in such a briskly definite manner that Beard didn't have time to say goodbye. He always set himself to walking in the same way that he might sit down to write. He did it with so much vigour that he appeared to be illustrating how to do it.

He was in a hurry but, as always, he avoided Hungerford Stairs. It wasn't in his immediate proximity but still he swung himself away from it. Even here, he could feel his chest tightening and his eyes smart, slightly, at the onset of tears. The stairs were magnetic, still. It was like a story told at night: one that kept pulling you towards an ending that was almost exactly the same as the beginning but it was worse, because of all the effort that had been taken to advance away from it. He pulled himself more firmly upright and took determined steps towards the site of the new square. It was surrounded by a hoarding that, despite the notices of "Stick No Bills" and "Bill-Stickers Beware," was covered in advertisements.

This was another habit: the way that he always had to check without wishing to appear as though he did. He liked to see his name in public places. Mr. Van Amburg And His Lions were, apparently, going to be present at a ball. He would have liked to have known which one but that would have meant him stopping and peering in a way that gave away how excessive his interest was. There was an advertisement for Madame Tussauds and another for a dwarf in a cyclorama (and in a top hat, presumably). But, no, as far as he could tell, he wasn't here. He had often said this to Catherine: that he wanted to be Somebody. But first, it seemed, one had to keep flinging one's name at the general public. One's self-regard had to go hand-in-hand with a clownlike underlining of that self-regard. The trouble was that it felt, it all felt, necessary. It stemmed from the stairs, and the life that he had lived adjacent to the stairs. From Warren's Blacking Factory, and from whatever it was that made him, even now, feel as though he could eat all over again.

Inside the House of Commons, he did his best to apply himself but something dragged at him. Not the warehouse, nor his own hunger: something else. His mind had closed around it in the same way that, noting furiously, he made his consonants crowd out his vowels. In shorthand, what you were left with was something that felt like a closed concertina, and his mind was like that all night. He walked home and had his tea. He made himself bask in everything: in his place at the table, his wife and her pretty sister and the food and forthright furnishings. But part of him knew that he was willing himself to do this. He talked about mulberries and linen. He goaded his wife into making puns. But there was an unwonted tightness in his legs and upper thighs. He kept playing with his hair. Once, he looked out of the window and, when he came to himself, he didn't know what he was supposed to be looking at. It was a mild evening, and that seemed incorrect somehow. The pallid light seemed dull and innocent.

The same something nagged at him all the way to Yarmouth. Pleaded with him, almost. It was gathering, like wool, into something tangible. Nothing satisfied him: not the room; not the evening meal; not the glass of brandy that, in his usual fashion, he made last for three-quarters of an hour. In the morning, he stood on the beach and wondered at the flatness of the landscape. Everything seemed to be one thing. It was as though someone had dipped their finger in the sea and drawn the sand and the horizon and the sky in shimmering drops of water. It was a beautiful, uneasy dance, he saw, whose antagonist was a pier that was so down-at-heel that it appeared to be scribbled upon the horizon. Charles smelt the sea and it was like hearing something. He found himself straining upwards, breathing into the currents of the air. He stared at the point where the ship was supposed to have gone down. It wavered so, and seemed so very insignificant, that it felt incongruous to have travelled all this way to see it. All of the drama of the scene had been smoothed over by the sea and the sun and the sand, which held no imprint of the bodies that had been dragged up here two days ago. Tragedy; drama. It all depended on where you stood. He became impatient with reality. If he had written it he would have kept the wreck in sight. There would have been one spar, like an admonitory finger, poking above the waves. A crowd. Perhaps a body or two. And a woman, definitely; a girl, rather, whose hair was being driven backwards into her face. No tears: a fierceness of expression that made it look like she had decided to defy the elements. What was she going to do? Dive into the sea herself? Grab the corpse that was lying beside her and try to blow it back to life? Charles started to laugh.

"Like blowing up a balloon."

His shoulders were going now. Write that. And then perhaps she should do the hornpipe. A mile away there was a church and he had seen the bodies. They looked like soap. God and the sea had carved them into a memorial. Even the vicar had cried. He, Charles, had bowed his head and spoken in a respectful murmur that had been amplified by the vault and the dome of the roof into what in his imagination sounded like the voice of a huge paterfamilias with a broad chest and ruddy cheeks. Charles saw an invisible handkerchief; the way that it wilted in his hand. Thick whiskers, and a watch chain like a question mark. Reporter; writer; maker of comic images—how very removed he was. Outside, he had torn into the cheese sandwich that his landlady had gently put into his hand. She felt that he would need some sort of sustenance. Beard had gone off to talk to the families and Charles stood in the hall, trying to arrange his face into the right expression. Meanwhile, here he was, imagining the hornpipe. Laughing, it seemed, directly at the sea. He felt a lack of connection with just about everything and he had the sense, just for that moment, that the whole world was a set of painted flats. That it was like a deck of cards that one could shuffle one way and then another. He was both scared and invigorated. He was, he suddenly felt, both cliff and someone standing on a cliff, and he knew now what he had been trying so very hard not to think about. Sarah. Her face. Her dress. Her rear, tick-tocking like a pendulum. He saw how very carefully he had arranged things for himself. How thickly his house was furnished; how eager to accommodate him he had taught his wife to be. He saw how it enabled him to do whatever he chose.

But, in many ways, whatever he chose was inimical to what he had chosen. How could you keep plunging forward when you also wanted to be tethered to the ground? He wanted to go home and nuzzle his wife at the same time as he wanted to plunge, with all his clothes, into the sea. Only the sea was not for plunging. It was so quiet this morning. Charles wanted to irritate the surface. He wanted to bash at it until it spoke to him. He wanted to run, shouting, around the bay until he'd gathered a substantial crowd. More than anything he wanted to walk the London streets. He wanted to go where he wasn't wanted. He wanted to *make* himself wanted; to live one of the many lives he knew that he could live, with an eye on the bolt-hole that he called home.

CHAPTER FIVE

HE HADN'T SPOKEN the whole truth when he told Beard what had happened. For one thing, he hadn't told him that it had started on the pavement while he was lying on his back. Sarah had shaken her head and he had seen that her shoulders were as bare and white as slices of the moon. He felt his stomach tighten. He became aware that he had another erection and he was careful as he was standing up to make sure that it was appropriately covered. Excitement was like another suit of clothes. It dulled the pain so that it was more like a faint buzzing out at the edges of consciousness. He could feel himself feeling it from far away.

She closed the window but he could see the way the candle lit the interior of the room. Sarah did something with her hair that made it seem to melt into her head. He knew that watching was a way of staying where he was; that he should make a run for it before she came downstairs. He rubbed his forehead, and it was as though he was illustrating to himself how badly he was hurt. It was a form of self-justification. He flexed his legs from side to side and, when she came to the door, he looked at her stupidly for a moment. He found that he was swaying slightly, and that this was a way of pretending to be drunker than he was. He wasn't sure who he was pretending for. He pointed at the scaffolding.

"I fell."

"You did."

Her dress, the same dress, hung from her like dirty washing. She had wrapped a shawl around her shoulders. Now she was eyeing him blankly; not quite suspiciously. He shrugged and smiled and made a gesture with his hands that acknowledged that he should really be somewhere else. But it was also a question. He was ashamed of himself, but there it was: he was asking what she wanted him to do.

She was looking at him as if he were livestock and he found to his surprise that it was arousing. But disconcerting, too. One's usual experience was that the girl would perform for you. It was part of the unreality of the thing. What you paid for, not that he had paid often, was the hygienic palliation of release. But what you also wanted was a fantasy. It enabled you to feel as though you had been put to sleep, somehow; as though your conscience had been lulled by the equivalent of Eastern music. Indeed, the brothel that he liked best was tricked out like *The Arabian Nights.* There were huge jars and bowls of sherbet and the bareness of the walls felt like a provocation. One of the girls, his favourite, had the figure of a dancer. She used to roll her stomach for him, although the East End touch, the quivering of laughter that was like running water, complicated this somewhat. He could never tell if he liked it. He liked *her,* but that was the problem. The more real she became the less able he was to tell himself that he was dreaming.

He wasn't dreaming now. The alcohol was receding. It was like the tide going out, and what he was left with was the bareness of plain reality. He was staring at a slum girl. There was the noise of a pub nearby and it was difficult to tell if what was happening was a party or a fight. He was covered in mud, but he was still dressed like a dandy. He had rings and he would, if it wasn't so tactless, have taken them off. And no, actually, it wasn't true about the plainness of reality. Because desire was reshaping everything. The shadows dancing out at the edge of the candle's flame were a manifestation of what he was feeling. The houses were nothing; the voices were nothing—they were all ready to be snuffed out by whatever happened next. He saw her begin to smile. She was looking down at his trousers. He found himself placing his hands in front of them and stammering something. Or nothing. He couldn't tell.

"Is Sir coming up or ain't he?"

She had laboured the word "sir." She had seemed to examine it even as she was saying it. It was like a fake coin. Or a shared joke. It appeared that, yes, he was coming up. He found that he had lost the ability to stare with pleasure at her arse. It was part of something larger; the same thing, it seemed, that made the walls reel drunkenly in candlelight. From somewhere inside the house there came the sound of water slowly dripping into a pail. It wasn't reassuring. His chest, he noticed, seemed to have lifted up towards his neck. His knees shook. He found this disproportionately irritating. He barely saw the room they were entering for the emotion that made him say, "Now look—" But she was already talking.

"I'm not a brass," she said.

She was sitting on the edge of the bed. She seemed to have shrunk somewhat. Here, in the steadying candle, Charles could see that she had applied rouge to her cheeks. She had done it almost negligently: it sat there like paint, and it functioned more as a challenge than anything else.

"That doesn't mean that I don't entertain occasionally."

She gestured to where the world outside seemed to be flailing in the wind and rain.

"This ain't Pall Mall. And a girl likes her comforts. But I'm telling you: I'm not a whore."

Her voice was the voice of the streets; it had the croak in it that you got if you were touting your wares. They were like cracked bells, those voices. Charles had been listening to them since he was a child. But there was a warmer voice underneath. It was almost mellifluous. She thumped the bed.

"And don't treat me like one."

Her room was cleaner than you might expect. The mantelpiece and the fireplace shone with a dull burnish that was reassuring. There were bare boards and a plain deal table and two chairs. There was another mirror placed next to the wall beside the window. It was free-standing and incongruously stately. What Charles wanted was the confidence to improvise. Where had it gone? She was beautiful, that was the trouble. Overpainted, yes, and reduced to something smaller and more vulnerable, even as she so forcefully stated her terms, but beautiful nonetheless. She gave off a form of heat. He refused to sit, however. He raised his hands, palms outwards. This part of his story had been true: his mouth opening and closing like he was floundering on a line.

"Take off your coat, won't you? You're soaking wet."

His mind was like a spinning top. It was base, he felt, to calculate but his brain seemed to be calculating for him. How much should he give her? What could they do that didn't compromise his life at home? Should he sit down? He was almost at the point where he might take her hand and lean towards her. Almost. The fact that he could consider it meant that he couldn't claim that it was involuntary. He was nothing if not disciplined.

"I beg your pardon. I don't ..."

He made a strange gesture with his hands. It looked like he was squeezing an accordion. Even as he was doing it, he was finding an analogy for it. He was a monkey, he saw, on a barrel organ. He was attempting to communicate but he was also sorrowfully aware of the limitations of his own nature. He found himself wishing for a piece of paper so that he could write it down. This made him want to laugh, which in turn gave him a little more confidence. "I don't know why I followed you."

Enunciation. That was the key.

"I am a married man." He displayed his wedding ring. Sarah was nodding wearily. She had heard this before. "It was a moment of madness."

"A moment."

"Alright. An hour." He grinned. "An hour of madness. Look at me."

"You are a fucking sight."

Even as he sat beside her on the bed, Charles was aware of the fact that he was performing a ruefulness he didn't feel. Even as he was putting his head in his hands he knew that he still wanted to touch her breasts. But he also wanted to escape. The room was horrible. No. Functional. There were none of the comforts that Charles so relied upon. He was excited and repulsed in equal measure. There was also something that he couldn't put his finger on. It was to do with Sarah's sense of equality. Not her mental equality, exactly, so much as her physical confidence. She didn't draw away when he sat beside her on the bed. She didn't retract into something smaller that you might wish to tease out of itself. But she didn't attempt to seduce him, either. Either would have been like songs that he knew how to sing. Instead, it was a little like being with a man. Charles retreated into comedy.

"I feel," he said, "like something you might put into a pot. My toes are like cabbages."

"Whose fault is that?"

Her voice had softened slightly. She studied him.

"How long?"

"My toes?"

She laughed. She did this like he did it: she threw her head back. Again, there was a confidence in this that Charles found disconcerting. It was as though her head left her body behind to fend for itself.

"How long have you been married?"

"Two months."

"Oh God."

She laughed again but continued to look at him. It was, he saw, *shared* laughter. They were like two people in a lifeboat.

"That poor woman."

"Yes. Well."

"And you ..."

She made little scurrying motions with her fingers.

"You looked at me, and?"

It was a real question. There was something tender in the way she asked him; she really wanted to know. He modulated into gallantry, but not excessively. And not untruthfully.

"It was your face."

"My face."

"Not just your face."

"'at's better. No rumpty-tumpty, please. No patter."

"It was both."

"And you were drunk."

"I was."

"But you're not now."

"No. At least, I don't think I am."

He gestured to the room, and then outwards to the slum and the faint rumour of voices in the pub.

"I think all of this has sobered me up."

"Don't tell me you're out of your depth."

"A little."

"No. Not you."

"And this you know?"

"Look at him. Bridling."

She peered into his face and smiled. She touched his hair.

"Does your mother know you're out?"

She was older. Not so very much, perhaps, but older in a way that wasn't to be argued with. All that experience. Charles found that he envied her. But he was also sitting rigidly to attention. One could attempt to dominate a woman or else one could wheedle with her. But this made him feel slightly feverish. Lightly, she touched his knee.

"Go home."

He didn't want to, but he did. He stood for a moment outside her door, pretending to himself that he didn't know which way to walk, but it was his own heart that he was orientating. He felt the rain, obscurely, as a commentary and it continued to argue with him as he walked back. He refused to be ashamed and he was already, ten steps away from Sarah's house, turning the whole experience into something else. It had, by the time he got home, become an anecdote that he couldn't tell.

But now he was outside the pub again. A couple of months had passed and the night was warmer. There was no fire, and this made it look more prosaic than it had seemed in memory. The inside was no longer mysterious and neither was it welcoming. It seemed to shrug you off, so that you felt that it would rather have been in an alley or in a village somewhere else. He couldn't hear anything from inside. He had dressed down; he still wore a waistcoat, of course, but there were no rings on his fingers. He had told Catherine and Mary that he needed "verisimilitude." He had made it sound like a joke, or almost a joke, but he had also made it sound as inevitable as the tides. This is what one did: one soaked up the streets. But that was for writers. Now he was very much a human being. He tried to discipline his breathing and then gave up the attempt. He rode it instead. He walked into the bar like he was on a horse.

And she wasn't there. The grate was, and the same old men. And Grimaldi. He looked raffish, but he also looked terribly tired. He had turned from his table to the bar but he seemed only to have moved his upper half. It looked, from his face, like he was lifting his body rather than simply turning it. Charles stood irresolutely in the doorway. Grimaldi was still a delightful sight; he shone, still, with the nimbus of past glamour. But you knew that he was also going to be exhausting. Before Charles could make a decision, he saw him turn back. He saw that it took him a moment to focus on him. Then he nodded just as though Charles had gone out briefly to take the air.

"Here he is," he said.

His face was still mobile, even if his body wasn't. He held a deadpan in the same way that a real pan might hold water that was about to boil. He took out a handkerchief and did a bit of business on the seat beside him, making the cloth lift and settle like a bird. Then he vigorously brushed the seat.

"Come on, Boots."

"Where's—"

"Davey? He's got the night off."

"Orf." It was part locution and part performance.

"He's, um, *revivifying* an old acquaintance. There'll be a lot of noise from that quarter, I should imagine. Here. Sit. Sit."

He made a courtly gesture, revolving one hand rapidly while pointing with the opened palm of the other.

"No. Davey's still young enough for that sort of thing. Me, I have an Italian physique. Strong as a bull. Until you're not."

He grinned.

"Sod's law. I'm a low comedian. We're meant to do pratfalls and all of that. But things break. They seize up. They come off you and roll away."

His voice had leant so heavily on "low" that it was like his thumb was on it. Now he was fingering his bottom lip. His upper lip was poised between a pout and a moue of disgust.

"I should have been anything, really, but a performer. But it's fate, see. When I was this high—a *sprat*—I used to tell jokes to my tin soldiers. Dirty ones. You try explaining your tin soldier's erection to your mother."

His face had assumed a careful balance between bewilderment and knowingness. Then his features seemed to retreat; to contract into something duller and more pragmatic. It was like he had stepped back into himself.

"No," he said. "Really, I was beaten. Beaten for standing up. Beaten for sitting down."

Either this was earnestness or he was performing being earnest. He wanted Charles to feel it, his pain. There was something disproportionate about the way that he was peering steadily at him, watching his reaction. There was something inscrutable about it.

"Anyway."

He had become somebody else again. He was doing an extraordinary thing with his mouth. It seemed to be tasting itself.

"Talking about erections."

He raised and lowered his eyebrows rapidly. Then he cocked his head to one side and fixed Charles with what appeared to be a winsome stare. He batted his eyes.

"Not saying? Coy. Very. Still, I don't blame you."

He rubbed the bottom of his nose with the back of his hand. It was like rubber, his nose, and it reminded you that there'd been a time when his entire body had been like that. Not anymore: he sat like a South Sea Idol now. Only his expressions ebbed and flowed and even then they didn't seem to have a lot to do with him. He was drunk, Charles saw. Just before he put his hand back on the table there was a moment when it hovered there, like the handkerchief.

"Our Sarah didn't say anything, of course. But there was a glint in her eye. Lummie, those arms. I envy you."

He was patting Charles's arm for emphasis.

"Although, she can get fucking cross. I was a little scared for you. I thought: a dolphin in a sentry box."

Charles stiffened slightly. It was his own simile, but it was no longer innocent. He inclined his head then tried to smile. Grimaldi nodded.

"Dignified. Some Boots. I've been reading you. Where is it? Here."

He flourished a copy of *The Morning Chronicle*.

"Sam Weller."

"Ah."

"Yes. Ah. He doesn't look like you, does he? *You* do, though. I've seen a picture of you, Charley. You and your ringlets. You want to be careful, mate. I mean, *I* like you. But there are others in here who are going to think you're a copper's nark."

He had leant in—*swung* in—to talk into Charles's ear. Charles smelt his breath, and something else: the flop sweat of an exhausted horse. He didn't flinch. He made himself stay exactly where he was. He was looking steadily into Grimaldi's eye.

"And you? What do you think?"

"What do I know? I'm a slap-and-tickle man. A bit of local colour. 'as what I think. You're here for Joey the Clown. Although I find you've done a clown."

He wielded the newspaper like an auctioneer. Charles tried to breathe as steadily as he could. He found that he was leaning backwards. Grimaldi struck a pose and cleared his throat.

"'He had been skulking in the lanes and alleys of London. I was dressed to leave the house, and was crossing the stage on my way out, when he tapped me on the shoulder. Never shall I forget the repulsive sight that met my eye when I turned round. He was dressed for the pantomimes in all the absurdity of a clown's costume. The spectral figures in the Dance of Death, the most frightful shapes that the ablest painter ever portrayed on canvas, never presented an appearance half so ghastly. His bloated body and shrunken legs—their deformity enhanced a hundredfold by the fantastic dress—the glassy eyes, contrasting fearfully with the thick white paint with which the face was besmeared; the grotesquely-ornamented head, trembling with paralysis, and the long skinny hands, rubbed with white chalk— all gave him a hideous and unnatural appearance, of which no description could convey an adequate idea, and which, to this day, I shudder to think of.'"

It wasn't in this paper; it had been in an earlier edition. Grimaldi had recited it. Proudly, almost. His top half gave a bow. It was like watching a puppet, the way that they seem to lean slowly into each individual movement.

"It took me a day to learn that. And I can't even read; not properly. I had Davey recite it over and over again. Poor bastard. He was hoarser than I am by the end of it."

He paused. Charles eyed him in the same way that you might eye a snake.

"And, see, I'm not a critic, Charley boy, but I do like 'skulking.' 'Repulsive' is good. It's very good. But 'skulking' is better. 'Skulking' is *much* better."

Charles went to speak, but Grimaldi grabbed his arm.

"You'll get your turn. Now listen. I want to ask you something."

He had fierce hands.

"Why does he have to skulk? To skulk repulsively, mark you. And how do *you* get to be dressed to leave the house? All smarmy, in your best bib and tucker."

"It isn't me."

"No. I expect it never is."

"I didn't—"

"What? You didn't what?"

Grimaldi was looking keenly at him. Charles saw himself being thrown to the men around the fire like a scrap of meat. But Grimaldi was shaking his head. He appeared to be working something loose.

"I think you'd better buy me a drink," he said.

"Gladly."

Charles rose on rubbery legs. He had put his hand lightly on Grimaldi's arm, and now he wanted to leave it there. But he also wanted to run. It would have been easy to escape Grimaldi. But what about the men slumped by the fireplace? Never trust a cut-throat not to have a turn of speed. Then there was Sarah, of course. Her absence hummed as loudly in his head as if she had been present. He leaned on the bar partly because he felt the

need to be propped up. The other thing he could have done—
the thing he nearly did—was smite his own forehead. You
walk into a bar and there, sitting right there, is Joe Grimaldi.
And everything else goes out of your head. Well, nearly, until
you spot the barmaid and then, of course, your head becomes
entirely empty, right up until the moment that you're reminded
that you wrote about Grimaldi's son. His son. What had he been
about to say? That he didn't mean to? That he hadn't meant any
harm? He wanted to punch himself in the face. But there were
enough people around him to do that for him. When he got
back, Grimaldi nodded. He took a huge draught of beer. He
flicked one end of his handkerchief aloft then wiped his mouth
with it, and all this time he was looking Charles in the eye.

"Funny coincidence, innit?"

"It isn't meant to be—"

"Him? Come off it. We've all done that. 'His Majesty? Lord
love me, no. Somebody else entirely.' Don't give me that."

"That isn't what I meant."

"I nursed him, you know. I did. I encouraged him. I wrote
letters, and I'm *shit* at letters."

He had tears in his eyes. His neck no longer seemed able to
support his head. His face seemed darker, too. It was partly
sorrow; the way that it can seem visibly to smother you.

"And you're ..."

Grimaldi made an eloquent gesture. His hand went lilting up
and down, encompassing Charles's clothes and the abundance
of his hair.

"Look at you. Was it fair? Was it?"

Charles had been around lodgings and prisons and rookeries
enough to know how dangerous defeat could be. It was like a
fire that had been damped down. One spark would do it.

"I didn't know," he said. "About your son."

He spoke as calmly as you would to someone in an alley. Or to a child. He found that his voice had deepened. He had filled his chest with air and now he was making his voice rock backwards and forwards.

"I didn't, Joe. One hears ... things. I go to theatres. I *like* theatres: I used to want to be an actor. In truth, I still do. You hear stories."

His fingers were flickering in front of him. They seemed to be delicately prevaricating. He had no idea what he was about to say.

"And I embellished them. I am truly sorry. It was only afterwards, after I met you, that I discovered that it was your son. It must have been upsetting."

He was ashamed of the emptiness of the word even as Grimaldi had pushed his glass off the table. He had the sensation that the beer was burning him in some way. Grimaldi was shouting "Liar!" and now his hands were at his shoulders. Charles thought, for a moment, that he was about to strangle him but, looking in his eyes, he saw what he should have noticed earlier: a kind of fear.

"You rub his nose in it, and then you rub *my* nose in it. You turn up all fucking spruce and you sit here and ... what? What are you doing? Tell me!"

He was shaking him. Charles's teeth were rattling. There was a swift blurring by his right side and he tried to throw himself away from it. He thought: a knife. His whole body seemed to flare upwards at him, like an elephant's trunk. All he could see was the impasto of Grimaldi's face; the reds and blacks and whites that were, this close, so similar to the way his face had been painted in the past. He considered using his own glass on him. He could do it, he thought: could employ enough violence to make the difference.

But then he heard Sarah's voice.

"Alright. Joey. Off. Come on. Don't soil the cloth, mate. He's only just bought it."

She had placed a hand on Grimaldi's shoulder, and once again it looked like he was a marionette. His body juddered to a halt, but it seemed to do it in stages. His hands were the last things to understand what was expected of them. Charles felt them lose weight and heft before Grimaldi decided to lift them up. Grimaldi's eyes had retreated into their sockets. His face had become slack. He was looking down at his lap like he'd soiled himself. Only his breathing was passionate. It seemed to lift him off his chair and place him down again. Sarah was saying, "What did you do?"

She had rolled her sleeves up to the elbows. She had dirt on her arms and she smelt slightly brackish. She had been down in the cellar, Charles divined, but she looked like she had gone much farther down than that. This was Charles's sense of her: that she had returned from far away and that, now, she was bearing news. He looked expectantly up at her.

"Nothing," he said.

Grimaldi raised his head. He gave him a look that was so cynical that it would have brought down the house. But Charles saw that there was no more violence in him; that he had no stomach for it. He sat there like a dog that had been told it wasn't allowed to bite you. All he had left was his incongruous skill at making faces. It was working, too. He was communicating his superiority so convincingly that Sarah now assumed that Charles was lying.

"Alright," she said. "'op it."

"But—"

"Fuck off. Go on."

Grimaldi shook his head. He placed one hand on Sarah's arm. Amazing how gently he managed to do it. It was just like the last ten minutes hadn't happened. His hands were talking to her, and she was looking down at them. She was listening to them.

"I want to hear him," he said.

He was rubbing at his nose again. He was squaring up, but it was more a way of settling back inside himself than of attempting to appear to be intimidating. His lower half was useless. He had to assert the autonomy of his upper half to gain his own self-respect.

"Go on," he said.

He patted Sarah's arm.

"He knows what I want. No gammon. Let him."

Charles was uncomfortable, and he realised that it was partly because Grimaldi was no longer performing anything. This, in turn, was like an imperative. Because now he was expected to extend the courtesy. Briefly, he looked out of the window. The late-evening sun told its own kind of truth: it scraped away the everyday until you saw the way that nature, even here, burned fiercely with its own fire. He was gentling his hair, he realised. He had left a pause. There was still a part of him that knew that a pause was an excellent thing to leave. What was he about to say?

"I didn't know."

Grimaldi made a noise that sounded like the noise a horse makes when it refuses to take a jump. Charles showed him his opened palm.

"About here. About you."

Another pause. But this was like the pause you took when you were waiting for a fire to light. He found that he was telling the truth, but he didn't know if the truth was going to illuminate anything. He was, he knew, helplessly articulate. He had to wait for the gift to flare outwards, seemingly of its own accord.

"I walk endlessly," he said. "I can't seem to do anything else. I write. As you can see."

He was surprised, all over again, by the note of pride that he could hear when he began talking about his writing. He shrugged, mock-helplessly, diminishing the trade that he knew must look like no trade here.

"I sit at the desk and I scrub at the page and there's a point at which I can't sit still. I walk through the night. I've seen everything. Prisons. The Houses of Parliament. They're not so very different. And I found you by accident. You were like an amazing gift. And then."

He gestured towards Sarah. She was studying him. He didn't think she knew what she was listening for, except the false note, like a false coin, that was going to give him away. Her crossed arms pressed down unforgivingly on her breasts. Her face seemed to have been folded inwards. Useless, he knew, to try and make her laugh.

"I followed her home. And nothing happened."

"What do you want? A refund?"

That made Sarah laugh, and Charles felt almost physically rebuffed, like he'd been pushed firmly in the chest.

"No. No. I simply mean … Oh, I don't know. I don't know what I mean. I didn't know. I didn't come here to taunt you. I haven't got a notebook. There is no newspaper in the country, I assure you, to whom I'd want to relate any of this."

"'Whom.' Fucking hell. And my JS? You stumbled upon him, did you? He was just there. On the cobbles. And you tripped over him. Because I keep wondering."

He was looking up at the ceiling as though he could find the answer there.

"What aren't you saying? This is cobblers, all this. You don't just ..."

His hand fluttered upwards and downwards. It was like the handkerchief; like a bird. Sarah placed her hand, again, on Grimaldi's shoulder. The mention of JS hadn't surprised her. They had talked about it, Charles could see. The thing that he had seen in her face was simply the contempt she felt for him.

"Joe. Joey."

She was calling him back. Grimaldi's anger was indistinguishable from anxiety. It was endemic; something that wore and wore away at him. Even a fireplace—a chair leg or a lamppost—could frighten you when you were in this state.

"Gossip," Charles said. "Just green room gossip. And, I swear to you, it wasn't maliciously meant. I forgot. When I saw you. I didn't put two and two together. I was too excited. It was like Christmas, seeing you."

"You forgot."

"Yes."

Grimaldi was shaking his head so rapidly that it looked like someone was shaking it for him. Sarah was minding him in the same way that you'd mind a saucepan, she was looking at Charles and then at Grimaldi anxiously, until Charles did something inspired. He hung his head. It was ridiculously theatrical. He might just as well have got down on his knees. Was he? Penitent? He thought, on balance, that he was. He was only exaggerating something that he could, if he prodded himself, discern inside himself. But of the fact that he was exaggerating there was no doubt. When he looked up, he saw that Sarah was pushing her cheek outwards with her tongue. Grimaldi couldn't see it. Then she mimed "gammon." Grimaldi, though, was rubbing at his own forehead. He was mastering his breathing. He looked at Charles for a long time.

At last he said, "She's right. 'op it."

Sarah was nodding. Charles nodded too. He stood as slowly as he would have done if he had really had to face a snake. He looked, briefly, into Sarah's face but he saw nothing there.

Nevertheless, he stayed. He lingered on the corner, hiding behind a tree. The night was so warm that it pressed, like bedclothes, against his face. He was tempted to take off his waistcoat but it was too much a part of him for him to feel as though he could. Instead, he sat on a wall and tried to look like he was waiting, casually, for someone who knew that he was there. The pub stood obliquely to his right but he was vividly aware of it. He felt it squeezing at his heart and thumping loudly in his head. But it was strangely quiet, too. The voices that he could hear seemed, from where he was sitting, to be lowered conspiratorially. He didn't look at his watch; he was too intent on staring at the door. His legs were tingling. He had a strange floating sensation in his arms. But he waited, deliberately, like a dog waits, with almost no thought in its head apart from food.

At half past eleven he saw a shape emerge. It was oddly lumpen. It seemed to bulge outwards at the front, like a pigeon. It had two heads. He realised that Sarah was carrying Grimaldi. She did it almost casually: there was no staggering or swaying from side to side. They were both laughing.

Grimaldi was saying, "Mind the togs."

"Come off it, Joe. They're hardly togs any more, are they?"

"I'll have you know that these were once the height of fashion."

"Oh do please fucking shut up."

Charles didn't know what to do. Announce himself? He thought, on balance, that he'd rather not. He kept parallel to them, and it wasn't long before they ended up at a doorway on the other side of the road. It wasn't quite dingy. It was respectable but slightly down-at-heel. Sarah didn't bother with a key: she kicked the door open and then walked, with her sailor's roll, into the hall. He saw their shadow, one misshapen thing, and then she lit a candle. The two of them, her and Grimaldi, billowed over the walls. It looked like they were dancing. Or simply revolving. She all-but-threw Grimaldi over her shoulder and Charles could hear him cursing and gasping for air. He appeared to be drowning in the great wave of inky black that had engulfed the room. Sarah was administering something and Charles found, with exasperation, that he was aroused again. It was her effortless pragmatism; the way that she appeared just to be doing something. His wife had a look almost of pained surprise whenever she took something out of the oven. She hadn't prepared it, of course. But she liked to give the impression that it was a gift; something that she had laboured over just for him. Charles expected to be ministered to like this but it was about as erotic as watching a wool puppet. Sarah had agency. It was enlivening.

Grimaldi slipped further down into the sofa. He was already asleep. The shadow was like one enormous wing. It was either protective or threatening, you couldn't tell. It was like something out of a dream, but then so was Grimaldi. Sarah wasted no time on watching him. She doused the candle and barrelled out, barely stopping to close the door behind her. Charles didn't bother to try to hide. He couldn't have even if he'd wanted to;

he just stood there firmly planted in her path. He had, he found, almost no control over his face. She stopped, and for a moment he thought that she looked scared. But then he realised that she was amused. Her face was taut with the desire to make a joke.

"Oh Christ."

"I—"

"Couldn't resist. I know. I'm like Asprey's."

She was brushing repeatedly downwards at her skirt. It was a nervous gesture, and he felt something more dangerous than arousal: a sudden uprush of sympathy. No. More. Of identification. She was still talking. Her face belied her action. It was brusquely, and humorously, dismissive.

"Only you're just a window shopper, aren't you, Charley?"

He didn't know what to say. She took a step towards him.

"Sam Weller this. Sam Weller that. You're cutting quite a figure."

She seemed to thrust her face into his own, but it was just the quality of her eyes: their bold, affronted resolve.

"You're a personage, Charley."

"I know."

"You do, do you?"

She had folded her arms.

"See, I'd say that, when it boils down to it, you don't know anything."

"I don't?"

"You don't."

"What don't I know?"

His stomach was churning somewhere far below him. There was something fluttering in his ears. He had the strangest feeling that she could tell all this. He would have touched her if he'd have the nerve. She smiled. Her teeth flickered briefly, once, just like a knife.

"Do you really want me to show you?"

He found that, yes, he did. He tried to nod but she had already taken his hand and was leading him back the way they'd come, into the dark.

CHAPTER SIX

CATHERINE'S HAND WAS halfway to the marmalade jar when Charles shouted, "Stop!" She let it hang there, absurdly, while she waited for what was going to happen. Charles was both looking and not looking at her. He appeared to be staring at her shoulder. His eyebrows had made furrows over his nose. He looked, whenever he became like this, just like a child. Mary said that, once, she had wanted to give him the sugar tongs to rattle with. Catherine had snorted with laughter but had then had to gather herself and express a certain amount of guarded sympathy. Charles worked terribly hard. He had a family to support. Etc., etc. The family was notional so far but even so. Besides, neither she nor Mary would have dared to actually do it. One felt buffeted; one felt aggrieved. But the best one could manage was a look that was both quizzical and obliging.

"Am I not," he said, "to be master in my own home."

He had banged the table on that "not." Mary was looking at him quizzically.

"Why, Charles," she said. "Whatever can you mean?"

Charles was attempting to control his breathing. He was looking down at the table now, his hair trickling along his chin.

"I mean ..."

He didn't know what he meant. It couldn't, surely, have been the marmalade. Had he wanted Catherine to wait? She knew that it was better not to ask. He would moderate his tone because of Mary's presence. She was grateful that she was there, but it was also infuriating. She hated not being able to ask him what the matter was. Mary could, partly because she wasn't implicated thoroughly enough in Charles's domesticity. Charles applied the same discipline to his comfort as he applied to everything else, but Mary wasn't expected to provide it. What she provided was different: verbal, playful, almost flirtatious. Catherine held on to that "almost" in the same way that Charles would have held on to the sugar tongs. The best she could manage now was a tone of voice that took Mary's surprise as a starting point but then displayed, as it were, its familiarity with deeper waters. It was a mixture of incomprehension and concern and then, below or above that, an *all-encompassing* concern—it was (it was expected to be) almost motherly—that showed the distance between a wife and a sister-in-law. In this ameliorative weakness lay her strength, she knew, but even as she said "Charles" she couldn't help but feel that she was at a disadvantage not only with Charles but with the two of them. Charles required earnestness. He needed you to cosset him in the same way that you might carry a boiled egg. But he didn't enjoy it.

Now he was studying the table. He shook his head, once, and his hair shivered in sympathy.

"I'm sorry," he said. "That was ..."

His hands moved inwards and outwards.

"... otiose."

He grinned, and Mary laughed. Word games. This was enough for Mary. In any case, it was largely for Mary's benefit. Now he had made himself look at her own face. It was, she knew, as round and boiled-looking as a pudding. Her cheeks flared pointlessly at the slightest provocation. She wished, sometimes, that she could scrub away at her cheeks until they had more definition. This was the effect he had on you.

"The table," he was saying. "Good Lord, woman. Why are the cruets over *there?*"

He couldn't reach the salt. Just that. She tried to smile.

"Oh *Charles.*"

"Look," she was saying to her sister. "Listen." Her "Charles" could only be forgiving because it acknowledged the things that made forgiveness necessary. His behaviour was excessive. This is what she was saying. But she was also saying that she understood him. But not, she knew, in the way that he always wanted to be understood. Now he was rubbing at his eyes. He made an extraordinary gesture, waving both hands above his head, palms outwards, like a comedian. But the intention wasn't humorous.

"Cruets," he said. "Good God."

Mary was looking at him and smiling.

"It could be worse," she said.

It struck Catherine, not for the first time, that Mary's Charles was much nicer than her own. She was so eager to be seen to understand that she encouraged him. Charles, the Charles that Charles wished to be, was safe in Mary's hands. They juggled his temper between them like a hot potato. Catherine sometimes wondered how much of this was deliberate. It was galling, the way that the two of them had their tongues pressed humorously against their upper lips.

"Imagine," Mary said, "if there was only one. Can you *have* one cruet?"

And they were off. Even Mary's breasts were jiggling cheerfully. Catherine wanted to slap her. But she also wanted to thank her. And to warn her. Marriage wasn't like this. Whatever this was. Harmless, she told herself. Carefully, she took the salt and pepper and placed them next to Charles's arm. She did this without saying a word and then stood up. She wasn't quite sure why. Self-abnegation, she supposed. The desire to be seen to be the thing he wanted her to be. Help-meet; lapdog. She clumped angrily over to the window. She pretended to look out, allowing the heat in her cheeks to calm to a slight glow. There was some comfort to be found in stroking the curtains; in reminding herself of the way that the flat seemed so necessary to both of them. She was aware of the silence and of the way that they must both be looking at her.

"The maid," she said. "Across the way. No cap. And three buttons undone. I should have thought."

And she burst into tears. Ridiculous, she knew, even as she collapsed onto a seat. She was nobody for a second: an expression of grief; no more. But grief for what? She couldn't have told you. She felt Mary's hand on her own, and Charles's cool palm against her forehead. So typical of Charles, she found herself thinking, to take charge. It was, partly, his way of showing affection. Mary was saying "tush, dear" and patting her hand and she was annoyed to realise that this—all of this—was what she needed. If they had been alone, Charles would have called her "titmouse." He would have cradled her head. Mary might have placed her head on her shoulder. Or else she might have ruffled her hair. She was the only person who had ever done it. All of this was implied in what they were doing now.

"I am not ..."

She was attempting to sit upright.

"Shhh. Sister, shush."

Mary was squeezing her hand. She was communicating her own strength. Attempting to infuse it, she supposed. She felt gratitude and resentment in equal measure. What she had been attempting to say was that this wasn't her. Although, perhaps, it was. Charles was so protean: a firecracker held in the hand; a sullen weight; a hilarious entertainment. Sometimes she longed for simpler pleasures. She would have liked to have had a husband who just sat down. But, no, it wasn't that. It wasn't this: the three of them. She loved her sister. What she had felt was more like being at the beach when a wave forced you onto the sand. She looked at Charles, whose face had assumed the distance of the family doctor. He had moved his hand to her stomach. She wanted to laugh. He had arranged his face not so much to pretend concern as to communicate it without ambiguity. To embed it.

"And when did you last ...?"

He didn't know how to say it, but, of course, he didn't have to. It had been on their minds for weeks. It was irritating, the assumption that this was purely physiological. But it was also thrilling.

"Charles. Not for—"

She counted on her fingers. She placed her hand, protectively, on her own stomach. It wasn't larger, of course, but her hand so wanted to find something that the skin felt tauter. There was a confused notion in her mind that, what with it being stretched so thinly, it was quite natural that she had burst into tears. She accepted Mary's ministrations with the dull, pleasant languor of someone who was entitled to them. Charles, meanwhile, was pacing up and down. "Oh Lor," he kept saying. "Oh Lor." He looked like he looked when he was writing one of his novels. He had to do this: to apprehend a thing by imagining it thoroughly. Mary was clutching at her hand.

"This is—"

"This is premature, Mary dear."

Catherine eased herself upwards, already carrying her body as though it was both heavy and preternaturally light.

"And the two of you must wait."

She looked meaningfully at Charles.

"You must wait."

But he must plan. He *must* be active. She consented to allow him out of the house, to look for ... something. She didn't know what. Neither did he. Mary accompanied him. She wanted her to. She wanted to be alone with the sense that she was taking up space in a different way. The idea of a child was inhabiting her in almost the same way that an actual child would. She didn't know whether to stand or sit; both, she realised, were going to become more complicated. Holding onto the window frame, she stood and watched Mary and Charles support each other down the street. Mary was clutching his arm, and laughing, but she found that she was able to watch this with a new equanimity. She was carrying a new life. It was her trump card.

***

Mary was clutching his arm and laughing. Charles felt several things at once. He wished that she wouldn't press her breasts against him. They were different to Catherine's. Not in their size, he felt (he had been *most* careful not to check), but in the careless way she handled them. Catherine would never press herself against you. Even in the dark, there was a moment of reluctance before she tilted them towards him. They were her secret, still, rather than theirs. Mary, in all innocence, would forget that there was meant to be a space between you. Her innocence was touching. You didn't want to draw her attention to it, but Charles could feel himself recoil under the necessary stillness of his skin. It wasn't appropriate. He felt this most strongly, even as her warmth seemed to be thawing something that he didn't know was frozen.

Because, of course, there was also the delight that she always engendered in him. A lightness, far removed from the careful manoeuvring of his marriage. She would pull him away from hansom cabs; would literally yank him, which made it feel like walking around London was a game. It was a would-be-perilous adventure, like teetering along a sofa and pretending there was a drop beneath. London felt sillier. Friendlier. You noticed different shops, and you noticed them in a different way. Fish, gleaming like mirrors. Their silly pompous faces. The eagerness of dogs. The mud, as slippery as a skating rink. He called her "sister" more often than he needed to, but it was partly this that caused it: the shared vision of two people who were reluctant to be anything but children.

Which in turn engendered a feeling of protectiveness that was so unmixed that it felt, sometimes, like a blow. How could you go about the world so extraordinarily unprotected? Catherine was clumsy; her wrists and arms were muddy with bruises. But she seemed, paradoxically, to be always careful. She approached the oven almost at a crouch. Mary was as elegant and lissom as a candle's flame but she was also as unselfconscious as a puppy. Once, to draw his attention to something, she had banged on a window; he had had to drag her away. She seemed to welcome everything. Yesterday, she had bent down to look at a flower by the roadside. Sunlight was making a river between one side of the road and the next and, when she stood up, she appeared to have gathered it, all of it, in her arms.

Oh, she was such a pleasure. She embraced life in the way that he did when he was at his best. She laughed like a man would: unselfconsciously. Catherine was always nagging her about her stays, which she refused to tie as tightly as she should. She was impulsive, true, but she was also his angel; his better, purer spirit. He didn't want to think of her as a woman. She was his ideal, rather. And she understood his work. Just now, her fingers were pressing his upper arm.

"But what does he *do?*"

"What do you mean what does he do?"

"He can't just *be.*"

"No, that's the point. He can."

"What? Be a Boots? How will that work? Will the story always have shoes?"

Charles laughed. He could feel the drag of his hair and saw, with a sudden lift of pleasure, the way that he must look. Glossy, almost, like a pampered animal.

"He's a *character*, Mary."

"Don't tell me that you're just going to trot him out."

"Yes. Well. That's the general idea."

"Isn't that—"

"What?"

Her nose was slightly ponderous. She had a habit, when she was thinking, of staring down it like it was a plumb line. Your heart went out to her. She was reluctant to hurt his feelings but she was also reluctant to spare them. It made her face look costive. Furtive, almost, although what you responded to was the way that her furtiveness was making her uncomfortable. She appeared to be holding it out for you to examine.

"Um. Self-defeating?"

"Good Lord. What do you mean?"

"Don't do that, Charles. Don't rear up like that."

Her fingers pressed his arm. Her breasts, he knew, the way they were squeezed against his jacket, were a profession of innocence.

"I'm not."

"You *are*."

She laughed.

"But Weller brings such life to things. You don't want to simply dangle him there, do you?"

"And what do you propose I do with him?"

"Do? Oh."

Her eyes went roaming over the house fronts. She was considering it. She had, as it were, sifted the irony and had chosen to address what he had asked her properly. She shrugged. It was charming; the kind of movement you might make if you were dancing.

"Love, probably. A marriage. He mustn't die."

She was rapidly shaking her head. Catherine might have detected something mannered in this gesture; something knowingly childlike.

"Death's a horrible way to end a novel."

"And love?"

"Love's what we all expect, Charley. You mustn't cheat us out of that."

She smiled and went dancing down the street. Her dress went billowing around her. Charles watched her somewhat ruefully. He felt like he had been bested in an argument but he didn't know how. Indulgently, he waited until the wind appeared to blow her back. He looked at her with affectionate irony.

"And a child?"

"Of *course* a child."

She began to move his arm, rapidly, up and down. He could see himself—could literally see himself—as a water pump. It was an image of beneficence that he felt suited to. Your humble author. The man who dispenses something like largesse.

Something necessary and life-affirming. He only needed to half-attend to Mary while she told him how very pleased she was. He felt something that he often felt: an emotional cross-current. He had provided his wife with a baby, and this had provided his sister-in-law with obvious delight. But how did he feel? How was it going to affect him? He was aware that his mouth had turned resolutely downwards. Mary squeezed his arm.

"Don't sigh."

"I'm not."

"A writer needs a child."

"Does he?"

"Of course! How will you *know* otherwise? You can't stay an emotional Boots all your life."

"That doesn't even make sense!"

"It does, too."

She stood and surveyed him. Her hands were on her hips and, for a moment, it was like an image in reverse: Sarah, but drained of all her knowledge and abilities.

"A man needs ballast. You do. You're like ..." She appeared to be straining, physically. She wanted so very much to produce a simile. "An untethered balloon. There are weeks when you're away and I wonder if you're going to come back. I half-imagine that you're off to be a pirate."

"Dear Mary."

He sketched a gesture which would, in other circumstances, have ended with him stroking a woman's cheek, or hair.

"I will always come back."

"You will now." She grinned. What had she guessed? It was like being presented with a trapdoor. He looked carefully into her eyes. Nothing. Her innocence was as visible as the sun behind her on the window pane.

"Come on," he said. "A crib!"

"A crib!"

He led her forth. They were like children playing at soldiers. He sneaked a quick look, sideways, and wished ... He didn't know what for. To be somebody else. But that, as far as wishes went, was as familiar to him as breathing.

CHAPTER SEVEN

IT WAS LIKE rowing. The more you exerted yourself the quicker and further you seemed to go. This had not been his previous experience. There was something ungentlemanly in expecting a woman to approach a crisis; it presumed a level of feeling that she might not be willing to express. The best one might expect was an acknowledgement of something stirring, gently, within her: the slow lowering of eyelids, say, or a slight tightening of the hand. Prostitutes knew this, and some would seem to commune quietly with themselves but to do so obviously. They would squeeze their eyelids shut or allow their hands to grab the side of the bed. They were perfectly aware that you didn't want to feel as though you were swimming against the current.

Sarah swore. She gulped in air. She held onto his shoulders as though she was about to drown. She also took a frank enjoyment in his body. He had always ignored it. It was his mind that needed tending: if he was tired or out of sorts he would force his body out onto the streets until his mind had settled down. Now he watched with a mixture of tenderness and curiosity as Sarah's head descended into his groin. She attended to everything and gave it sentient life. His body seemed to rise up in its entirety, like a loaf of bread.

Afterwards, Sarah studied him. She wouldn't do what Catherine did; wouldn't wait, expectantly, for the show of affection that she felt she was now entitled to. Had she done well? That was what Catherine's look implied. Did he love her? Had she given him pleasure? Sarah was much more conscious of her own. She looked at him like they had robbed a bank together.

"You flinched."

"I did?"

"Just at the start. You were scared."

"I was."

He looked up at the ceiling. There was a stain that reached from one side of it to the other. He might, under normal circumstances, have tried to find an analogy for it but he found that he wanted to leave it as it was. He shrugged.

"I always am."

"Of me?"

"Of this."

His hand went wavering over the blanket. It was thin—it was barely a blanket at all—but it was clean. It wasn't sticky to the touch. He didn't, when he was with Sarah, want to go home and bathe immediately afterwards. He was quite happy to lie here and to allow the conversation to drift sideways.

"Pleasure," he said.

She nodded.

"I guessed. The first time."

She laughed.

"You didn't know what to do with yourself."

Gently, proprietorially, she cupped his testicles.

"Poor Mrs. Charley. Gets a thimble-full, does she?"

Charles attempted to sit up. He went to speak but she placed a finger on his lips.

"Alright. Alright. I'm sorry. No Mrs. Charley."

Something passed, briefly, across her face. It was like a door that had opened and closed so rapidly that all you were aware of was the blur of it in motion.

"Watch me," she said.

She rolled out of the covers. She gave you the impression that this, the bed, was her element; that she was so familiar with it that she could use it like a tumbler might a trampoline. Her breasts were beautiful but they were as compromised by gravity as his own hair or his father's arse. This seemed to him to be unfair. He wanted them to float, like soap bubbles. He had developed tender feelings for them: he felt an urge to hold them up for her.

And, of course, she was entirely unselfconscious. Charles wanted to approve of this. He saw it as exemplary. But he also wanted to close the curtains. She was facing him, now, in the same way that she hoped later to face an audience. The first time she had done this Charles had said, "Imagine Mrs. Siddons."

But she didn't know who Mrs. Siddons was. His laughter had offended her. It was the terribly serious way she stood there and the way her arms went grappling outwards. Charles had learned to take, or to seem to take, this seriously. Now she was saying,

"Art thou afeard
To be the same in thine own act and valour
As thou art in desire? Wouldst thou have that
Which thou esteem'st the ornament of life,
And live a coward in thine own esteem,
Letting 'I dare not' wait upon 'I would'
Like the poor cat i' th' adage?"

Not saying. Declaiming. She had such a tight grip on herself that Charles was almost frightened for her. She was in a fury of concentration. At first, he had assumed that this had something to do with trying to remember what she was saying. But she had recited this whole speech at least five times, word perfect, and he realised that the way she spoke the words—the slow dropping of them, as from a roof—was how she thought she should speak them. Did she understand them? He didn't want to ask.

"Sarah," he said, "try breathing more slowly."

"What do you mean?"

"Like this."

He placed a hand on his chest and attempted to communicate relaxation.

"You're saying everything through gritted teeth."

"Wouldn't you? She wants 'im to murder the king, not go to the bleeding shops."

"No. But when I—"

"When you what?"

"When I act."

"What do you mean when you act?"

"When I act. I do. I act."

Her hands were resting on her thighs. She looked at him suspiciously.

"You never said."

"No. Well. I didn't—"

"Fucking hell, Charley. Not one word."

Charles was newly aware, as he shrugged helplessly, that he was naked. There were times when their situation would become apparent all over again. It was generally when one of them got out of bed. Then the size—the *brevity*—of her room came home to him. He noticed, once again, the way that her table tilted drunkenly. The shard of mirror on the mantelpiece. There were times when it was like a jaded eye.

"I didn't want to bring my home life here. It felt disrespectful. To you."

"Of course. To me."

She rolled her eyes and then she paused. This was something that Charles loved about her: the way that she sometimes seemed to think with her whole body. What she was, *prima facie*, was an actress, even if she couldn't act.

"What do you mean your home life?"

"That's where I act."

"At home?" She laughed. "Of course you do. And this is the whole family, is it? All tripping up over the furniture and going arse over tit on the linoleum."

She reminded him of Joe. The second syllable of the last word had been extended so that the whole word seemed ridiculous. He found that he was actually hanging his head.

"Most of them."

"Coo. You're priceless, Charley. You're like …"

But then she ground to a halt. She looked sideways, out of the window. She seemed to be studying another, invisible self—the part of her that would have liked to pummel him with her fists—in order to calm it down. Eventually, she said,

"I dunno."

She sat on the bed. She had managed to look both combative and defeated.

"I dunno what you're like."

She had leaned over and was thumbing his hair away from his forehead. At the same time, she was studying his clothes: his waistcoat, perched there like a tired bird of paradise, and his immaculate trousers.

"You're like one of your own illustrations."

He threw her on the bed. Because he wasn't. He was flesh and blood. Imagine Augustus Minns with an erection. Imagine him with this ... creature wriggling on top of him. Afterwards, he watched her face as it appeared to make its way back to him. There was a moment when she seemed, suddenly, to see him; when her gaze encompassed him in a way that felt almost like love. Charles didn't know what to feel about this. He welcomed it. Provisionally. It was all provisional.

"'Dwell I,'" she said, "but in the suburbs of your good pleasure?'"

Before he could express his surprise, she grinned.

"You'll come?"

He nodded.

"If I can."

But he knew that he would. He was frightened for her, and for himself: he was scared that he might be disappointed in her. He almost wanted to be. It would simplify matters.

Not that he acknowledged that they were complicated. It was a bright day in July, the heat like the back of a heated spoon upon one's arm. He walked home in the early afternoon, beside the Thames. The sun appeared to be hitting sparks out of the surface of the water. If he could have put it into words he would have told you how he identified with it; how he admired the muscular way it dominated its surroundings. Because, of course, it wasn't part of them. This, it seemed, was how he had always lived.

Sarah was necessary. He nodded, once. The word took care of everything. One's wife should not be troubled by one's grosser needs. And if, indeed, one felt a certain fondness for the provider of those needs, then all to the good. His romantic feelings for his wife were not reduced; were amplified, in fact, by one's having placed her so firmly in that category. Meanwhile, what happened between himself and Sarah was not, strictly, a transaction. It was a form of succour. He found that he was grinning. If he had been the kind of man who talked about this sort of thing, he would have come down on the first syllable in the same way that Grimaldi would no doubt have done. He was still thinking about Grimaldi, about the way that his charisma seemed to float free of the man himself, when he rounded a corner and found his father at the door.

He nearly turned around. Instead, he tried to make himself look taller. His father's father. Approaching with a show of openness, he took his hand. His father placed his free hand over Charles's in an attempted blessing.

"My boy."

He had contrived to look as respectable as possible. One had to look carefully to see the places at the elbow where the jacket was attempting to give up the ghost. His hair was carefully pomaded, and his stomach tugged against his waistcoat. He looked like Charles, but Charles preserved in aspic. Charles *in potentia*. The thought made Charles shudder.

He said, "I trust that everything is in order."

It sounded more formal than he had intended. More disapproving, too. He peered at his father with what he hoped looked like concern. He was also keeping a careful distance. His father brushed, unnecessarily, at his hat. It was a familiar pose: he was standing, hat in hand, in what was essentially supplication. But he never allowed himself to seem humble in any way. Even his teeth appeared to announce themselves.

"I have," he said, "been for—"

"A perambulation?"

Charles hadn't been able to resist.

"Quite so."

Did he know, his father, that he was being ridiculed? His eyes were as opaque as the black buttons on his jacket. His smile buttressed his face. Charles was, as always, both exasperated and impressed. Affection was struggling feebly against the need to have this done with as quickly as possible. Ambivalence: it was his birthright. He led his father in and straight into the drawing room. He took him to the desk, unlocked it and produced a five-pound note.

His father was saying, "It is hard, Charles, to be deprived of all of the concomitant advantages."

But he wasn't listening. He could, out of habit, nod in all the right places but he also said, "Father, I have to work."

He steered him downstairs; he all-but-pushed him. He could hear Catherine say "Charles?" and he ignored that too. There was too much to be done. He left his father by the open door like this was a perfectly reasonable thing to do. Absently, he patted him on the shoulder but then he ran upstairs. Newspaper articles; sketches; Pickwick; an operetta. A way of thrusting forward, yes. And of keeping the wolf from the door. He was not—he found himself thinking this most emphatically—his father. He bent over the paper on his desk. He should have written in the morning but had, instead, taken what he had called, mock-jovially, "a constitutional" all the way to Sarah's house. Now his tongue was pressing eagerly against his upper lip. He wrote.

"There is no month in the whole year in which nature wears a more beautiful appearance than in the month of August. Spring has many beauties, and May is a fresh and blooming month, but the charms of this time of year are enhanced by their contrast with the winter season."

His hand was travelling across the page so smoothly that it was hardly as if he was writing at all. The next issue was going

to appear in August. Tying it in so closely with the seasons
gave him the same sense of satisfaction as if he was tying his
shoelaces or knotting a cravat. But there was ambivalence, too,
in the way that he was escaping to a place that was entirely
fictional while his wife was downstairs beating at a rug. In the
way that the drawing room felt like a refuge and a prison. In the
way that he looked at Mary's bonnet; in the way that his pleasure in her was not, could not, be unalloyed. He must be rueful;
fond, reluctant and constrained. And Sarah? He found that he
couldn't settle. That he was pacing up and down. Never to feel
one thing; never to be at rest. He was bounding down the stairs,
but there were his wife and father, talking snugly at the door.
He felt a repulsion that almost shocked him. Nevertheless, he
said, "My dear."

"Charles. Look."

He wasn't sure what it was that he was meant to be looking
at. His father had the same half-sorrowful, half-hopeful expression of a spaniel that had been kicked. Charles felt guilty but he
also felt the desire to do it again, harder this time. His father's
hand was rubbing at his stomach.

"Half a stone," he said.

"Ah."

Charles nodded encouragingly.

"Abstinence does you good."

"Enforced abstinence, Charles. Enforced. A man's spirit
dwindles at such a time; not just his—"

"Paunch," Charles said.

"Yes. Well. If you must."

Catherine looked at him disapprovingly. Or, at least, as disapprovingly as she could bear to. Her chin had tightened slightly.
Her eyes had looked swiftly into his own then lowered bashfully.

She had—he told himself she had—an exquisitely pretty face. Even when it was flushed it wasn't flushed in the same way that Sarah's was. The colour was like a glaze.

"Your father is after a position."

"A position."

Charles looked steadily into his father's eyes.

"What sort of position?"

His father avoided his eyes. He looked off into the middle distance like he was considering the question. His foot was flirting with the scraper but he still took each breath like he was asserting his right to take it.

"It would need—"

"Need."

"Yes. It would need to be sufficiently remunerative. Your mother ..."

He appeared to be holding something in his hands. An invisible weight; something like a person or a dead animal. He tilted his head to one side. Charles shook his own head, rapidly, like he was freeing it from something: responsibility. Already his father was sliding from the doorstep onto the street. He patted Charles on the shoulder.

"Take your time, my boy."

If you watched him closely, you could see how deliberately he sauntered. It was really a pronounced awkwardness, but it had been slowed down until he looked almost relaxed. Charles wanted to throw something at his back. He thumped his own forehead, and, yes, true, he was displaying himself doing this—it was meant, partly, to be funny—but it was also genuine frustration that caused him to do it.

Catherine said, "You are—"

"I am a fool."

"His son."

"What he *needs*, Kate, is to pay sufficient attention to the relationship between his, um, remuneration and his outgoings. I have nearly been to jail."

"That is an exaggeration."

"You think so?"

"I do."

"I held surety for his debts."

"Which you were perfectly capable of paying off."

"Yes, with a Herculean effort. I have contracted a fever; had rheumatism of the face."

"Charles."

"I will *not—*"

"Charles."

She placed her hand on his arm. For a moment, it was like a poultice. He might have allowed himself to settle into her ministrations in the same way that one settled into a hot bath. When he did this, he liked to give the impression that it was for her. Today, he would not give her the satisfaction. The calm and knowing softness of her hand was too much a part of everything else. It represented the weight of home and of his professional responsibilities and his feelings, too, which refused to settle anywhere. Was there nothing that he did not have to carry? Nothing that did not have to be prodded and weighed or at least loved and found wanting, continually, so that he always felt like a bird that was flying and alighting; flying and alighting. Again, he shook his head. He did a strange thing with one hand; a gesture of blessing that was as useless as his father's. Then he was off.

He was out on the streets again, attempting to soak up London just as though he was what he claimed to be: a recording instrument. He had never abandoned his work before. He made the best of it, watching the cabs as closely as if that was the purpose of his day. Their shabbiness; the way that the drivers cocked their fingers when they greeted one another; all that straw. It did him good. He had written about them and would write about them again. When one came round the corner it felt like he had imagined it into existence. He mingled with the people on the street, pretending to be one of them. It was like being in a diorama: ladies and swells and hawkers and those worn-out, starving, houseless creatures that he had already written so much about. He felt superior to all of them. He felt as though he contained them; he felt, certainly, that he could reproduce them at the drop of a hat.

On the main thoroughfare, horses glowed black and bronze. The shadows of the slums oozed out onto the streets beyond. Not just the shadows: there was refuse everywhere. Even that had its own kind of life. In a shop window, an illustration seemed to be juggling its own colours while, on the street, there were pugilists, rope dancers, children leering at a bowl of fruit. Everything mirrored everything else. Everyone flowered outwards in the sun. He saw, as if for the first time, that people seemed in the continual habit of rubbing themselves against each other. That the slow, languid look of a prostitute was mirrored in the way a lady peered through her lorgnette. That one could perfectly well be going nowhere, just angling on a street corner for whatever one might catch. Had he ever done this? Angled? He didn't think he had. Nevertheless, when he saw people embracing, he felt like he had created them, too. He sketched another blessing, but with considerably more feeling than he had the last one. He nodded gravely, tempted to intone something that was both grave and suitably comic.

By the time he was back in the East End, he had calmed down. At least, he told himself he had. Sarah had said that she was performing in a penny gaff but what he had imagined was what he wished to see: a gin palace or an ornate public house with a room at the back that was big enough for a proper performance. Tonight, as he approached, he saw that its interior was like the bright flaring interior of a gas lamp but that it seemed to become smaller the closer you got to it. It was a shop with, outside, a raucous and aimless crowd. Not everybody was entering; some were simply loitering or smilingly soaking up the atmosphere. The balance of power had shifted. He couldn't entirely remain aloof. He had the uncomfortable feeling that he was part of things. His ... what? His mistress? His lover? Whatever she was, she was performing here. Her reception depended on the auspices of this man, the one who was growlingly tearing at a brick of tobacco. Or the woman who was standing next to him. A feather hung from her hair. She had a mouth that was so vividly red that it was like the stage representation of a wound. She had too many teeth, and Charles felt implicated in them somehow. It was as though they were his; as though he was hers.

It cost, of course, a penny to get in. There was no room to stand. Better to wait at the bottom of the stairs and look up at the queue that was forming for the gallery. There was a stretch of canvas in front of it that functioned as a door. To the left of him, he was aware of a swilling motion—a soup made up of bodies and hats and smoke. There was a smell that was terrific but cheerful, too. A band, squeezed up on a table in the corner, were so tightly packed together that they were almost unable to play. The ceiling had been painted with awkward clouds and what he might have done, if he were trying later to bring it all to life, was concentrate on the cheeriness. It was certainly there: an atmosphere of festive celebration. But he felt too anxious and out of place. There was a palpable savagery in the air. There were knots of boys, all smoking pipes. They observed the crowd with an air of superciliousness that was would-be-threatening. One boy was jingling his change, and each jingle felt like a palpable assertion, like he was prodding you on the shoulder. The queue, meanwhile, seemed to throb with an energy that, he knew, would have to be discharged somewhere. People were clutching fruit. It was an ominous sign.

At last, the crowd from the first show came out. This was in single file, but there was hardly any room and the shoving was done with such gusto that it looked, from where Charles was standing, like a fight. Then there was the fight to get in: boys, mainly, hurling themselves against each other so that they looked like a nest of rats. One leaned over and bit the ear of the boy beside him then scuttled past the woman who was collecting the money, allowing his companion's howl to distract her. Charles found that he had almost entirely lost his sense of humour. As he shuffled his way inside he saw that there were other boys thumping each other out of the way so that they could get to the seats in front. You could half-see the stage through all of the smoke, as well as the whitewashed beams of the old upper floor. The walls of the theatre were made of the barest bricks but the paper of the sitting room upstairs was still on the walls. Two jets of gas were placed on each side of what was meant to be the proscenium and boys were lighting their pipes at it. The gallery had been hastily constructed and you could see the boards bend under the weight of those who were sitting up there. Or not sitting. They were leaning over the edge and cat-calling. Girls were calling back. Charles felt terribly conspicuous. He sat on the edge of a row and polished his hat with brief, rapid and feeble strokes.

He would have loved to have loved what he saw. It was like one of his own sketches. There was an old piano, almost as wide as the stage, that was as decrepit as Sarah's house. This gave it a rueful kind of dignity: it was like an old racehorse, used to being stared at, that had ended up in a stables that was woefully down-at-heel. The man who played it was wearing tails and had such a collection of rings that they seemed to influence his playing; his hands appeared to be forced by the weight of them onto the keys before he was properly ready. He was accompanied by an actor who was so drunk that he swayed from side to side. This seemed to be what the audience expected. They waited for the furthest reaches of his outswing and then threw rotten tomatoes at him. After a while, the backdrop appeared to have been soaked in blood. He stopped singing for a moment and looked queasily back at it. This only encouraged the boys in the audience to redouble their assault.

At one point, the pianist wheeled around and shook his fist, but the stool was too much for him: it whirled him back into the same position and he looked lost for a moment. He stared at the piano like it were somehow at fault. The singer was still singing. He was wafting his hand up and down in front of him. Charles felt the ghost of a laugh but it hung there in his throat. He felt a compassion that was really just the compassion that he was prepared to feel for Sarah later on.

He expected something terrible to happen. As the night progressed, as it seemed to reel drunkenly from one performance to another, he became more and more certain that Sarah would come a cropper. He almost couldn't bear it, although it wasn't only compassion that he was feeling. It was embarrassment, too. She was, from the start, powdered to such an extent that she looked already dead. She was doing a kind of sleep-walk, even in the early scenes. But her instincts as an actress were similar to her instincts as a barmaid: what the performance in her bedroom had left out was how conscious she was that the audience was watching her. She seemed to be presenting her acting as a gift. Each gesture was proffered with an accompanying gap for your response. Once or twice, she almost smiled. She smirked, certainly. Macbeth was a big man. He had huge arms and stranglers' hands. But he had a tiny voice. He hurled it around but, in the end, it was unequal to the task. Hearing it recite Shakespeare was like watching a sparrow thrumming around a three-story house. At first, the audience were willing him on. As was Sarah. Charles was egging him on for Sarah's sake. He knew how seriously she had prepared.

In the end, she started to make faces. To *project* them. You could see her, trying to make herself inconspicuous—or, at least, trying to try to—at the side of the stage, but you could also see her give in to the instinct to give the audience exactly what it wanted. The dagger was invisible. When Macbeth asked if it was there she made a point of peering at him, incredulously. When he had seen the invisible Banquo, she hustled him off like she had just called time. She belaboured him; she did it deliberately. It was, Charles saw, a kind of plea. She was demonstrating that she knew what the audience wanted to do and that she agreed with them. That she was one of them. One or two of them cheered. He wasn't quite disappointed in her. Nor was he embarrassed. She had confirmed something, merely; a difference in temperaments. She was part of the streets. He felt as superior to her as if she had been a rope walker or a pugilist. Afterwards, she clutched his arm.

"I am so furious. I *am*, Charley."

She was still holding on to him. She did it like a wife.

"He ruins everything. We have to kick him into position."

As she mimed a kick, he felt his arm move with her. This Darby and Joan business was making him want to wriggle with discomfort. He couldn't extricate himself. He didn't want to hurt her feelings. She felt it anyway. She stopped and looked at him.

"Too much, is it?"

She pulled out her arm.

"Dead weight, am I?"

"Sarah—"

"Don't 'Sarah' me. I mean it: don't name me, whatever you do. You might have to start thinking of me as a human being."

It would have been better if she had marched off. Instead, she continued to stare at him. To stare into him. Charles felt himself blush.

"I didn't mean—"

"No, of course you didn't."

She wouldn't stop looking at him. She had both hands on her hips, and her chin was jutting forward slightly. Charles felt himself recoiling.

"You're tired," he said.

"Don't patronise me."

"I—"

"Don't." She looked him up and down. "You pompous little poof."

"Oh, this is ridiculous."

It was frustrating, this trying to gather words. They were like recalcitrant wool. And what were his hands supposed to be conducting? He was gesturing as elaborately as his father had. He was wishing himself elsewhere so fervently that he could feel the clenching of his jaw. She was still staring at him.

"Me, you mean. I'm ... what? What am I?"

He stood there uselessly, wishing himself away.

"Trade? A bit of rough? You don't like my teeth. Or is it the noises? Too loud, is that it? Tell me."

He felt like she was advancing towards him. If anything, though, she was holding herself aloof. She had retracted, like a snail. He was aware of a certain amount of tenderness; of wanting to pull her to him and stroke her hair. But, at this precise moment, what she was saying felt like the simple truth. He found himself looking briefly over her shoulder; it felt like his body was preparing to make a run for it.

"I am known."

"You are what?"

"Known. I am known. I can't just—"

Sarah had thrown her head back and now she was laughing up at the sky. It was deliberately provocative. The thought of the vulnerability of her throat went through Charles's mind in the form of an unwanted picture. Now she was looking at him with a mixture of hatred and disgusted pity.

"Listen to yourself. I hate to tell you, Charley, but no one gives a monkey's who you are. Not round my way. You're just my bit of posh. Them."

She pointed back at the theatre.

"They think you're prey."

She levelled her eyes at him.

"*So* small. You don't think, surely, that I see anything in you but the promise of future gifts?"

What was it in her enunciation that was so belittling? Each consonant was so carefully rendered that he felt reduced to something in a pantomime. A sidekick. The speed with which she had decided to attack him seemed to have robbed him of himself. His anger was strangely separate—it was possible to feel unmanned, he realised, and to want to overpower somebody at the same time. He wanted to wrestle her to the ground.

"And you?" he said. "What do you think *you* are?"

He wasn't sure what he was going to do. Not grab her throat, certainly, but grip her arm, perhaps. Shake her. Even as he was taken, seemingly, and whirled out of himself by the feeling of anger, he was aware of the pleasure in it. He lunged across whatever it was that lay between them and grasped her shoulder.

"Listen to me. I am Charles Dickens. I am. I. Am. Known." With each of the last three words, he had squeezed her shoulder a little more tightly. "I have worked and worked and fucking worked to be the man I am. You have no idea. Truly: none. I have sat in a coach and four, covered in mud, and transcribed somebody else's words until I was sick. Literally. I have smiled amenably at more lawyers than you'd care to know in a lifetime. I have *wooed* publishers. I have put my mouth against their ear. Big ravenous beasts, like sea monsters, they are. And right now—at this *precise* moment—my writing is about to lift me up like a balloon. You do not have the imagination to conceive of the vistas that are opening up for me. So I suggest, with the greatest of all possible respect, that you shut—"

"Up?"

She pushed him away as hard as she could. "Shut up? Bedswerver." Contemptuously, she looked down at her breasts. She wiped his spit away. "Besprawler. Come on. Make me." She was looking at him, almost, in triumph. It was a strange, a wild, form of welcome. They held themselves as tautly as if they were about to dance.

"You think I won't?"

"I think you can't."

"You," he said, "are nothing but a cheap, over-inflated fucking—"

And she was on him. She had his head in her hands and was trying to push him onto the pavement. She curled a leg behind his and attempted to topple him over but he bumped his back against the wall and found that he was able to push upwards at her. Her arm went around his neck and her teeth were snapping at his ear. He tried to wrestle free, but she was too strong for him. Her body insisted on itself; on its right to be exactly where it wanted. All he could do was do what she had tried to do to him. He put one leg behind her and pushed her backwards. She went flailing over and he found that he was allowing himself to fall on top of her; that his hands were in her hair and that he had lifted her head upwards, just as though he was going to batter it against the ground. He was snarling, too, he realised. It was only then that he became aware that he had an erection. More: that he was holding her down with his entire body. He both could and couldn't hear the footsteps that were approaching them. A voice said something and Sarah shouted, "Piss off, will you? Can't you see we're busy?"

Charles lifted himself onto his arms and saw the affronted wobble of a retreating back. The man was huge—fat eagerly crowded the space beneath his arms. His arse appeared to be wagging at them in admonishment, and it was this, Charles felt, that was too much for him. He had to roll onto his back and laugh. Laugh, indeed, with such gusto that he was rolling from side to side. Sarah was laughing, too, and now they were both rolling, one over another, because they couldn't seem to help it, snorting and hiccupping and travelling almost by accident into a patch of wasteland at the corner of the road. It was dark here; it smelt of shit. There was a dog somewhere. It added to it, all this: it made it more exciting, true, but it also gave them a context; almost a home. It was like being in the foreground of a painting. Her breath was like thunder in his ear.

"No more suburbs for you, Charley."

Her hand was at his trousers and now her mouth was everywhere. He was tearing at her clothes. The warmth of the night was like sustaining hands. And, really, wasn't nakedness a blessed state? Known; they were known. Bucking, half-naked, free, he held the woman that he loved and found that he was at one with her and with himself and with the pulse that he could always feel beneath the raging tumult of the streets.

CHAPTER EIGHT

THE PAIN BEGAN at three o'clock in the morning. The flat was dark but he had known, as soon as he got into bed, that Catherine was awake. It was in the quality of her stillness; the way that, as he stretched himself carefully along the sheet, she didn't move. He lay staring at the ceiling. He didn't want to think, but it appeared that his body was thinking for him. There it was: that throb. It happened periodically, and, despite his attempts at stoicism, he always dreaded it. Once, in the factory, he had had to lay down in the straw while Bob applied warm crockery to his side. It was, more than anything, the humiliation that he remembered. He had tried, even then, to hold himself aloof. He had attempted to draw himself away but, of course, pain follows you. Then, as now, he ended up writhing and moaning. Twitching. Catherine leaned across and placed her hand on his forehead.

"Charles."

It felt like somebody was wringing his kidneys with both hands, but he could still hear the tenderness in her voice. The pain seemed to answer her. He became conscious of it as a response, somehow, to his predicament: guilt roaming his body like a wolf. But then, as always happened, he merged with it. In the morning, all he could do was hold onto the bed. The pain had receded and left him clinging, half-afloat, to the coverlet.

101

He was too scared to move. Catherine had dressed. It distanced her, a little, but it also made her easier to apprehend. In bed, Charles had been uncomfortably aware of their shared humanity. Now she was taking charge: she was leaning over him and looking carefully into his face. Her eyes were so innocent of implication that he could hardly bear to look at them. Her hand was on his arm, and he was aware, again, of how complicated a procedure this had always been. She was beautiful. No: pretty; she was made beautiful by the gentleness of her glance. It seemed to tug her face along with it, so that, for a moment, it was *all* gentleness. A light suffused it. But there you had it: it was otherworldly. An ideal. She was always—always!—so very trustworthy.

"I believe it has passed," he said.

"Charles. Dear Charles."

She appeared to be tracing his face. Her mouth was held in suspension, like a drop of water. It was difficult to know what expression it was trying to communicate, or perhaps not communicate. It was almost pert. Her dress kept moving stiffly along with her. There was no sense of a body; no heat. She tried again.

"You test your strength too much."

"You know that I have to do it."

"No. I don't. You don't."

Was it unconscious, the way that she was gently rubbing her belly? Either way, it was a reminder: house and home. Charles's own stomach was in a knot.

"Who else will provide for you?"

"You provide enough."

She was stroking his forehead. If Sarah had been doing it, it might have been a prelude to something. Or else an exploration.

But Sarah seemed very distant. What disturbed Charles most was the attentiveness, not just of Catherine but of everything in the room. The chest of drawers; the wainscoting; the washstand, with a towel draped like a napkin over the side. (It seemed, to Charles, to be waiting, just as Beard's hat had been.) The room had a sense of rightness that no other room had ever had. What he was trying to ignore was the feeling that that rightness had a moral dimension. It demanded something from him. That boy, the one writhing in the straw, could only have dreamt of all of this. He was so sensitive. So ambitious. If he could have looked in the window now it would have seemed to him that Catherine was ministering to him, like an angel. He would have dreamed of being here and he would have bound himself to all sorts of promises in order, one day, to live up to it. Charles felt like he was about to cry. He took his wife's hand in his own.

"My dear sweet Catherine. What must I do?"

"Take a holiday, Charles."

"A holiday."

"Charley. Your face."

"I have so much to do."

"I don't propose you stop entirely."

She was winding and unwinding his hair around her fingers. It was a child's game, done knowingly.

"Where do you propose we go?"

She smiled. "Why don't you choose?"

She was still tugging at his hair. For a moment, he longed for Sarah. It was like a gust of wind: if he had let it, it would have thrown him out of the room. But then it was gone. His wife was all tentative, mellifluous persuasion. All sweetness. And, suddenly, he was scared. Catherine's touch; her smile; the innocent ruddiness of her cheeks; the sun coming through the window and lighting up the rug so that it seemed about to speak, or sing; the geranium on the windowsill. To risk all this ... No, last night's pain had been a purge. A door. He stroked his wife's cheek. There was a kind of serenity not only in the motion but in the cheek itself. It was so smooth. Sarah's was like a nutmeg grater.

So they ended up in Petersham, in the Dysart Arms. It was almost the country. The inn was sympathetic; all nooks and sudden corners, like Charles's imagination. Their room was light and airy. Upon the high fourposter bed, he tried, all over again, to love his wife. It was like coaxing a flower to open, because, of course, they never fully did. There was the same tranced fascination, true, but there was also the sense that she was trying to accommodate herself to him. She was awkward about the baby and there soon grew a tacit understanding that it was probably best if they simply lay there, making plans. Once, Charles had looked down at his groin. He had looked carefully into Catherine's face but she had seemed to misunderstand; had placed the cover over him to prevent him from being embarrassed.

Most days, they walked slowly through the meadows. Her arm was looped through his. The first time, she had said "Darby and Joan" and he had nodded and smiled. She was awkward (she was always awkward) and there were times when he saw the child as a counter-balancing weight; the kind that you find inside a toy and that makes it move in ways you wouldn't expect. Gravity was difficult for Catherine at the best of times but now she seemed to live in an element that wasn't, strictly, part of the world around her. Charles was touched by this, just as he was touched by the way her finger seemed to be swelling around her wedding ring. She had a new seriousness—she seemed to be listening to something that Charles wasn't able to hear and he found that he was jealous. When she smiled at his jokes he felt as though *he* was the child.

He swam. He woke up at six and marched down to the Thames. The light was pearlescent; the trees and greenery prelapsarian. There was a moment, as it were, of innocence and then, when you plunged in, it was all effort. Charles went decisively from one bank to the other. When he came out, he felt briefly shorn of something, but then his life would reassert itself. Pickwick; sketches; the play. An immense restlessness would come upon him and he would have to walk or run or march back to his room and write.

Now he was back in London. He leaned back in his chair.

"I am incorrigible."

"You say this with some satisfaction."

Beard was smiling. But he was also frowning. They were back in the same oyster room. It seemed as if all London was outside rattling the windows but it was really just the wind. They had stood on the doorstep and looked at the clouds gathering above their heads.

"Self-knowledge, call it."

Charles stabbed at an oyster, but it resisted him. Beard was tugging at his gloves. He did this so slowly that he appeared to be skinning himself.

"The idea, surely, was to get some rest."

"How is that possible? I have so many deadlines."

"You create so many deadlines. You're like a man who insists on running a race by putting obstacles in his own way."

They were the best reporters in town. Or, at least, on *The Morning Chronicle*. They had been yoked together so often that it was like a marriage. Beard reminded him of Catherine: soft-hearted and accommodating but with surprising reserves of capital. He sometimes made Charles uncomfortable, but it was something that Charles permitted. It was his *droit de seigneur.*

"My dear fellow. What would you? I have an improvident father. I have a wife; a child on the way."

"And a thirst for glory."

"Well. Yes." He smiled. Glory. It assumed some sort of annunciation. "I like to make a flare. But so do you."

"Not in the way you do. I always hope to illuminate." Beard's fingers seemed to be sparkling on the table. Then he smiled. "But you want to cause a conflagration."

"I will, too." Charles downed his wine. He picked up the bottle and stared at it for a moment. He appeared to be asking it a question; then he poured himself another. "Watch me."

"I am."

Beard meant the wine. Charles shrugged.

"An expectant father."

"And how is she? The expectant mother?"

"She is, um, *radiant.*"

"And this troubles you?"

Charles was rapidly scratching at the hair above his ear. It was a kind of metaphor: he was all itch. He shrugged. Then he visibly sighed. Beard studied him.

"Ah."

He looked down at his food. His bald spot made him seem older. Charles was embarrassed. When Beard looked up he thought: Is he about to recommend a remedy? Could one do that, even with a friend? Had Beard? Gone to The Cut or the Haymarket Walk Past and availed himself? One didn't ask. Beard was still carefully marshalling his oyster.

"But the peace and quiet," he said.

"Yes. Well. That too."

"Like Dingley Dell."

Charles looked out at the rain. It appeared to make London grubbier. Strange that it felt so much like an invitation.

"Sometimes I hate Dingley Dell."

A confession. But Beard nodded.

"Of course."

"Of course?"

"It is only one part of your nature, Charles. And then you blow it up into everything. You are convivial to a fault, but that's the thing about conviviality." Beard took a sip at his own wine. He looked both tentative and smug. "It's all *outward*, d'you see? It's for other people. You overwrite."

Charles made to protest, and Beard held up his hand.

"I don't mean like that. I mean you ..."

Beard was searching for the right word. He was fastidious, and only a little nervous. Charles could be savage. He knew that about himself, and he rather liked it.

"You put your thumb on the scale. Like those child lovers."

"What child lovers?"

"In your sketch. 'They have dreamt of each other in their quiet dreams, these children, and their ...' What is it?"

Dickens was grinning.

"'Their little hearts.'"

"Their little hearts. Which will never recover, apparently. 'When will there come in after life a passion so earnest.' You don't believe that nonsense."

"I do!"

His voice was louder than he had expected it to be. It was the wine. He felt as though his arm were continuing his gesture outwards.

"Sometimes."

"Shame on you. And you with your adequate education."

Was it? Adequate? While still a child, Charles had seen every-thing. He had walked from factory to lodging house by way of the Marshalsea and he had seen so many acts of degradation that he was surprised they weren't imprinted on his skin. But that was the point: he had only seen them. They had, even at their worst, been like the illustrations in a picture book. He had already known his Hogarth; it wasn't such a terrible shock. Once, he had walked past an alley in which three men were taking it in turns. The woman was laughing, but she was obvi-ously drunk. Charles knew this because of his own parents. There was always the point when someone's face became so heavy that it was like a paint brush being dipped into the air. He stayed and watched; they didn't seem to mind. He wanted to defend her, but he also wanted it to carry on. He was both disgusted and aroused. There was still part of him that was sifting through the consequences of that arousal.

"It isn't the same," he said.

"What isn't?"

Love and sex. Or writing about love and sex. He wasn't sure what he meant. He shrugged. Beard looked at him shrewdly.

"And the *cocotte*?"

"An aberration. Nothing more."

"So you haven't—?"

"Good Lord, dear fellow. No. No, no."

But once outside he knew exactly where he wanted to go. He had physically to grip himself. Out loud, he said, "Talk about Herculean."

He wasn't sure if he hadn't done this deliberately, to prove to himself that he was drunk. He shook his head and made himself watch Beard, who was walking towards Fleet Street, past St.

Clement Danes. He had one of those strange moments when he saw two things, remarkably unlike, as mirroring each other. Beard was foursquare, just like the church. He was upright and, in some ways, impervious. He envied him, not for his after-noon's employment so much as for the way he walked. Striding between the horses and pedestrians, he looked determined, yes, but also essentially untroubled. Dickens rubbed rapidly at his brow. The rain had stopped but the wind was still playing ducks and drakes with the London streets. He could feel it, but only theoretically. It was the drink. There was a part of the day that was beyond him, like a difficult argument. He wandered up and down the Strand.

He didn't want to see Black, now. He was too drunk. Not that it mattered, but it didn't do to negotiate with an editor when you were in a weakened state. Instead, he made himself look at the familiar shops as though he had only just come upon them. Barley sugar; ironmongery. There was always something to be seen, to be *truly* seen, if you focused your attention. What was barley sugar like? Gas lamps. Guttering stars. Even as he was doing these exercises, he was aware of Sarah in the way that one would be aware of a stomach's incessant rumbling. Petersham suited Catherine: its quietness and would-be serenity enabled Charles to live, always, with her in mind.

London, though, wouldn't let you alone. The noise of horses' hooves and of cabs thumping against their axles was newly prominent, now that he had been away from it for a while. It forced you to square up to it; to throw yourself energetically into whatever came your way. That, the energy, became the point. It became who you were. London haunted you. Even when it was directly in front of you, you were constantly embracing it and warding it off. He thought, again, of Sarah: of her face and breasts, the way they seemed to rest, knowingly, in his hands. He shook himself, literally, and took out a comb. He stood in the street, his legs slightly apart, and watched himself order his appearance in the window of a wine merchant's. Always this need to assert the thing he was. Always this loneliness. Only, of course, what right had he to be lonely? He filled his chest and made himself say "my wife; my wife; my wife." It had a refreshingly martial air, and he delivered himself up to it. He began to walk with deliberate purpose from alleyway to alleyway. There was a chandler's, a butcher's, and now a jewellers. He stood there for a moment and soaked it up. The drops of rain seemed to amplify everything in the window, so that it danced in front of him. There was about the glitter what felt like an irrefutable, impartial truth. It was like a balm.

He found that he was still saying "my wife" as he walked in. The noise outside didn't diminish to any great degree but the light was like the light of a bower, or a cave. It wasn't gloomy so much as plush; it was like velvet, soothing and framing all of the things that were on offer. The man behind the counter pushed himself forward slightly in what was meant to be a bow. It was carefully calibrated, Charles saw. Dressed in his usual gaudy waistcoat and bright tie, he didn't look quite respectable.

"My wife ..."

He made a gesture that was strikingly similar to his father's. He looked like he was weighing her or weighing her up.

"She is expecting."

"Ah. Of course, sir."

Charles didn't know what that meant. He was a little offended; he hadn't said what he wanted to look at but the man was already at a cabinet, bending down to unlock the glass. Turning to Charles, he had a necklace draped over his fingers. Charles peered at it. What were those stones? He was insulted that the man had made an assumption as to how much he could afford. Illogically: he *could* afford it, and he couldn't go much higher. But he wanted to be treated as a man of substance. He pointed to something in mid-range; a series of loops, all seemingly made of diamonds. The man's reluctance was shrouded by the sombre eagerness that, Charles could see, was as carefully considered a performance as Sarah's Lady Macbeth. Nevertheless, it was visible, and Charles lifted his head slightly. He looked the man firmly in the eye.

"It's my first," he said.

"Ah."

The man proffered a smile. Charles had a vision of him actually doing this; of holding it out for inspection in his hands.

"I completely understand."

He was smaller even than Charles. There was a network of black hairs untidily arranged over a scalp that, in this light, looked painfully red. His nose was too prominent, Charles felt; it seemed to bully his eyes. Charles looked at him with a certain amount of contempt as he carefully lifted the necklace into the air. The diamonds appeared to make sense of the light. They seemed suddenly, the two of them, to be in league. The man ran the necklace through his fingers. He was talking, but it was unclear whether it was to Charles or the necklace that they were both watching as raptly as if it had been a woman.

Charles said, "May I?"

Reluctantly, but also eagerly, the man put the necklace into his hands. It trickled through his fingers. At first, it felt as though it was barely there but then it began to feel heavier. He didn't want to let it go. The man was so close that his breath was drumming in Charles's ear and, when Charles took a step nearer the light, he could feel him straining beside him. Too polite to move, he nevertheless gave the impression that he was about to leap on him. Charles wanted to say what he had said, once, to a man in a dark room in Clerkenwell: "Get your own." He was looking directly into the quiet fire of the diamonds. But he was also much too aware of the man's scalp, and the spurious polished brightness of his fingernails—the way that they seemed to mimic his stock in trade. They both knew that Charles could no more afford to pay for this than he could lift the shop onto his shoulders. The man, he strongly felt, was his antagonist. He smiled, began to proffer the thing then snatched it back and ran.

Ran into the Strand, past the Coal Hole Tavern and through two bewildered maids. He nearly collided with a drayhorse that was standing at the corner of an intersection that his eyes had refused to acknowledge. At first, he could hear the man behind him. His footsteps were like little prods in the back. He had heard "stop thief" once or twice and had expected something to happen: a blow or a foot stuck out to trip him up. But nothing did. It was too noisy out here. He was so conscious of the man that he had amplified his voice; could still hear it now that it had stopped. But, in reality, his shout had been sopped up by the blotting paper of the London streets.

Because, of course, London didn't care. He allowed himself to slow at the bottom of Fleet Street. His heart was battering at his chest and his hands were tingling. Nevertheless, he wasn't shocked at what he'd done. He had seen it done, had dreamed about doing it, often enough. He was beginning to discover what all thieves know: that the act is much more satisfactory than whatever you end up with afterwards. The necklace was still in his hand and he studied it, briefly, before thrusting it into his pocket. It was nice; lovely even. But he was beginning to wonder what exactly he had seen in it. He laughed and continued to laugh so long that there was part of him that felt a little frightened. He was drunk, but it wasn't that. It was so violently convulsive that it was almost like being sick. He had to stand, with his hand on his knees, and allow it to run its course. It was his familiar; the part of him that could stand so close to a house fire that he had, once, set his waistcoat alight. There were times when he felt as though he *was* the fire. He felt something like what he had felt on the beach: that he could, if he wanted, reach into reality somehow and tear it into a thousand pieces. Looking up, he briefly felt the same contempt for St. Paul's as he had felt for the shop assistant. It had the same round dome; the same smug look of benevolent rectitude.

But, then, so did Catherine. When he got back to the hotel, she was washing her hands. It was a ritual that she now allowed him to see. It was like going backstage. She had been dipping her nails in warm water, using a lemon to bleach them. Now she was trimming them into ovals, not too long, in order that they didn't harbour dirt. But they mustn't be too short, either: this made for stubby fingers. There were a whole set of instructions, from which she never seemed to deviate. Her hair was centre-parted. Smooth and straight, all the hair at the back was drawn into a rigid bun. The hair at the front, divided into two, fell down smoothly on either side of the face, in front of the ears. Her chemise was tube-like with short capped sleeves. Her arms were bare and her breasts were exposed, as were her lower legs. Briefly, he felt his lower body growl. But it was no use. She was immured inside her pregnancy. He sat carefully beside her on the divan. He was still a little drunk, and there was what amounted to a band of pain expanding and contracting around his forehead. But he would have been careful, anyway. It wasn't that she was delicate, exactly; more that he had an inner vision of himself as a troll, or as a Mr. Jingle: nothing but urge. At this moment, he still had London in him.

"Successful trip?"

"Yes. Yes, I think so."

"Oh Charles. Not more work."

"No, titmouse, not more work."

He stroked her ear. Now would have been the time. But the necklace lay, like curdled milk, in his back pocket.

"I saw Beard."

"How is he?"

"Eminent. He is developing a chin."

"Just one?"

She lay her hand on his.

"I can't tell if you look vexed or rested."

"Oh, the latter. I walked the streets. I looked. Prodigiously."

"I'm glad."

She patted his hand.

"Now you *must* be mine again."

She seemed to retract timidly as soon as she said it. It was, really, the opposite of assertion. Outside, the clouds were like a stagecoach, but the moon remained. It seemed to be getting surlier and surlier. Charles watched his wife loosen the skin at the base of a nail. She worked at it until, swiftly, she gave a tug. It came off like Sarah's skirt. Charles put his head on her shoulder. He placed his hand, lightly, on her swelling stomach. Sighing, he closed his eyes and watched himself put his hand on Sarah's breast.

CHAPTER NINE

BACK TO THE slum. Petersham had had the colours and the gently transient light of a drawing done in chalk, but Saffron Hill was all greys and browns. It felt to Charles like he was visiting a rookery for the first time. The shock wasn't so much at what was there as at the fact that he had something that he valued here. There was cloth stuck in broken windows and there were big piles of what looked like human waste upon the cobbles. They, the cobbles, were filthy anyway; a treacly black that he had never seen out in the London thorough-fares. Even today, in sunlight, it was more often dark than not. Everything was squeezed against everything else. There were houses, he knew, just a stone's throw from Oxford Street, that were so crowded together that they didn't have any windows at all. Here, the girls stared so blankly at you that they seemed blind. The children had a sidelong way of walking; they were ready to swerve out of the way at a moment's notice. Adults, you felt, were as unpredictable a quality as the weather. It was midday but it was strangely quiet. Not the settled quiet of his flat in Furnival's Inn; more the sullenness of the air that you felt before a thunderstorm.

That first night, he had had the feeling that Sarah had the whole house to herself. Absurd, of course. There were a whole tribe of them downstairs; they were as thickly crowded together as the boys at the gaff had been. Sarah always hurried him upstairs, and he had the confused impression of a crowd that looked, in their griminess and hopelessness, exactly the same as one another. Now, there was a woman sweeping the front step. This, too, was hopeless. The dirt was so thickly begrimed that the only thing that you could meaningfully do was put a chisel to it. He found that he was hovering just out of sight, so that he felt at a disadvantage. He had always felt, before, that he could side-step all of this if it were necessary. That some inherent superiority would save him if he ever needed to be saved. Now he felt like a potential housebreaker. It was a Tuesday, Sarah's morning off, but he couldn't bring himself to ask if she was in. He couldn't bear to be seen. Not that he thought, for one moment, that he would be recognised. It was a more intimate feeling: that, if someone took notice of him, they would see everything, his heart and lungs and stomach, all wound so tightly that he felt like he was going to be sick. Even the air rubbed against him in the wrong way.

The woman had disappeared, and he saw Sarah at once. She had been watching him; he had been so intent upon the sweeper that he hadn't noticed her. Her face looked bruised but it was merely red. Charles waved. He could feel the tautness of his own face. His chest, meanwhile, was stretched as tightly as a drum. His wave had been ridiculous: a broad half-circle.

She flung her window open and said, "Go away." She had emptied her voice of all expression. Still miming, he tried to express how sorry he was; how much he had missed her; how much he desperately wanted to see her. She shook her head, briskly: no. She turned her back and went to close the window, and Charles found that the pressure on his chest was suddenly unbearable. He started to run towards the house.

"Sarah!"

She turned and looked back down at him. He would so much rather that she was angry. This, the stony blankness of her face, was something that he couldn't seem to bear.

"I ..."

What could he say? Two months. He shrugged.

"You can explain," she said.

"No."

He looked steadily into her face. He couldn't bring himself to look into her eyes.

"I can't."

"It's not hard, is it? Cold feet. The bosom of your family. You're hardly the first."

The coldness of her tone had an effect on Charles that was almost physical. He found himself yearning upwards. Becoming angry, too. He had brought the necklace but had been unsure if he was going to give it to her. Now, with a desperate flourish, he lifted it out. The contrast with their surroundings was so severe that it looked like the clumsiest of illustrations. It glittered there like an insult. She almost screamed.

"Put that thing away!"

She was looking rapidly from side to side and making rapid downwards motions with her hands. She watched him drizzle it, like icing, into his pocket. Now he *was* angry.

"You idiot," she said.

"You do not seem to realise—"

"What? What don't I realise? How much *trouble* you went to?" Charles had intended to retreat into a cold formality, but he had sounded more like a child who was readying itself for a tantrum. Sarah was staring down at him. One arm was holding the window open. It looked as exaggeratedly muscled as a snake.

"Sarah."

He held his arms out in an embrace.

"Don't. Don't you dare say it."

"Sarah."

"I'm warning you. Bedswerver."

She had mimicked the slight muddiness of his w's. Her face had contracted around the word so tightly that her face had reddened even further.

"Besprawler."

But she was the one who was spitting. He didn't care.

"I love you!"

Immediately, he felt ridiculous. Was he relieved? Appalled? He wanted to sit down or run away. Had he miscalculated? Because now she had wheeled back into her room. He heard her thump from one side of it to another, and he thought that she was going to come down. Her footsteps were as loud to him as the man's had been on the street. He heard her coming back. He didn't know what to expect. She had something in her hands and, before he could properly see what they were doing, she had emptied the contents of her chamber pot onto his head.

Her urine was still warm. It felt, at first, like an insult. Then he was wet; then cold. A September wind was being funnelled through the narrow streets, but he hadn't noticed it. He stood stock still. He was frightened that, if he moved, the wind and wet would combine to form something both painful and constricting. Already, the liquid was seeking him out. He tried to read her face, but it was making too much of an effort to conceal whatever it was that she was feeling. Was she going to laugh or cry? She shook her head. It was a different, rueful shake.

"Oh Charley."

She closed the window. He became aware of his predicament: stuck in the street covered in urine, each movement making him, despite himself, intimate with the wet and the smell and the seeming judgement of it, that he was a man who deserved to be covered in somebody else's piss. He hadn't felt quite this lonely since he was a child. But then he heard the door. She had opened it and now she was looking at him closely. After a pause, she cocked her head. He followed her upstairs. It was like walking in a nightmare, every step not so much moving you forward as further into the element from which you were trying to escape: a mixture of fire and water. She stepped to one side and allowed him to enter. Gently, with a determined deadpan, she helped him take off his clothes. He felt extraordinarily naked. It was like being a child, when you felt like your mother was about to tell you who you were. There was, he saw, a bucket and a cloth. She washed him, gently enough, but the cold water felt like a punishment. There was no dressing gown. She threw his clothes into the bucket and gestured to one of the chairs. He thought of the necklace. He felt as though it was drowning. But he knew enough to sit there, quietly waiting for whatever it was she was going to say.

She was walking, now, between her bed and the window. Her breasts swung tantalisingly beneath her dress. In any case, she had washed him imperfectly and the tang of her was beginning to arouse him. The feeling hovered there, like the beginning of a headache, but was dispersed by her austere nobility. Her shoulders were straight and wide; her hair made no concession to whatever bonnet she might later have to wear. Her face was leonine. It was stiff; unyielding. But it was also beautiful. She could, he saw, look properly like a queen. She flamed before him in the dull sepia of the outdoor light.

"I waited."

She was looking at the wall behind his head.

"For *weeks*. I still am. I still am, Charley."

She began to cry. He tried to stand but she advanced her palm so fiercely that her gesture pushed him back. He sat down, gingerly. It felt like he was balancing on the edge of something. The chair was uncomfortable, but it wasn't only that. He felt nervous, still. Feeble and vulnerable. Sarah had her head in her hands.

"Two months."

She shook her head, then she lifted it in appeal.

"You can't do that to a girl. You can't … do what we did."

Her hands appeared to be battling with the air. Was she beckoning to something or batting it away? Charles knew what she meant: make love. They had come back here after the street and made love, slowly, in her bed. They had both been so tender that, now, she didn't want to acknowledge it.

"You can't do it like we did it, you can't, and not say a word. Not visit; not write."

"Not write?"

"I can fucking read."

"I simply meant—"

"Oh there's nothing simple about you, Charley."

She appeared to gather herself. She slowly took in air.

"I'm sorry. About what I said. The others. There haven't been many."

She sniffed.

"Whatever you might think."

She rubbed the back of her hand against the bottom of her nose.

"And it was always me. Do you understand? It was always me who told them to fuck off."

He was intrigued. Forgetting he was naked, he sat a little forward in the chair.

"Why did you?"

"Oh, I don't know. It's silly. Fine dining. Carriages. I know what they think: that that's what you want. But it makes it worse. You come home and it's not your home no more."

Again, she sniffed.

"Anymore."

She scowled at him.

"Listen to me. Your fault."

She loosened her neck. Charles had once found this to be a gesture of incongruous grace. He no longer saw it so much as felt it. Sarah was scowling.

"And then you come along."

She pointed out of the window. Her breasts rose and fell and he felt his throat tighten in response.

"Round here, I'm considered something of a catch. I'm like—"

"A saveloy."

She threw her head back. It looked like air was being poured down her throat.

"Don't do that. Don't make me laugh."

She was still smiling.

"You need to account for yourself."

She ran her fingers through her hair.

"You really do, you know."

"No gammon."

"No gammon."

He looked out of the window. He was aware of a familiar urge: to polish his behaviour up to a bright sheen. Not that this meant justifying it, necessarily. It was more that he could present it to her fully grown, with its hair combed and its fingernails cleaned. Sarah looked at him almost in fear.

"*Don't*, Charley."

Known. He had forgotten. How did it feel? Like sitting naked in a chair. It was his turn to place his head in his hands. He was so used to thinking about an audience that he didn't know which words and which expressions didn't have their taint. I shall, he thought, at least speak slowly.

"It isn't that I couldn't bear to come. It's that I couldn't bear to stay away."

"Bollocks."

"It's true. My wife ..."

It felt like stepping off a cliff.

"... is having our first child."

He didn't dare look at Sarah's face. He stared, instead, at his clothes, drowned in a bucket. You wouldn't, if you hadn't been told, know what they were. Clothes, yes, but you wouldn't be able to identify the kind of man who wore them. At this precise moment, he couldn't have answered to that himself. He spoke as slowly and deliberately as if he were speaking in court.

"So, as you can imagine, there is a conflict of loyalties. If you *were*, um, a lady of the night, then this would not be so accentuated."

He wanted to punch himself in the head again.

"I'm sorry. So pompous. I wouldn't ache for you, I mean. I do. I ache. I watch myself. I look at it."

He gestured at his groin.

"And I think: Where is she? Why is this here? In this room. Because I know exactly where it should be. And that ..."

He wanted to signal to her: make me stop.

"Well, that might not be the most romantic thing you've ever heard. But it's true. All of me aches for all of you. I don't know what that means. It feels like love. I sit here, covered in urine, and it feels like love."

Meanwhile, his wife, rolling as gently as a tethered boat, waited at home. His flat was positively serene. You listened and you realised that you weren't able to hear the London streets. It was like being in a fairy tale. Two sisters, loving and accommodating, and a boy under an enchantment. In which case what was this? And if this was love what was the other? The entire situation was contained, he felt, in the way that his hands seemed to be pleading independently. And none of it could be spoken. Because, if it was, the spell might break. His eyes were wet. Sarah was studying him again. He could see something soften in her face. Not much: a muscle or two.

"Your child."

"My child."

Her hands were working at her forehead. Rubbing at it; remoulding it. She appeared to be shaping thoughts with them.

"You need some clothes."

And she was gone. He sat and felt his breath go in and out. His whole body rattled with it. He was doubly naked: still waiting, he realised, for Sarah to tell him who he was. Impatient with himself, he stood up and made himself survey the room. It was a sketch, no more. How could anyone live here? But part of him, he knew, was always here. Desperate to do something, he stepped over to the bucket and rummaged in his pockets for the necklace. There it was: as cold and unaccommodating as an eel. He fished it out and stood irresolutely in the middle of the room. It wasn't as though he could hide it about his person. In any case, that was unworthy. After everything he had said he owed it to himself as much as her to put up a decent showing. He slipped it behind the mirror just as she was coming up the stairs. He sat back in the chair and placed his hands over his groin. Sarah laughed, or else she mimed a laugh.

"Too late for that."

She threw a bundle at him.

"Yours," she said.

She grinned.

"For now."

It was nearly a joke. Why would he want to keep them? They were as rough as municipal blankets. He tried not to rub them, fastidiously, between his fingers. He put them on with an attempt at willingness and looked at himself in the mirror that was leaning against the wall. Was it or wasn't it a transformation? In some ways, this sudden lowering was what he had always expected. It was more a reversion than a fall from grace. He wanted to say: "I can't go home like this." Instead, he followed her out of the house. The clothes dictated how he walked: they rubbed against him, so that he found that he was hoisting his legs around an invisible obstacle. There was no belt for the trousers. Perhaps this was deliberate. In order to walk fast enough to keep up with her, he had to keep one hand on his waistband. His arms poked out of the sleeves. They looked as thin as if they belonged to someone else. The shoes that she had given him were no more, really, than bits of cloth. The street felt unfamiliar. It was obtrusive: it seemed to push upwards against him at every step.

Where was she leading him? She seemed deliberately to be taking him past all of the better shops. He realised that his money was in the bucket. Was he imagining the change of atmosphere? It wasn't quite that he was invisible. It was more that people were trying to give him the space to become so. He had not noticed, before, the way that street singers sang directly at you. Girls in shop windows would usually perform an understated ballet. Now, no one acknowledged him. Even when, as a child, he had walked these streets, the fact that he was a child had changed their relationship to him. Vendors would sometimes smile. Once, a woman had come out to watch him drink his porter. A phenomenon, she said. He saw how very inimical to London's sense of itself he was. It was like being a dog that had escaped.

He saw, also, how Sarah's walk was adapted to her circumstances. The slight sailor's roll was an aspect of her determination to get safely and quickly to wherever she wanted to go. She wouldn't pause. Once, they stopped outside a jeweller's. She gave him a look whose sharpness was really just an aspect of the hurt that he had caused her.

"Go on," she said. "Go in."

He might as well have been in jail. But the jail was here, outside; freedom was the ability to walk into the room he couldn't enter and make the purchases he couldn't make. Sarah nodded. Her smile was so perfectly balanced that Charles wanted to rub away at it with both hands. She placed her fingers in his palm but a shadow came between them. Literally: it came across them, spreading over their face and hands. The man was in a jacket of double-breasted check with a roll collar. His whole face was in motion: his leer was travelling across his face and one eye was winking, seemingly of its own accord. He was swaying slightly but it was difficult to tell if this was drink or an attempt to communicate his own importance.

"And your name is?"

He had turned his back on Charles. Sarah shook her head at him; at Charles. She smiled upwards at the man.

"Sarah. And yours?"

"Bill," he said.

Charles saw the muscles on his back crowd inwards as his chest expanded and his arms came slowly undone, like wings. Sarah was staring at him.

"I'm surprised you can remember it. You're not much, are you Bill? Why don't you piss off home and sleep it off?"

It was difficult to know what was supposed to happen next. It took a moment for the man to realise what she'd said. As his head seemed literally to be butting at her words, she grabbed Charles's hand. She nearly pulled him off his feet. She ran with him, down the road. Breathless, Charles tugged at her.

"Wait," he said.

"For what?"

"I could have dealt with him."

"My maiden aunt you could. Look at your trousers."

They had turned a corner. She dragged him into an alley then rested for a moment with her head on his shoulder, catching her breath.

"He's a scoundrel."

Once again, Sarah threw her head back. Her laugh so overtook her that he had to wait for her to speak.

"And you're not?"

He made to reply but she had placed her hand over his mouth.

"You're not 'Charles Dickens' anymore. Look at yourself."

He didn't need to look. He could feel it in the way that the wind insinuated itself between his jacket and chest; in the way that the pavement was pushing up at him.

"You're nobody," she said.

This seemed to give her enormous pleasure. He realised that they were reversing the steps that they had taken on the first night. Here were the same shops and the same trees, only this time everything, even the branches, appeared to be in use. The trees were framing the shops. Old and alluringly gnarled, they were confirming their status. Charles's stomach had congealed.

"Not the pub," he said. "Please, Sarah. I can't go in. Look at me."

Sarah had an expression that was so sardonic that it appeared to have the depth of an entirely different order of thought. There was wisdom there, but it was so tart that you wanted to back away from it.

"I am."

"I won't go in."

She ruffled his hair.

"You will."

"I can't."

But he did.

At first he thought that it was merely meant to be a penance. Grimaldi, of course, seemed delighted. Almost every part of his face conspired to make him look rapt with joy. His eyes were a puzzle: they had the blank gleam of a bird, or a monkey. But his shoulders shook with what you were expected to think was laughter.

"Oh dear. Oh dearie, dearie me."

He rapidly rubbed his chin. His eyes did a dance in his head. It was an old routine; something that his body and face remembered, even if you weren't sure that Grimaldi did. His face was a mirror but not of anything in particular. Of the zaniness of life, perhaps.

"Times is 'ard," he said.

It was a non-sequitur, like "here we are again." But, when coupled with Charles's dress, the idea seemed to delight him. He slapped the table, and Davey had to grab his pint. Davey was smiling too, but uncertainly. Charles had the impression that, if Grimaldi found it funny, Davey thought that he should too. Just like the first time, he had abandoned his hair to itself. He was big, though. Tough-looking, despite the tardiness of his expression. His eyes were like Grimaldi's in that they didn't seem to trust his face.

Sarah said, "Sit."

She pushed him down on an empty chair at the same table. Charles noted the beer that appeared to varnish it. They had been here for a while. He thought: be quiet. But it was unnecessary. He had sparked something in Grimaldi, whose hands, great knotted turnips, floated in mid-air. He was smoking a cigar. Its smoke came, hornwise, around his forehead.

"I used," he said, "to work with a fortune-telling duck." He leaned back in his chair. He waited for a second before he said, "Not that it could actually tell your fortune. Can you imagine? No, we used to have to prod it. Some nights we used to kick it. I used to stand behind the curtain and kick it hard." He didn't actually get up but, oddly, it looked as though he had. "At which point, it would squawk. People would shit themselves. It got to be like King George in the end. There'd be a queue and then this ... thing balanced on a velvet cushion. I wanted to give it a turban and some what-do-you-call-ums. Pantaloons." He shrugged, with his whole body. "I did used to fan it, though. It used—I kid you not—to nod, like this." He lowered his eyelids and rocked gently backwards and forwards. He produced a plume—an obsequious genie—of smoke from his cigar. "It always had the same dopey look on its face. It looked particularly stupid, I must say, even for a duck." He smiled at Charles. It was all in the face: he could look pitiable or comic or oddly matronly. Right now he was all superiority. "And you, mate, look just like it."

Charles thought: what will Davey do now? Because Grimaldi's animus was palpable. He hadn't seen him since the night that Sarah had carried him to his house. Cloaked in thick gouts of smoke, he seemed to *be* the animus. In which case, what was Davey? The ensuing act. Charles saw him with a knife. A small one, glinting for just a second before he pushed it into your stomach.

But then Sarah was sitting beside him. There was, he realised for the first time, a fire in the grate. It lit her so that he saw her with sudden clarity. No bonnet: her hair as loose as the dress that flowed from the top of her breasts down to her knees. Her mouth was doubly itself: bright red, highly amused and moist from drinking gin. She placed her glass, and Charles's porter, on the table. He looked at her enquiringly.

"Day off."

"Orf." Here, with Davey and Grimaldi, she had roughened her accent. Or was it that she softened it when he was with her? He had lost his sense of her. Alone, they seemed to contain each other. But here she belonged more to the place itself, to Grimaldi and Davey and the old boys who were brooding at the fire, than to him. He was beginning to be angry with her. How long was he expected to be repentant for? This, his jacket, was enough like a hair shirt to do the job, surely? Now she was making him sit and listen to her describe what had happened that morning. Grimaldi was shaking his head in genuine delight.

"Real piss?"

"Real piss."

"Atta girl."

He slapped Charles's arm.

"She's a Tartar."

Charles nodded, mutely. Davey was laughing too. It seemed independent of him, somehow. You could imagine him practicing it when he was at home. Sarah described their walk and the man who had accosted them. She hoicked up Charles's waistband and made them look at his shoes. She mentioned everything, it seemed, apart from the necklace. Charles thought: no more. He started to get up. He was desperate for his own clothes. For a comb, too; for the opportunity to remake himself at a mirror. He found that he was scared, not of Davey and Grimaldi, but of his own lack of definition. He was staring into the pub just like it was a gigantic mirror. He looked at Davey and he saw another self: the one that seemed to accompany him wherever he went.

But Grimaldi had grabbed his arm. It was not a threatening gesture.

"Oh mate."

He was patting his hand.

"I'm sorry."

Davey was looking from Grimaldi to Charles and back again. Grimaldi nudged Davey's shoulder and peered down at Charles's drink. Charles saw that he had almost finished it. Davey nodded.

"Same for me," Grimaldi said.

He batted his eyelashes.

"Pur-lease."

He had finished his cigar. He was tilting slightly in his chair, and Charles saw, again, how very harmless he was. He felt a gust of fellow feeling that was inseparable, really, from the effects of the first pint.

"You. Deserved. That."

Grimaldi pushed slightly at Charles's shoulder with every word. But he was grinning. His smile was like Sarah's: it sat there at a tilt.

"So what now, Romeo?"

And Charles saw what she had done. She had humiliated him; had thrown him, as it were, into the mud. But she had known exactly what she was doing. It had raised him, somehow, in Grimaldi's esteem. Or lowered him sufficiently, perhaps, that he was no longer a threat. In any case, he thought he saw, for the first time, some genuine fellow feeling in Grimaldi's face. Shrewdly, Charles rubbed at his hair. He hoped that he had disarranged it so that it looked like Davey's. Or, at least, like someone who was having to go at life with his head. He scratched, half-consciously, at the material of his trousers. He saw that Sarah was looking at him anxiously. He mustn't overdo it.

"I haven't the foggiest," he said.

His elbow was on the table. He felt that this, its contiguity with the dried beer and the ash from Grimaldi's cigar, would help his case. There was to be no touch-me-not-ishness.

"What I mean is ..."

He didn't know what he meant. He had heard the initial word as "wot," as though it was laden with a burden of associations that weren't entirely his. But they were, too. He thought of that little boy; of the way that he both refused to embrace the factory and tried so desperately to fit in. His tenderness for him clogged his throat when he said, "What can I do?"

He was more careful with his pronunciation. It was his own voice but rubbed free of the drawing room aplomb that he found himself adopting at his own fireside. He heard his own anguish as though for the first time. He was divesting himself of the responsibility, and, yes, the respectability, that were a constant burden. He had to stop himself from copying the mannerisms of the people around him. He wanted to thumb his nose; to spit on the floor then rub it in with his heel. He wanted to plunge his hand up Sarah's dress.

"I'm going to be a father."

He spread his hands. His feelings, he was saying, were self-evident, although he couldn't have told you what they were. It was a risk, but Grimaldi rose to the occasion. He pointed at Davey, who was carefully placing each drink in front of its owner.

"He has six," he said.

He lifted his fingers.

"Three wives."

Davey eagerly nodded his head. His face had opened out into an unexpected grin. He did have a knife, it turned out, but this was later: it was pulled out as part of a song that Charles only imperfectly understood. In the meantime, they got on like a house on fire. Or, at least, they seemed to. He was drinking constantly; his thirst, he found, was in keeping with his new love for his surroundings. Men came and went. They had dirty hats and grubby neckerchiefs and one had a huge cauliflower ear, but he was grateful to them all for enfolding him into their company. It became difficult to tell if it was light or dark outside. The pub seemed to be floating parallel to the street. Grimaldi had become extremely earnest. How many drinks had he had? He leaned into the table, pressing down hard on it with his thumbs. His voice had become husky, although his eyes, as always, kept their hard gleam. His face appeared to understand you; to gather you in. But his eyes seemed to be holding out for a contending and balancing principle. Himself. His hands went over his arms and legs like he was fondling them.

"My shoulder blade," he was saying. "Both arms. My foot. But it was purposeful, you see?"

He bore down harder on the table.

"It was art."

"Breaking your bones?"

"No, you poof. Suffering. My father beat me constantly. He used to stand at the foot of the bed when I was asleep and hit my leg. Like this."

Grimaldi slapped the table, hard. Nobody else in the pub appeared to turn a hair.

"A lesson, he said. He used to fuck everything that moved. It was all part of the training. Mine or his? Don't ask me, mate."

"Well, if you're going to start talking about fathers."

"Gahn. Your dad?"

"My dad."

"Folds the newspaper in the wrong way, does he?"

"He was imprisoned for debt." Charles said this with a kind of pride. It was like disclosing a good poker hand. Of course, he was drunk. Even as he said it he could feel how he might respond when he woke up in the morning. But that didn't matter now. What mattered was this new sense of collusion. Of seduction, almost. "I was put out to work. A little labouring hind."

"You've said that before."

"I haven't. I might have written it." He grinned. "In my head. Even my wife doesn't know."

"Why doesn't she?"

This was Sarah. She wasn't drunk in the way that Charles and Grimaldi were. She watched her hand distrustfully as it picked up a glass. She appeared to be willing it to do its job. She had retreated into the deportment of a lady, or "a lady"—it was still hard, sometimes, to credit her with finer feelings. The drink had simplified things for Charles; he wanted to push her into a corner. But now he saw something naked in Sarah's eyes. It was the keenness of the pleasure that his remark had given her. He felt uncomfortable. But he also felt a delirious pleasure of his own. Nakedness. Being known. There was a lot to be said for it. He shrugged.

"Her father knew Sir Walter Scott."

Why was this so very funny? The four of them laughed for longer than was strictly necessary. Oh, it was delightful. All of it was: the tightly bound environment, the warmth, the close proximity—especially Grimaldi's, whose pert, ambivalent regard Charles was gratefully aware of. Sarah was smiling at him in a new way. She seemed, almost, to approve of him. After she had gone out to the lavatory, he patted Grimaldi on the arm. He made himself do it; he was still a little scared of him.

"I've got something for her," he said.

"You dirty sod."

"No. No no no no no."

His fingers did a sinuous little dance.

"A necklace."

"Oooooh. Clever boy."

Grimaldi was rubbing his hands together.

"How much did that set you back?"

"Ah. Well. Now."

It was irresistible. Grimaldi was hanging there like a fish on a line. And Davey, obviously, was a villain. He wanted to give them something they could fix their teeth into. He wanted them to look at him in the same way that they looked at each other.

"I didn't *exactly* pay for it."

Once again, Charles was behaving as though he was drunker than he was. Even now, after four or five pints—an amount that, in the context of his own drinking habits, felt almost mythical— a part of him was closely watching how he was behaving. He saw how he bore down, almost sloppily, on that one word and he assumed that it was a debased form of theatricality. He was adapting himself, as he always did, to the prevailing tone. What he didn't see was the way that this, the plunge, was meant to excuse his indiscretion to himself; how his obvious drunken- ness made it all-but-involuntary.

"There was one. Which I could afford. *But.*"

He tilted his hand from side to side. Wincing, he drew in an obvious breath.

"It looked like spit."

This was Davey. His face had changed. He looked as eager and as fiercely focused as a dog at its bowl. Charles smiled and nodded in appreciation of the simile.

"Yes. Dribble."

But, for Davey, this was a judgment of value rather than a matter of expression. A moral judgment, almost. Grimaldi's head was nestled on his hands. His thick, lugubrious mouth was pushed as far forward as a duck's bill. It was busy confirming the drollery of the situation but his eyes were clamped tightly on Charles's own.

"And then?"

"And then he pulled out this, this, sparkler. Gorgeous it was." Davey nodded.

"And the bloke was on you like a suit."

He looked mournful, almost sardonic.

"He was."

Charles was nodding eagerly.

"I was here, and he was here."

Once again, he patted Grimaldi's arm.

"I couldn't afford it. He knew that. He was like this."

He danced where he was sitting. He threw his arms from right to left and back again, like he was trying to stop someone from escaping.

Davey's mouth smiled. His eyes, though, were entirely serious. He nodded. What Charles was saying seemed to confirm some universal law. Grimaldi was still looking directly into his face.

"And you scarpered."

"Yes."

Grimaldi threw himself backwards and clapped his hands. Even now, his eyes were fixed on him. They were expressionless still, although his face was jubilant.

"Oh fucking hell. That's perfect. The famous author."

Charles immediately wanted to take it back. He had expected some measure of approval; a delighted confirmation of his own recklessness. But Grimaldi saw hypocrisy. Perhaps stupidity. This wasn't necessarily bad; this, too, was a universal law. But it was less than Charles required. Davey, meanwhile, was shaking his head.

"Daylight robbery."

He took a long drink of porter, but his face ignored it. He was still staring at Charles.

"'as bad."

He seemed to sympathise. Charles found that he was irritated.

"No. No. Well, alright, yes. Yes it was. But it was more of a ..."

How did you translate *jeu d'esprit?*

"... a prank."

Grimaldi was taking his handkerchief out of his pocket. He wound it around his neck then pulled sideways at it. He crossed his eyes and stuck his tongue out of his mouth. Davey was saying,

"And he definitely seen your face?"

Charles nodded. Davey shook his head. His hair looked like it was agreeing with him.

"Scragged," he said.

He was looking seriously at Grimaldi.

"He'll be scragged."

They both began to laugh. Davey turned back to Charles.

"I thought you was supposed to be brainy."

Charles saw, at last, what Grimaldi's eyes were expressing. Relish. It was the same frank enjoyment that he had shown, onstage, when someone had fallen out of a window. Charles was trying to stand to one side of what he had done and see it from another angle. If he could somehow redescribe it then it might feel benignly humorous again. Grimaldi was squeezing his hand.

"Mate, if I'd known you was poor I'd have saved a space in the pawnbroker's window."

Davey laughed. He was shouting,

"He used to! He used to!"

He mimed Grimaldi miming. There he was in the window, his arms and legs tucked in like a disconsolate chimpanzee. But Sarah was walking back. She was stepping as carefully as if she was balancing something on her head. Grimaldi said, "Does she—?"

"No."

Grimaldi nodded, and then he winked. It was not a gesture that was intended to inspire confidence. He had done it with such gusto that his ear seemed to come round to meet his nose.

"We'll vouch for you," he said. "You were here all day. Wasn't he, Davey?"

"Oh certainly."

Davey, it appeared, was now on solid ground. His lower lip was pushing at his upper in a show of rectitude.

"Most certainly."

He patted Charles on the shoulder. They were all bound to a common enterprise. It made him feel a little sweaty. Sarah plonked herself on his lap and there were songs. Davey did something brief. Charles, his head in Sarah's hair, only half-heard it. It was obscene, evidently. Sarah wouldn't sing. When she shook her head, the rest of her shook alluringly in Charles's arms. He himself was prevailed upon, and he stood unsteadily on his feet. He made what he could of "The Cat's Meat Man" then lowered himself carefully back onto his seat. He had leant forward confidingly and conducted the table but he had felt like a child who was being indulged. His clothes seemed not to give him any purchase. When it was Grimaldi's turn he paused. The inference was that what you were going to get was something properly nutritious. He rubbed his palms together. He seemed to aim, then throw, the song at the bar.

"A little old woman, her living she got
by selling her codlins, hot, hot, hot.
And this little old woman, who codlins sold,
tho' her codlins were hot, she felt herself cold."

Charles had never seen anyone's face express so much self-satisfaction. Grimaldi's hands were gathering everybody in: Sarah, himself and Davey and the entire pub. It was working, too. The old men at the fire were smiling. The barmaid, a drab little thing compared to Sarah, was swaying slightly from side to side. They were all warming themselves at Grimaldi's song.

The barmaid tucked a stray hair behind her ear and stood up a little straighter. It looked like something was going to be expected of her. Grimaldi's face said: "Here it comes."

"So to keep herself warm she thought it no sin

to fetch for herself a quartern of—"

And the entire pub, Charles included, shouted "gin!" Grimaldi's line was "Oh, for shame!" He did this with a glorious show of censoriousness. Both eyebrows came swooping downwards. His hands were on his hips and he was doing the duck's pout again. He looked neither male nor female and this contributed to the sense that they were all giving two fingers to the world outside. Charles felt his two strongest impulses cohere: the urge to be part of a family—a central part; someone who was so inextricably caught up in it that he could barely breathe without it—and the desire to take the world in his teeth and shred it.

Soon, it was time to go and there was a protracted set of farewells; a warm overcoat of farewells. Outside, brisk clouds went scudding across the sky. Gas light appeared to be breathing in time with the woman beside him. It was, as she was, only intermittently illuminating. Now, she was all body: something that had to be half-lifted through the London streets. In Holborn, she pressed him against a wall. She stared at him until, all at once, she seemed to recognise him. Softly, she stroked his cheek.

"My Charley."

She placed her teeth around his lower lip and tugged at it. This seemed both gentle and fierce. He waited for her to finish.

"What's 'scragged'?" he said.

"Hmmm?"

"Scragged. What's scragged? Davey said it to Grimaldi."

"Oh, he would."

Once again, her face came back from wherever it had been.

"It's hung. He will be too."

Her hand was resting on his erection.

"Speaking of which."

She giggled, placed a pert kiss on his nose then danced away. When they got home she yanked him up the stairs. His clothes, he briefly noticed, were still in the bucket. She threw him onto the bed and sat astride him, yanking her dress impatiently over her head. She wouldn't let him take off his clothes, just pulled his trousers down sufficiently for her own needs. Her breasts swinging from side to side, one fist pressed tight against the wall and the other holding onto his hair, she appeared to be angrily in charge. Charles was too drunk to do anything but observe her warily and he could see, far back behind her excitement at her own tyranny, the tenderness and fear that flickered like an unprotected flame. She seemed, the whole time, to be asking him a question that he didn't know how to answer. At last she roared: threw her head back and let out a noise that must have carried out onto the streets. Victorious, she waited for her breathing to catch up with her. But she was also stroking his face. She was studying him. He held her breasts just like he always wanted to and tried to meet her eyes, but it was like looking into a furnace.

"That."

She was moulding his cheek in the same way that, earlier, she had been moulding her own forehead.

"I want you to feel like that."

"I do."

"Yes," she said, sadly, "but you also feel about a hundred other things as well."

It was like watching Catherine gather wool: she seemed to tuck in and tidy her own face. She smiled. Then she bent down and bit the tip of his nose.

"Now tell me about that necklace," she said.

CHAPTER TEN

THE NEXT AFTERNOON, he spent two hours at Grimaldi's table, watching Sarah work. There was an excess, almost, of bonhomie. His head was thumping and, when he touched his forehead, it didn't feel like his. It was cold and somehow shrivelled, like he and Grimaldi had switched places. When he left, he could feel Davey's gaze on the back of his head. It was so very intimate that he wanted to pull his collar up.

He was in his bedroom when Mary knocked. He had been fumbling in a drawer, trying to find a pen, and now he wheeled around with a look that, in the mirror, reminded him of peeling stucco. What you were meant to see was the veneer but what you saw instead was the unhappy arrangement of the reality underneath. He was still ill. What he wanted, most of all, was to lie down on the bed. But he had gone two days without writing. His deadlines were like eggs that he was failing to juggle in the air.

Mary stood at the door. It wasn't quite shyness but she didn't seem prepared to look at him in the usual way. She ignored his smile.

"I have written to Mary."

"To Mary?"

"Mary Scott Hogarth. You surely remember her."

"Oh yes."

He was about to imitate the way she walked. But Mary dipped her head. She appeared to be ashamed of her slight smile.

"Don't Charles. I have been praising you."

"Well, of course. I am a fountain of goodwill, am I not?"

He made his arms plume above his head. Once again Mary seemed to be fighting her own smile.

"What you are, Charley, is beyond redemption. I feel slightly hypocritical, I must say. Catherine tells me that you came home last night dressed as a rude mechanical. Your normal clothes, she said, were sopping wet. This morning you swept out of the house and now you smell of drink. Again."

"Mary."

"Don't stop me, please. Charley, what's wrong? She is the dearest, sweetest girl. I know she can be troubling. Who better? But you must remember that she is carrying your child."

"And when do I forget?"

"Now you are bristling."

When she was cross, or awkward, Mary reddened. There was a light dusting of pink on her forehead and at the base of her throat. Her stays were properly tightened and this had brought her breasts into play. The phrase came to Charles like an obscenity. He tried to concentrate on her face.

"Mary, it was a *jeu d'esprit*. I met with Beard and we caroused. Or rather *I* caroused."

"And the clothes?"

"I can't remember. I was drunk. It was an aspect of my drunkenness."

"Yes, but *why* Charley? Why do you feel the need? My sister is in tears again upstairs and you do not seem to feel your usual solicitude."

He grinned.

"Yes. Flowery. But *you* try talking to a writer."

The fact that he had made her cross was, he discovered, more pleasurable than not. This, too, he wouldn't allow himself to acknowledge. He sat on the bed. Then he patted it.

"Mary. My darling Mary. Please sit down."

She did so, throwing up her skirt. She did this as pettishly as if it was for Charles's benefit. Charles took her hand.

"Listen to me. I love your sister."

Her skin, unroughened by domestic work, felt new.

"I will always love your sister. And, yes, perhaps I have felt constrained. A little. I am, after all, a man, despite the many occasions that you have taken to point out that I am essentially a clothes horse."

There it was: her smile. He found that he was as motionless as if he was hunting after it. Or her. He didn't want to scare her off.

"I am," he said, "a creature of fixed habits. I must walk. I must laugh."

"And you can't laugh here?"

"That isn't what I mean."

"You mean you must be made to laugh."

She had a ruefully tolerant air; it seemed to bind the two of them together. He ran his fingers through his hair.

"I feel as though I have to take a breath. The writing. Its grip is almost literal. I have to escape it. And you will say: how hemmed in, then, must Catherine feel? And you will be right."

He had lifted her hand. He became, all at once, as conscious of it as if it had been a stranger's. Carefully, he placed it on the coverlet.

She was saying, "There's no point, I know, asking you to alter this. Or you. I know that you will try and I know that, within hours, you will be absolutely impossible."

Catherine would never have found the courage to say this. She would think it, and he would know that she was thinking it, but it would only be present in the lowering of her shoulders or in the way that, sighing, she picked up an item of cutlery. Mary presumed equality. Her youth was irrelevant, or it nearly was. It made her integrity seem all the more charming. Charles felt something; a vibration. He made himself ignore it.

"I will barricade us in," he said. "I shall build a moat."

"Charley, be serious."

"Mary, what would you have?"

"You, Charles."

There was a tiny pause. She briskly shook her head.

"She would. She wants you back. We know, poor helpless souls, that we can no more tether you than keep a horse. But your actual living presence when you are here would be a start."

She raised her hand.

"Not when you are writing. Charles, please. Don't look like that."

Her hands were slightly larger than you might expect. You could see them work their way through what were supposed to be elegant, feminine poses. At rest, they reminded Charles of girls who stood in terror at the side of a dancing class.

"You are so immured," she said.

"Ensconced, I think you mean."

"I don't. You are bricked-in."

Frustration suited her. It seemed to give her body purpose.

"Pretend, if you must, to be anxious about her. Make her laugh."

"I am. I do."

"You don't. You've stopped."

His hand was rubbing his chin. His face had a characteristic look. It was both excited and diffident. He was listening for something.

"Perhaps—"

"Oh, Charley, no. Not a plan. She's lying in bed, now, barely able to lift her eyes."

"Exactly. Mary."

He clapped his hands.

"A theatrical."

"Good Lord. *No*, Charles."

"Think of it."

"I am."

"For Christmas."

"No."

"But *think*."

He was no longer looking at her. He was staring out of the window.

"She broods, your sister. Always has. She needs to be taken out of herself."

Now his thumb was rubbing against his forefinger. It looked like he was trying to produce a spark.

"The scenery, Charles. The rehearsals."

"Oh, the scenery can be produced elsewhere. The rehearsals are just rehearsals." He shrugged. "They are simply what's necessary."

"And you will write it. Along with everything else."

"I think I can cobble something together, yes."

He was pacing up and down. He grinned down at her.

"It will be *prodigious*."

Mary had given him up to his enthusiasm. She shook her head.

"Can't you just hold her hand?"

He wasn't listening. Not entirely. And he did, anyway: he held her hand almost immediately. He held it every day but he couldn't quite bridge the gap between her feelings and his own. This had very little to do with Sarah. His absence from her, now, was like the time he spent away from his desk. He felt less himself, it was true, but whatever happened next would happen. It was there, in suspension, waiting for him to bring it to life.

The last thing she had said to him was, "A week. I can stomach a week."

"And if it's two?"

"Oh, then I'll sleep with someone else."

He had searched her eyes. Her mouth was tilted in what he thought of as her Cockney grin. It was like the palm of her hand. Or like the rough grain of her voice. They seemed to enjoy pushing you away. Nodding, he said, "You won't."

"Because you know."

He didn't, and so he worked more feverishly than usual. One thing bled into another. The humour of Pickwick became the humour of the theatrical which became a sketch which then, via a route he couldn't begin to apprehend, became the humour of Pickwick. He often felt like he was giving a deposition. This, ladies and gentlemen, is my sense of humour. These are my good spirits. Honour them.

London deliquesced and reformed in exactly the same way that it was doing now, on the foggy streets. He had gone to the pub yesterday morning but she wasn't there. He had told Davey to tell her that he would see her at her house on the following day. It had given him pleasure to do this. He was proud of possessing a woman who was seen as something worth possessing. She was popular, too. Her standing increased his own. Their relationship had become, already, part of the life of the pub and had cemented his position there. Whatever that was. He seemed, in one of his strange transfers of feeling, to *understand* the fog. It both was and wasn't itself. It pushed itself into your face, but, in essence, it was barely there.

Charles inched his way along the street. You literally couldn't see your hand in front of your face. What you relied on was the way that mass, and the absence of mass, communicated what was around you. There would be a building's confiding shoulder and then a boundless space. His instinct, always, was to plunge but he was held back, first by the crowds that formed the edge of the road and then by the noise of coaches, hansoms and their horses. By their shapes too: the way that they seemed to gutter at the heart of the fog like the thickest part of a flame. The sound was magnified into that of a dream heaviness: endlessly falling barrels or else a sentient thunder. He didn't like being cautious, and he didn't like admitting to himself that he was scared. The vehicles spoke to his stomach; they made him want to step back, although this, too, was not so easily defined. Step back from what? To where? Even in sunlight, you couldn't properly differentiate the road from the road's edge. What he did, and what he hated doing, was rely on the crossing sweeper. They had an instinct for it. Perhaps it was simply an excess of bravery brought on by hopelessness. Charles wanted to hold on to them, but he never did. It would be a loss of nerve. And, anyway, they were too dirty.

Mary? He had forgotten. His thoughts were all concentrated in his eyes. But, then, his eyes were implicated in his thoughts. Fog nuzzled the buildings; it stroked his feet. It was bosomy and blowsy. It lay, like a cat, and licked itself. Concupiscence lay all around him. He thought that he was walking towards it, but he was hurrying away from it too. He might have been inclined to give the fog a moral dimension, as though it was something lurking in the body politic. But it wouldn't wash. Neither could he, now that he entered it, have described the rookery to himself in the way that he would be inclined to describe it later, at his desk. He could see, already, how he might turn it into a fairy land. Fog, in his hands, might provide an ambience that was suitable for Ali Baba: a flickering fantasy from which you might expect to see an angry vizier or, yes, an elephant rushing out. But Saffron Hill appeared to have been annulled. Or perhaps it had been properly defined. It had never existed, not in the way it should. The houses were only houses insofar as they were inhabited. They were only shelters in so far as people sheltered there. Nothing seemed permanent—the walls were like rotting teeth, with an excess of saliva surrounding them. The street only became a street when you decided that it was.

The fog wasn't as thick by Sarah's house. She was looking out of her window but she hadn't seen him yet. He examined her with familiar feelings of love and tenderness and helpless ignorance. Who was she? Who did she imagine she was? Who did she imagine that *he* was? She was wearing yellow: it was like a buttery sun hitting the window all at once. Her hair, he saw, had been tied back and she had made herself up carefully. She looked hopeful. You might have said that her face was unguarded if it wasn't for the way that she was balancing her expression, like a hot coal. It felt cruel observing her like this. He stepped loudly underneath her window and she grinned. She did this before she looked down at him, and it was, in its own way, an assertion: that she paid such close attention that she recognised his step. It was a different, more girlish grin. He saw her and Mary both at once, and it made him slightly breathless. He pushed Mary away. If he could have told you what he was doing he would have said that it had been a random thought;

no more. But it lingered in the gentlemanly way he raised his hat. He found that his face was smiling for him.

"You look nice."

"Some writer."

She curtsied.

"I look beautiful."

Her deadpan didn't quite fit. She was obviously pleased. He could hear how lightly she walked downstairs. He wanted to see her in the necklace but he was also grateful when he saw that she wasn't wearing it. Her bare neck seemed to emphasise her dress, which gestured towards an innocence that, through the absence of stays, it then denied. She had on a pair of shoes that she seemed to have saved for the occasion. They were too tight for her. As she swayed up the stairs he could see how her feet struggled inside them. On her table there were strawberries. There were two glasses of red wine. It was touching, the way that it was all slightly wrong. No one had pulled the leaves from out of the strawberries. There was no sugar. Charles nearly laughed. How pampered he was. He smiled, in a show of pleasure. He took her hand; he knew that the moment demanded it.

"Now this is *lovely*."

He made to pick up his wine and a handful of strawberries. Half of the wine was already gone and this encouraged him to try to move her body towards the bed. She grabbed his wrist.

"Sit, Charles."

They were first to behave like storybook lovers, then. Charles saw that there were napkins. He wondered if she'd stolen them from the pub.

"You're honoured," she said.

"I am."

"This dress has been to Ascot."

"On its own?"

There was something they were both grasping for: a style of conversation which might flow more easily between them. Sarah, he saw, thought that the ambience was enough. Provide a space for what you want and what you want will fill it. But Charles didn't know what to do with the polite distance that she seemed to have encouraged. Nothing that he would have done, back in his courting days, seemed to fit. He was reduced to a tender, playful irony that he knew was not enough. Soon, he thought, he would be making swans out of the napkins.

"Tell me," he said.

"What?"

"You never have."

"Explain myself, you mean." She grinned. "Are you going to take notes?"

"I'm genuinely curious."

He didn't know if this was true or not. He didn't feel comfortable. His chair, the way it wouldn't settle on four legs, reminded him of how far he was from home. Perhaps he simply wanted her to feel familiar.

"Charles. Look around you. It's not something that you have to ponder over."

"You are so beautiful."

"I don't know what you mean. That I'm out of place? Listen, you can find this ..."

She gestured at her mouth, and then her eyes.

"... everywhere."

"I know."

"You don't. Bless you. You think it's special, don't you? Like virtue. By rights, I should be a virgin." Smiling, she popped a strawberry into his mouth. "And when you write about me, I'm sure I will be."

The strawberry's sharpness felt like an aspect of Sarah's own. Before you bit into it you expected sweetness. Charles shook his head.

"How could I possibly write about you?"

"You'll find a way. I obviously don't belong here. What was it, Charley? A shipwreck? My father's gambling? Was I with child? Lawks."

She put a hand over her mouth."

"Was it my father's? The rotter."

Smiling, she ruffled his hair.

"Poor lamb. Completely out of his depth."

She sat back in her chair and watched his face.

"I wasn't with child."

Still watching, she seemed to come to a decision.

"Once. He touched me once. I kicked him so hard that he didn't dare do it again."

She grasped his hand.

"Beauty just happens, Charley. Like rain."

She kissed him, lightly, then pulled away.

"Do you want to meet him?"

"Who?"

"My sainted dad."

Before he could answer she had moved quickly towards the door. She opened it and shouted, "Dad?"

No answer. For a moment, Charles thought that this was a joke. But she did it again.

"Dad!"

Now he could hear a scraping and the slow drag of boots. Someone had come to the bottom of the stairs.

"What?"

Wot. The voice was feebly querulous.

"I want you to meet someone."

Charles heard a sigh. The man came effortfully up the stairs and, as he came in, Charles saw how feeble he really was. His legs were like chicken's legs. His arms retained the faintest memory of strength. He had red eyes, a hawklike nose and a mouth that kept trying, and failing, to say something. It was his clothes, Charles thought, that he must have worn; what he was wearing now was almost exactly the same as the outfit that Charles had been made to wear. He took in Charles's waistcoat and top hat and seemed especially taken by his tie pin. Charles found that he wanted to give it to him, but only, really, in the way that you might tip a waiter to get him away from the table.

"This is Charles," Sarah said.

Her father's head appeared to be too heavy for him. He advanced it in the way that a cat might, asking to be stroked. His teeth, when he opened his mouth, were barely there.

"Charmed, sir."

Oh, it was horrible. The breath; the way his voice came sliding obligingly out of his mouth. What did this have to do with Sarah? He was saying something about his humble home, and this, too, was a shock. It made Sarah seem dependent upon him. The man could hardly bear his own weight. The reversal diminished her. Meanwhile, his eyes appeared to be furtively attempting to attach themselves to Charles's. Charles felt himself backing away.

"And how many of you are there, Mr. ..."

He didn't know Sarah's surname. It came to him with the swift horror of a plot reversal. He saw her father register this and saw how it seemed to confirm what he had already thought. His smile became even broader.

"Cooper."

His lips appeared to be fondling themselves. It was like watching someone vigorously rub their hands together, but in nightmare form. Charles had experienced this in dreams: lobsters for hands; macadam for a tongue. He felt something like the same sensation; that he had been put together ineptly and that his parts were drifting away from him.

The man was saying, "It's easily forgotten."

His eyes were flooded with a horrible consanguinity. Nevertheless, he bowed his head.

"Eight, sir."

He looked, somehow, definitively bowed down. His hands appeared to be gripping each other for support.

"Times is 'ard," Sarah said.

She had grinned but now she turned upon her father.

"Stow it, will you? He hasn't come for you to put the bite on him."

Her father's eyes began to boil. It was disconcerting to see how he continued to smile while his voice had the tautness and the keenness of someone who was preparing for an argument.

"So why *does* he come?"

"Enough."

"I'll—"

"What? You'll what? Go on now—sling your hook."

Her father turned to look at Charles.

"Girls, sir. Ungracious. Do, please, stay. I'm sure you'll be made to feel comfortable."

He seemed to ooze his way out of the door. Charles was made to feel ashamed of his clean fingernails and clothes. He felt like he had failed a test. Sarah was closing the door behind him. She didn't look upset. The opposite, in fact. She nodded at him in satisfaction.

"My father the pimp."

Charles didn't feel the comfort that he felt he should have got from the closed door. Outside, the fog made Sarah's room feel like the pub: a bubble kept aloft by dint of a conspiracy. But there was no comfort in that either. He was rubbing at his nose. The strawberries no longer looked invitingly domestic. They no longer looked like anything.

"Why did you show him to me?"

"Show him?"

She was assessing him.

"This isn't a menagerie."

"You did. You displayed him."

She sat down, heavily, in her chair. She leaned across and breathed into his face.

"Charley, why do you come here?"

"What do you mean?"

"Why do you? Is it just to spend an hour hanging by your fingernails?"

Charles tried to gather his thoughts.

"Is it to test yourself? To dig up something juicy?"

She appeared to be choosing where to place a strawberry. Up and down. It was a form of punctuation.

"Is it the sex? Is that it? Because—"

She held up her hand. He had been about to speak.

"Because I love you."

She had never said it before. She seemed struck, suddenly, by the truth of the words that she had spoken. "I do. And this. This room. It's what I amount to, Charley. You can't just come." She grinned. "Well, you can. But you have to come *here*. You have to know what it is. You have to be here, with me." She smiled. "And him."

"'This thing of darkness I acknowledge mine.'"

"Yes." She thought about it. "No. Nearly."

Again, he tried to speak but she was already continuing.

"I don't acknowledge him. I won't. I get this room because I work. I pay for it. Otherwise they'd all be in here, rubbing themselves against the furniture."

"And he thinks ..." He didn't know how to put it.

"What?"

"That I—"

"That we fuck? Darling, he can hear."

"No."

He was shaking his head too rapidly. The inference was suddenly too terrible to contemplate. It took her a moment to catch up.

"That you pay?"

"Don't."

He was looking down at his feet. He felt her hand capture his chin. It was both rougher and less rough than his wife's. Less rough because more graceful.

"Look at him. He cares. No, darling, he doesn't think that. He wishes you would but that's a different matter entirely."

"I've always tried to avoid this sort of thing."

"Don't lie."

"Not prostitutes. How else would a man learn anything? No. I mean ..."

What did he mean? She stood and came around the table. She took his hands and lifted him onto his feet.

"Life," she said.

She picked a strawberry.

"I wonder what we can do with this?"

She looked at him almost kindly. She put her hand behind the mirror on the mantlepiece and pulled the necklace out. She fastened it then stepped out of her clothes. Afterwards, she allowed him to cradle her in his arms. She was looking up at the ceiling. Before, the necklace had excited him: it had felt like the two of them were stealing it all over again. But now it was their guilty secret. Neither was accurate. He hadn't told her anything.

"I always wanted to be a ballerina," she said. She stared into his eyes. "Don't laugh."

"I wasn't."

"You were about to."

"No. No. I wasn't. You are always so graceful."

He meant it. Like neatness, only sexier. She was allowing a smile to spread across her face.

"This is like beauty, is it?"

He shrugged. He did it carefully, so as not to disturb the arrangement of her limbs over his own.

"What did you expect? Mooing?"

"It's just—"

"Knocking things over with my tits."

"Your fingers," he said. "They dance."

He made his fingers flicker. He meant around the bottles behind the bar. Sarah looked down at his groin.

"You don't complain."

"You are a lubricious woman."

"Thank you."

She bit his shoulder. She wasn't particularly gentle, but he wouldn't have wanted her to be.

"A ballerina," she said, "and then I wanted to go on the stage. I did the usual when I was little. I sold matches, then watercress. You try to make yourself look grubbier. You stand there looking like you'd ask for something if you only could. Do you want to see?"

"Of course."

She lowered her forehead so that her face appeared to be all eyes. She had pushed her mouth outwards and her cheeks appeared to grow fatter against her shoulders.

"That's very good."

"I used to practice in the mirror. I made a living."

She waggled her hand from side to side.

"*Almost* a living. But it's miserable, of course."

"I can imagine."

"You can't, Charley. I know you think you can but you can't."

Before he could speak she said, "And I'm not going to tell you."

Her face was inscrutable.

"I ... advanced my career. Now I make faces inside."

"And do you like it?"

"Bar work? It's better than the streets. And think: I was only selling matches. Mostly."

She was toying with his right hand. She was pulling up one finger and then the other. Her face was impassive but her fingers couldn't rest.

"My sisters. Well there. They will take money. They do."

She was biting her lower lip. Charles said,

"What do you mean? Mostly?"

She shook her head, rapidly, like she was freeing herself from something.

"Don't, Charley. Don't ask me, please."

Her face was more serious than he had ever seen it. He had seen it angry, of course, and passionate but he had never seen it so denuded of expression that there was almost nothing left except for loss. Nor had he seen this: the way that the muscles of her face were working so strenuously to deny it. He saw her struggle to make her eyes and mouth cohere; to look at him with what passed for hope. At last, she prodded him in the chest.

"I'm a cut above. I work."

"And act."

"If you can call it that."

"I do. To me you do."

"You think it's stupid, which it is. I might as well be a bear. They might as well prod me with a stick." She sighed. "'Macbeth.' Only it isn't, is it?"

"It could be worse. I did O'Tello once. I was meant to be Irish."

"In your house, was it? Lots of … How do you describe them? Ruddy faces. All beaming at you. You and your—"

"Yes. Alright."

"Your wife. Why can't I say the word?"

"It shouldn't trip so easily off your tongue. I can hardly say it myself."

"Perhaps you should."

He shook his head.

"No. Here isn't the place for her."

"Among the poor and needy."

"That isn't what I meant."

"I bet she doesn't use a bucket for her clothes."

"Sarah."

The leg farthest away from him was moving swiftly up and down.

"Does she even get cramps? Or does she pay somebody else to have them for her?"

He went to move closer to her but she pushed him off. She was pressed against the wall now and he saw that, in the extremity of her anger, she looked almost scared.

"Everything! I tell you everything!"

"Not quite."

"Don't you split hairs with me."

"It isn't the same."

"Why not?"

Sternly, he said, "Because I have so very much to lose."

Attempting to rear backwards, Sarah pressed herself even more firmly against the wall. It had been an attempt to say something definitive; to end the argument. It was supposed to be similar to the way she used her palm. It was only now, when he saw her face, that he realised how much he had hurt her. He said "Sarah," softly, but she was already saying, "And I haven't, have I. Just this."

She gestured to her room. In the fading light of late afternoon, it appeared to be something that they were both failing to imagine. She began ticking things off on her fingers. "And the pub. And the penny gaffs. And a family. Nothing."

"The child, Sarah."

"The child." She shook her head. "Do you not think I'd have one if I could? Christ, I'd have *yours*."

Where was she going? Too late, he realised that she was straddling his chest. She had begun to pummel it.

"I would not hurt your *fucking* child!"

This wasn't mania. She was proving a point; no more. Nevertheless, her hair was as wild as if she was in a storm. Charles felt sorry, and ashamed, but still there was part of him that wanted to extricate himself, the way that he would if his hand was in a dirty glove. This made him feel even more ashamed. Sarah was crying.

"I might as well be a fucking whore."

"Don't say that."

"At least if you paid me I'd know what I was getting out of it."

Once again, she gathered her face together. It was impressive: an assertion of a will whose strength had allowed her to negotiate God knows what. Charles didn't want to think about it. He saw the darkness of the streets; the shadows looming from the alleyways. He saw her for a moment at the age of eight. Despite his writing's careful nullity, he knew exactly what might have happened to her. As always he wanted both to hold her and to run away. She was looking down at him like she didn't know what to do with him. He was as much, and as little, a problem as his clothes had been. Then she inhabited herself again. She sniffed. It wasn't unattractive. It made her seem innocent, almost.

"Charles, do you love me?"

When he tried to speak she placed her palm over his mouth.

"Wait," she said. "You can't—"

Briefly, she struggled with her hair. She was attempting to persuade it to lie down.

"You can't just say it. Do you understand? I'm sure you have. I'm sure you've said it to all sorts of people. Or else you haven't. You've avoided it. You've said "esteem" and "tender regard." Well, you can't do either of those here. Tell me exactly what you feel. Be brave. I dare you."

Her face belied her words. It was more naked than he had ever seen it.

"Please."

Love her? Of course he did. Right now he did. How could he not? But every word that he might say seemed sullied with misuse. It also seemed inaccurate. Instead, he stroked her cheek, looked into her eyes and nodded. It wasn't enough. He saw how she was still waiting for something tender. He took a breath.

"I do."

An unfortunate choice of words. He loved her, at that moment, with all his heart. When would there come, in after life, a passion more earnest? But he still wanted to take it back. Sarah was nodding. Silly, he supposed, to have expected that she would throw herself upon him.

"Then you have to *love* me."

She was still straddling his chest. She looked down at him from what appeared to be a position of superiority. She paused. She was marshalling her thoughts. Eventually she said, "I want to see it."

"What?"

"Your house."

"Oh Sarah. No."

"Why not?"

"It isn't a house. It's a flat. You won't see it if we walk past it."

"Who says I want to walk past it?"

She was holding onto his chest hair; tugging it so that it almost hurt.

"I want to see inside."

"That isn't possible."

"Why isn't it?"

"How can I possibly take you inside my flat?"

"You don't trust me."

"It isn't that."

"You don't. You think that I'll be out there at all hours, weeping and groaning. Or that I'll nick something. Or shit in your bed."

"There's always someone there."

"So what? I could be anyone."

"Like who?"

"You choose."

He found that his hand was searching for a comb. He reached under his arm instead and made it look like he had an itch.

"It isn't itself at the moment."

"What *do* you mean?"

"We're getting it ready. For a theatrical. The whole place is going to be upside down."

"For Christmas."

"Yes."

"When else?"

She wasn't looking at him now. She was imagining it. She stepped off the bed and began to busy herself around the room. It was impossible to tell what she was thinking. She finished the last strawberry then stacked the plates and cutlery. Charles presumed that they were washed in the same bucket that she used to wash herself. Once again, he was struck by the incongruity of his situation. Not even when he had been forced to live in lodgings as a child had he stayed in a room so small and badly appointed. The house itself was like the toilet in the factory: you wouldn't want to go near it after dark. But the room was comfortable. It wasn't even that she was in it. It was that she always gave it sufficient attention. She was like a potter, smoothing and tending something as it threatened, always, to dissolve. If Charles was no longer moved by this it was because he had become a part of it. But not entirely: watching her walk naked around the room was arousing him. It was because, for that moment, he was estranged from her.

"Your thoughts?"

She snorted.

"My thoughts? That there are people who can stage a play in their own homes."

She had begun to polish the mirror. Charles wasn't sure if she knew that she was doing it.

"God. Those gaffs. You take your life into your hands. But you have carols. You have pastries and games."

When she wheeled around it wasn't quite balletic. It was more another assertion: that she intended to be undeniable.

"I want to be in it."

"In what?"

He knew perfectly well what. He shook his head.

"Don't be ridiculous."

"Am I? Being ridiculous?"

"Sarah, think about what you're saying."

"I *am* thinking. I'm always thinking. I don't get to do anything else."

"But damn it, woman."

He had sat up and now he was enumerating points; he was ticking them off with his index finger on the sheet beneath him. She wouldn't be dissuaded. He was almost certain that it was a whim. Something womanish: an impulse that would not survive the evening. But his resistance goaded her into a stubbornness that refused to be reasoned with. It became, in the end, something that she felt that she should have by right. She threw a plate at him and, as it shattered behind him, he wondered if this wasn't a prelude to some kind of passionate renewal. Against the wall perhaps? On the floor, beside the bucket? But it was no such thing. She was all fire then she was stone. She didn't turn away when he tried to hold her; just stood there, immobile, and suffered his embrace. She wouldn't even watch him leave.

He didn't brood upon the argument. She could hardly have meant what she was saying. Almost as soon as he left, his head was with Pickwick and Weller. His right hand was making little adjustments in the manuscript that he was about to write.

But his father was in the living room. There was no one else there, although Charles could hear the noise of pots and pans in the kitchen below. His father was standing with his back to his desk and, just for a moment, it was humorous, almost: a parody of his younger years. Had he ever been disciplined? He must have been, although he had been such a sensitive soul that his body had administered most of its own punishments. His father was not a disciplinarian. His face, these days, was a corrupted version of Charles's own. He had the same pride and determination but they seemed to come at you sidelong; they had to make their way through all of that deference and charm. His face was getting fatter and it looked like there were two of them: a placid outer one and an inner one that knew no rest. He was working the brim of his hat. He seemed, when he stepped slightly forward, to be dancing in one place.

"Hello, old chap."

"An unexpected pleasure."

The words seemed not to want to make their way between his teeth. When it came to his father, there was always something clotted in his response. He found himself speaking with a terse, reluctant attempt at casualness that sounded like someone else. His father tried to smile.

"Come now," he said. "Cannot a man decide to see his son?"

"Yes. Yes. Of course."

Charles pointed to a chair. His father very carefully sat down. He took the top half of each trouser leg and tugged at them, fastidiously.

"Your book."

He was nodding rapidly.

"Successful. Very. Witty, too."

"Thank you."

Was he about to put the bite on him? For once, he seemed at a loss for words. He had placed his hat beside the chair and now he was rubbing the top of his head. He was looking down at the floor. When he looked up, he fixed his eyes on a point just to the left of Charles.

"This is difficult, Charley," he said. "I am not ..."

He waved his hand in a gesture that should, really, have accompanied a generous amount of eloquence.

"... a Pharisee. I am a man of the world."

Again, he gestured. He made a rotund-looking curlicue that Charles knew from his youth. It was the acme of good breeding; of argumentative élan. Charles wondered where he got it from. Usually, by now, he would be rocking slightly. He would have produced a tone that had both the thrum and the momentum of the traffic on the London streets. Now, though, he had paused again. Both hands appeared to be whipping up something in front of his chest; invisible cream, perhaps, or a froth of water in the bath.

"One expects," he said, "that a man will formulate a view of life that is both generous and expedient. That he will not, ah, *refuse* experience. After all, it is usually impressed upon him that he must experience everything. And, of course, you are a writer."

There was a slight panic in his eyes. He seemed to be watching helplessly as the words ran away from him.

"You must—"

"What must I do?"

Charles was beginning to lose patience. He found, these days, that he often spoke to his father as though he was his child. He indulged him, but with a lack of patience that, even to himself, seemed somewhat Teutonic. His father flinched. He pointed his head towards the floor then slowly lifted it. It appeared to have gained weight.

"This is difficult, Charles. I have friends. They come from all walks of life and they are, as you may imagine, scattered all over the city. I have something like fifty eyes and ears."

He said this with a certain amount of pride. But then his face dropped. Literally: his mouth and his eyes seemed to have become tired of themselves. It was like Charles's face: a cornucopia. But now his solemnity came entirely from within; it hadn't been thrown over it like a cloak. What *was* the matter with him? Charles felt a little frightened. His father was awkwardly thumbing his nose.

"And you were seen."

"And I was seen. Where was I seen? Seen doing what?"

Charles had leaned forward slightly. He was hoping that his natural impatience would work in his favour. What, he seemed to imply, could he possibly have been doing that could merit all of this fuss? His stomach had tautened alarmingly, however. His face, he knew, looked colder and more forbidding the more that his stomach tightened. He had to stop his hand from reaching for the comb in his waistcoat pocket. As it was, he had already taken the hair at the front of his head and flung it backwards in irritation.

"With a woman, Charley. You were seen with a woman."

"Father, I know many women."

"Not like this. This, apparently, was outside a penny gaff. You were ..."

He couldn't finish the sentence. He was rubbing at his forehead, punishing it with his fingers in exactly the same way that

Charles would do. After a pause, he spread his arms on either side of his body with his palms pressed upwards. It looked like he had wings, but in reverse. Never had either of them seemed so earthbound; so unequal to life's circumstances.

"Have you lost your head?"

"To her?"

"No, no. Yes. Possibly. That wasn't what I meant."

He was leaning forward now. He was as innocent of mannerism as he had ever been.

"On the grass, Charley."

He was looking at him man to man. He had never done this before. Charles wanted to get up.

"On a scrap of wasteland. A married man. There are—"

"Places."

"Yes. Places. And times. And means."

Charles felt as though shame had covered him from head to foot. He attempted to stand upon his dignity.

"Father, this is not—"

But his father had thrust a finger between them. He was wielding it like a baton.

"I do not think that it is your turn to speak."

No one, apart from Charles, could be as angry as his father. He had once flung himself at a mirror, mistaking it for an intruder. Now he glared furiously at Charles and Charles could do nothing but allow himself to take it in. How much weight would a parental injunction have? He was almost curious to find out. He watched, a little disappointed, as the fight went out of his father's face.

"I hope you know what you are doing."

Charles nearly said, "I don't." The need for his father's understanding was like the twinge of an unused muscle. He wanted, just for a second, to throw himself into his father's arms. He saw everything, suddenly, in a big heap: a barmaid with whom he was having sex; a stolen necklace; Grimaldi's animus, still there, like a quiescent snake; Davey, who looked like he wanted to pick him up by the throat, not out of animosity so much as for his own amusement. And the sex again; the public nature of it. He felt, for a moment, like he wanted to unburden himself. But one doesn't use a muscle that one doesn't trust. The moment lengthened until he could stand it no longer.

"Do you need money?"

Immediately, he could have kicked himself. It had been a form of self-assertion. An acknowledgment, too, of the filial feelings that he found himself unable to express. But it was too sudden. When he usually asked this question, several expressions would appear on his father's face at once. Greed, yes, and embarrassment and fear and a distinct rage against the world and a coyness that made him seem flirtatious. Now, though, he just looked hurt. He looked almost dignified. He glanced down at his hat and scratched his cheek. He grinned, but in a way that was entirely without humour.

"I do. As you so rightly intuit, Charles, I always do. Thank you."

And he stood up.

"But not just now."

He walked with real dignity towards the door. He seemed about to speak but then he changed his mind. Placing his hat upon his head he nodded, briskly, once. His face was appalling: all injured pride, leavened with real concern. He looked, Charles thought, like a returning ghost who had been sent to warn someone who could do nothing with his feelings but hoard them carefully. He tried to speak, but that was the point: he couldn't. Then his father was gone.

CHAPTER ELEVEN

Sarah said, "Who's Mary?"

He was only half-aware of what he'd said. He was already pushing the word as far away from him as he could. It had been like touching a hot iron, or a turd that had been mouldering in the street.

"You called her name."

"Did I?"

He was having to be as careful with his voice as he was being with his face. It had to display its own kind of immobility.

"A slip, I assure you. The only Mary I know is my wife's sister."

"*Do* you now?"

"No; no. Truly. She's my sister-in-law, that's all."

"Who," she said ambiguously, "would want your life?"

Her face had an immobility of its own. It resembled Grimaldi's deadpan, but the effect was not meant to be the same. It was true, in any case. Who indeed? His feelings were so complicated—so hopelessly, endlessly entangled—that he couldn't put them into words. He chose to pretend that they didn't exist. Sarah had slid from underneath him and now she was tinkering about the room. Even her arse communicated how annoyed she was. There was a briskness to the way it ticked from side

173

to side: as Charles observed it, it kept saying "no." But not for long. She loved him; it was as simple as that. Soon she would be in his arms again.

She hadn't mentioned the flat. Charles thought that he might have got away with it. Or, at least, that he would be able to counter whatever blow she felt disposed to aim at him. He had seen her twice, and both times she had slipped the necklace on. She appeared to think it was something of a wifely gesture, even though, for Charles, it felt deliciously transgressive. He couldn't tell her this, of course. He wondered why he wasn't more concerned. A capital crime! He would have given it back but he wasn't sure if that wouldn't have made it worse.

He had lain awake at night—he would, if he had not been with Catherine, have torn his hair—but then he hadn't. He had got used to what he had done. He had given the necklace to Sarah. Time had passed. This is what he told himself, most strenuously: that, if the man had known who he was, he would have tracked him down by now. Charles had avoided the Strand at first, but now he didn't. If the man should accost him in the street (he said this to himself with especial emphasis) he could simply shrug and say he didn't know what he was talking about. Charles put great store in his ability to carry something off. But it was more than that. It was all of a piece. Sarah; the necklace; rolling like an animal on the grass outside the penny gaff—it was difficult to separate them in his head. He felt entitled to get away with all of it.

Meanwhile, he was even more determined to protect his domesticity. His father had genuinely shocked him. He hadn't been prepared to change but that didn't mean that he didn't want to put up a better show. He had been looking for a house; with Catherine, yes, but also with Mary. Moving Catherine around was like attempting to steer a galleon. She needed notice just to turn a corner. But without her the task would have felt pointless. They needed the extra room, of course; they weren't allowed to have a baby where they were. But could they afford it? And what was he doing, anyway, further embedding his life in bricks and mortar when he was so very present somewhere else? No, Catherine was a physical reminder of the necessity for space. She seemed, sometimes, to take up the entire room. The necessity for comfort, too: somewhere soft and emotionally velvety, like a jewellery box, to keep her safe. She was, her face was, still a jewel. It was a moral imperative.

And Mary? Mary was like sunlight. Her laugh was like running water. She brought each place to life. This wasn't always a good thing: one didn't necessarily want to hear about the hilarious way that a house was leaning sideways or the way that its windows seemed to be insistently opaque. She gravitated, invariably, to the best houses in the same way that Charles was drawn to rookeries. She perched on a window-sill, licked her finger, placed it in mid-air then *drew* the house that they were in. Then they both examined it in the air. Or else she drew a new one, garden and all. Her face participated in every facet of their future life. It frolicked in the garden; squeezed itself doubtfully into the scullery. But it stopped short of the bedroom. It skidded to a halt, and grinned. Charles could tell himself that he was planning it all for Catherine, but in his head he was able to inhabit it with Mary. Catherine was upstairs somewhere, feeding the baby. Mary was riddling the grate or playing cards. He always imagined laughter and, when he did, it was always Mary's.

He had reached what he thought of, without putting it into words, as higher ground. He was safely ensconced in his new plans. Immured, so that when Grimaldi said "scoundrel" Charles was unprepared. Grimaldi was different now. He sat there like a lion, expecting Charles to pay court to him.

"Sam Weller. Here he is."

He gestured graciously to the space beside him.

"Come on, Boots, pull up a chair."

He was alone, although Charles could see that Davey was at the bar. He was murmuring something to Sarah. Sarah was nodding, and smiling, but her eyes were fixed firmly upon himself. He was careful not to try to wipe the chair. He nodded, briefly, man to man but Grimaldi didn't wish to respond. He was looking Charles up and down.

"Where *do* you buy your clothes?"

He leaned over and took his lapel between his thumb and forefinger.

"I've seen ringmasters who are more discreet than this."

He grinned, then shuffled backwards into his chair. The thinness of his legs accentuated the size of his upper body. But his body was useless too. He was reduced to swaying from side to side like a parakeet. His fingers were as thick as potato tubers. He took aim with his cigar.

"How *are* things, Boots?"

Charles shrugged. What could he say? He accepted a cigar, and then a match. The taste of the smoke made him feel like he was holding his own: that he was sharing, to some degree, in what Grimaldi was experiencing. If Grimaldi could decide that it was pleasant then so could he.

"There's a theatrical I hear."

"Ah."

"Yes. 'Ah.'"

Grimaldi was scratching his chest. He looked like a monkey. This, the way he was taunting him, was monkey business. He stared deeply into Charles's eyes.

"You, sir, are a scoundrel."

He seemed delighted with this sally. Charles was bewildered, and then he remembered Sarah's laughter on the street. Did she tell Grimaldi everything? Charles squared his shoulders. He was about to make a riposte when he saw that Davey was teetering towards them from the bar. He had three drinks and he put one in front of each of them. It was significant, Charles felt, that his was the only one that spilled.

"There are," he said.

He squinted at Charles.

"Down it," he said. "You need to catch up."

Charles took a gulp; one that, he was prepared to admit, was bigger than usual. But he was damned if he was going to allow these people to tell him what he should or shouldn't do. He was angry at both of them. He felt as though someone had come behind him and tried to pull his trousers down. Grimaldi was waving his cigar. Was it deliberate that the smoke seemed to be smearing itself all over Charles's face?

"I was just saying."

"You were?"

"I was."

"Do you need to ..."

Davey waggled his fingers in mid-air.

"... go back? I do love a good story."

There had been something mock-courtly in the gesture. It had been vaguely literary—he could almost have been writing something down—and it seemed both pointed and sardonic. Grimaldi shook his head. This, too, appeared to be exaggerated.

The stilted nature of their exchange was amusing them. It was meant to be instructive. Intimidating, too.

"No; no. You know it."

"Ah."

Davey was eyeing Charles, with relish.

"I do, do I?"

He was trapped, just as he had been trapped before. But this felt different. When Davey picked up his glass, his hand was as lazy as a cat's paw. Checkmate. Grimaldi was rocking, slightly, from side to side again. If he could, he would have danced. Or leapt up and down.

"See her?"

He nodded his head towards where Sarah was doing something with the spirits at the back of the bar. Her hands had their usual dazzle but Charles could see, from the set of her shoulders, how aware she was of the three of them. Of him, especially.

"I do."

"You do, do you? Davey, what do you think? Do you think he does?"

"I don't."

"You don't?"

Davey shook his head. He had his own form of deadpan. His lips were pressed as tightly together as if he had just tasted something that he didn't like.

"I don't think he does. At. All."

Once more, Grimaldi employed his cigar. It was like he was lecturing; like Sarah was an exhibit.

"She," he said, "loves you."

He allowed a moment for them all to examine that. Davey was stony faced. Grimaldi was moving his head, slowly, from side to side.

"Remarkable," he said. "Me, I think you're a glass of milk."

He was studying him closely. He looked just like his father. All the business had left his face. It was just his: careful and serious and disapproving.

"Me, I wouldn't put you in a basket and throw you off the stage. I wouldn't catch you, neither."

He dragged, luxuriously, on his cigar and blew the smoke up at the ceiling. He watched it for a moment. It separated into gouts and tufts. His creatures. When he looked down, his face had resumed its usual expressiveness. One eyebrow seemed amused while the other had lowered itself over an eye. His mouth had set into a line. It looked like he was both angry and trying not to laugh.

"So this is what you're going to do. You are going to employ her."

"Employ."

"It's not a difficult word, Charley. Make use of. Utilise. And not when your legs are around her head."

Charles went to stand up but Davey held his arm. He held it lightly; delicately, almost. But it was sufficient.

"Look at him," Grimaldi said. "Sensitive."

He was pointing his finger at him. His hand appeared to be smoking, like a gun.

"I have promised her, my little impresario, that you are going to give her a part."

Charles groaned.

"Well may you groan. I don't envy you. Do you envy him, Davey?"

"I really don't."

Davey's face was still perfectly straight.

"I mean," Grimaldi said, "God knows how you're going to square it with the missus. Still."

Again, he shrugged. It was remarkably expressive: his shoulders seemed to go all the way up to his ears.

"Not my problem."

"I can't."

"You will."

"I won't."

"You fucking will. Davey?"

Charles was actually writhing in his chair. He was becoming, despite himself, more and more angry.

"I might," he said, straightening upwards, "be prepared to take a beating. I really might."

He punched his chest.

"I mean it," he said.

Davey stared at him and laughed. Or almost laughed: it was more of a violent propulsion of air. He rubbed his hand slowly under his nose.

"It wouldn't take a whole beating."

Grimaldi said, "He's a firecracker, ain't he? Listen, jack-in-the-box, no one's beating anyone. Davey. Tell him."

"Tell me what?" Charles was still angry. He was still debating with himself. Would he make an issue of it? He found that he wanted to punch Davey anyway. His face had a supercilious gloss; he was too lordly, for the moment, even to acknowledge Charles's presence. He was looking down at his fingernails. He seemed to be examining them.

"Colbert's. Just off the Strand. The geezer's going mental. Or he was. I have a mate who goes in sometimes. He wouldn't do what you did; he wouldn't be so fucking stupid. He goes in, makes little purchases and looks for weaknesses. Only there aren't none. Thing is, the bloke who runs it has no idea who done it. None. Who would be *stupid* enough ..."

He had pushed his lips so far outwards that it looked like he was puckering up for a kiss. He left a tiny pause, just in case Charles hadn't got the inference.

"... to do a runner from there? It keeps him awake at nights. He keeps thinking: who? No, really, who? He has no idea."

He pulled his fingers inwards and looked more closely at his nails.

"Yet."

Charles found that no words would come. It was like grabbing for a handle on a 'bus and failing to reach it in time—like being jangled over the cobbles without any means of support. Grimaldi nudged him.

"Boots. Consider. She doesn't know."

He jerked his elbow backwards.

"Lord love her, she has no idea. She thinks it was a ... a ... what's that word?"

His face was visibly searching his memory. It went roaming through show after show.

"Afflatus!"

He was delighted.

"Divine afflatus. Lifting you above the common herd. You just floated in there, didn't you, and gave over all your hard-earned cash."

He tilted his head.

"Well, I say hard-earned."

He had been edging ash off the table. Now he was wiping the surface carefully with his sleeve. He didn't look up until this was done. It was a way, Charles thought, of displaying that this was his territory. Charles was an intruder, and they were done. For now? No. Done. He might come in as often as he liked but this would always be the way things were. Grimaldi rubbed his chin.

"You're not as nice as your characters."

He grinned.

"But who is?"

At home, Charles tried to work. He tried to walk, round and round, but even this was difficult. Nothing would come. There was a timid knock on the door.

"Charles?"

"Yes Catherine."

"You seem disturbed."

"I'm working up a sentence."

There was a pause. He was listening for her footsteps on the stairs, but then she said,

"Your father was here."

"I have neither the time nor the inclination at present."

"No dear. Was. I was telling him about the play."

"Oh God. Don't tell me that he wants to be in it."

Catherine giggled. Her face was half-in; half-out. It was beginning to dimple. Charles might, on another occasion, have found this endearing. Now he thought: is she doing it deliberately?

"The thought," she said. "No, I told him he could do the door."

"The door."

"Stand there and look welcoming."

"Good Lord. Why?"

"He needs something to do, Charley. He is terribly sad. He misses you, I think"

Usually, Charles wouldn't—he couldn't—have let this go past. If it was a criticism, it was so vaguely implied that it was possible that Catherine wasn't aware of it. But Charles couldn't think. He literally couldn't. He waved his arm in front of him, as though he was inviting himself to walk. He *must* walk, the inference was. He must do it now.

Catherine nodded, and smiled. She closed the door gently. Charles had the giddy sense that the room was about to dance around him. Watching the door close, he sat in the middle of the room and cried.

CHAPTER TWELVE

THE FLAT WAS arranged as follows: on the top floor, a landing, a sitting room and two bedrooms. Each was interlocked with the other, so that, when Charles was working, you had to glide through the living room like a ghost. Downstairs, there was a kitchen, a basement and a lumber room. Catherine had to keep them all balanced in her head so that each room was always as well-appointed as the other. Charles did this, too. You could move an ornament in the bedroom and Charles, seemingly rapt in concentration, would hear you. He would make you put it back.

Christmas was different, but only by a matter of degree. Charles had, in a sense, made up Christmas as he went along. It had always been pleasant but Charles had set such store by it that it became rather more than the mild, and mildly familial, religious holiday that she had been used to. There were candles and games and such extraordinary piles of food—such heaps of fruit and nuts and toffee and carefully tended meat—that she didn't know, afterwards, what to do with it all. Charles's version of bonhomie was slightly frightening: he would thrust drinks into people's hands in the same way that others might issue a challenge. He became so insistent on the games that he wanted to play that a vein stuck out on his forehead. One couldn't just *be*. But that was what being was for Charles: to do, to do, to do. And to show. This is my flat. This is my wife and her lovely sister. And look: look at my trousers.

Catherine smiled. The flat was upside down, of course, and she was supposed to be grateful. The scenery hadn't fitted in the living room. Charles and his brother had had to saw away at it. Now it stood, somewhat disconsolately, against the wall. It was supposed to be a London panorama and, indeed, enough of it was recognizable to make her feel a slight degree of anticipation. Sunlight had been painted on the Thames and now it glittered in the candlelight like so much gold. Sawdust was everywhere, and Fred was looking at it suspiciously while listening to Charles. You could see the way that he wanted to be seen to defer to Charles in everything; the way that he smiled and nodded so enthusiastically that it was as though Charles was deaf. But, then, she did something similar, and so did Mary. Mary teased him, which only appeared to be different. She was approaching an age when this should stop.

Catherine watched Charles and she saw how hard he tried not to respond to it. She saw how his eyes lit up; how he pulled himself backwards, like a bow, in order to issue another sally. She knew that it had been almost entirely her doing when he stopped touching her. She thought that she could feel the child, the way that it tilted warily from side to side, and sex, she felt, would have been something of an assault. Still, she sometimes allowed herself to think that it had been Charles's doing. He had stopped getting drunk. He was everything she could have wanted: tender and softly spoken and solicitous. But he treated her like she was ill. He didn't seem to see *her* at all. He edged himself around her like she was a horse that was blocking the road. He did this with great good humour, but he only ever did this. He seemed no longer to want to participate in what her body was doing. Meanwhile, he and her sister tossed his mind between them like a bright ball.

Neither did his father know what to do with her. He behaved like she was liable to cry at any minute. (To be fair, she often did.) He studied her eyes and hemmed and hawed then cleared his throat. What came out, invariably, was something leaden and altogether too sympathetic. It was Christmas Eve. There was holly everywhere but he had eyed it distrustfully. He had looked even more lugubrious than he usually did. Now he seemed to want to guard the place. He kept sneaking a look around it, as though to check that nothing was going to run away. He insisted on standing by the front door. He had on his best waistcoat, a swallow-tail coat and a cravat. He had taken his hat off but, even so, he seemed much grander than she would have liked. He had nodded, briefly, at Charles, had tested the stability of the panorama and had grimly surveyed the actors and the maid who was attempting to clean the floor. When he was satisfied, he left the room as slowly as if he had been a captain checking his ship.

Catherine didn't know where she was supposed to put herself. Certainly not in the sitting room, where Charles was drilling the members of the cast. There was Fred and Charles's sister, who was at the piano. Her arms were already feathering the keys, so eager was she to dip her hands into them. Beard was ... what? A suitor? And was that Cruickshank? He looked particularly uncomfortable. Dear Mr. Browne had also been drafted in. He had the kindest of faces but he, too, looked a little lost. He was dressed, approximately, as a woman, with two shockingly bright circles of rouge plastered over his cheeks. His dress was so wide that he had to hold it down. Mary was a shepherdess. Of course. She was in curls. An innocent. Charles couldn't have borne to expose her to whatever indignities he had prepared for the rest of them. He had drafted in the extra maid; the one who was currently attempting to do something about the sawdust. It struck her that she should have been the one to tell her what to do but this was typical of Charles. The whole thing, the whole bright Christmas bauble, was ostensibly made for her but she might as well have been a puff of air for all the influence that she felt she had. Charles had his arms suspended above his head. Beard smiled.

"'Speak the speech, I pray you—'"

"Yes. Yes."

Charles looked like he was poised over a drop. It was all too serious for him to want to smile. This despite the fact that he was dressed not only in a waistcoat of wide stripes but also in breeches and leggings. He had a red handkerchief around his neck and had carefully placed an old white trilby at a jaunty angle on his head.

"Cruikshank," he said, "don't chew your lines. Browne. Sashay, please. You're not moving your hips. And Fanny: it needs to be broader. It's not a showcase."

Cruikshank was already slightly drunk. His face had a look of ponderous irony and, when he nodded, he seemed about to fall asleep. Browne nodded eagerly. He stood on one leg, raised an eyebrow and placed a finger against his lips. Fred laughed. Frances was studying her fingers. She was lifting them up and down as briskly as she could. Charles was instructing Mary,

"You're—"

"Completely innocent."

"Yes."

"Without a thought in my pretty little head."

"Well. One or two, perhaps."

"The notion of men hasn't occurred to me at all."

"I'm barely a man."

She sighed.

"I know."

"I'm like Dick Whittington's cat."

He grinned. She gave him a look that was so complicated that Catherine had to stare at the floor. She turned her attention to the woman who was still picking diligently at the sawdust. She was paying altogether too much attention to what Charles was saying. Her hands were remarkably deft: she had picked up a respectable amount, but she seemed to have no notion of what to do with it. Catherine noted the roughness of her complexion and the bold steadiness of her regard. At one point she had smiled.

"That'll do," Catherine said.

The maid stared at her for a moment, nodded and stood up. The nod was an affront; it made it look like they had decided something together. Her body was bold: it took up space like it had elbowed other things out of the way. She was negligent with it because she could afford to be; because it was slender enough to do exactly what she wanted. She would never have to lift it, carefully, out of a chair so that it didn't embarrass her. Catherine didn't reflect on this so much as feel it, and it was all-but-forgotten when she saw what the girl was wearing around her neck. It was a necklace, but one of such extraordinary beauty that it must—it surely must—be a replica. In every other regard, the maid was correctly dressed. If her stockings were a little grey, they were at least straight and her dress was neatly ironed. She had thrust her hair into a mob cap and even that, the irreverent way it seemed to slide around, seemed to suit her. But, no, it was the necklace that arrested your attention. It was like starlight; like a strange sort of personal advertisement. What was the point of bruiting it about?

"Come with me, please."

She was as conscious of her own dignity as if she had had a sheet thrown over her. She wasn't, she would never be, comfortable with servants. As she stepped carefully downstairs she was aware that she was holding her back and neck unnaturally straight. Her hand went to her hair, and it annoyed her; it made her voice sharper and more distinct than she had intended.

"In here, please."

The kitchen had been commandeered in exactly the same way as the living room had been. There was a bowl, and there were various bottles, on the table. Food was everywhere. The other maid was putting pigs' trotters onto a dish. She wasn't garnishing them so much as pushing slivers of lettuce onto them, and Catherine felt, just for a moment, the hopelessness of ever entertaining in the way that Charles expected. She was afraid that her face was showing this; that this knowledge would flow, somehow, between her and the maids, especially this one: the one whose face was so perfectly poised that Catherine felt sure that she was judging her. She looked at her more closely. No. Perhaps not. All that you could see, really, was a determined blankness. Catherine's instinct was usually to forgive, pre-emptively. She smiled and said, "I'll find you a decent broom."

"Thank you, ma'am."

The maid's voice was perfectly neutral. Her hands went to her skirt, unnecessarily, and Catherine saw that she felt awkward too. She had squared her shoulders and was looking at her warily. Catherine smiled.

"That is ..."

Her hand went out towards the necklace, and she saw the girl flinch slightly.

"I'm sorry. But it is. It's beautiful."

The maid smiled, faintly.

"It's a sparkler, ain't it?"

She was pleased but she was also, obscurely, defiant. There was a space that Catherine couldn't identify around the words. It was as though she was speaking in someone else's voice; as though she was presenting the words, the last two especially, for their mutual amusement. Catherine assumed that she was expecting her to ask her to take the necklace off. She might have, actually. What were the guests going to think? It seemed insolent, almost. But Catherine could see, from the way the girl was resettling it around her neck, how very important it was to her.

"A gift?"

"Yes ma'am."

"You're a lucky girl."

The maid only half-assented. She had lowered her head to one side. It wasn't hard to guess her situation. Some roué. Someone who Charles might parody for the stage. If it had been relayed to her, Catherine might have found the whole thing delightful. Or she might have distanced herself; have chosen to sombrely judge what she didn't want to admit that she was frightened of. But the girl's face was denying her the opportunity. It was too human; too intimately part of what she was telling her. Catherine didn't know what to say. She felt a pity that was both vivid and, strangely, comfortable. She found that she was grateful for the flat, for this cramped kitchen, and for Charles. The woman was older than her, which made it worse. Nevertheless, she felt motherly.

"You need to keep it safe."

The girl patted her neck.

"Safest place, ma'am."

Catherine believed her, although she couldn't quite imagine what she meant by it. Where must the poor girl be living? And where were her children? She wanted to touch her shoulder. No, what she wanted was to take the thing off her and put it in a drawer. Instead, she nodded. It was as though there was a seesaw, and Catherine had somehow inveigled herself into the air while this poor girl was still struggling on the ground. She was beautiful, if one were to avoid her skin. She was slender and there was a light that burned somewhere behind her eyes. It seemed to come flaring out at you and to attempt to breach the gap between you. Nevertheless, here was Catherine, still, floating above her. In a way, what this girl suffered enabled her to float. She felt something, again, like a maternal instinct: this, her feelings told her, was what it would be like when you wanted to take your child's hopelessness and helpless anger and smooth it all away. She couldn't, of course. Still, when she spoke she was careful to inhabit her own voice.

"What is your name?"

"Sarah."

A curtsey. Was it ironic? Faintly, perhaps.

"Ma'am."

Her expression of the word was so tentative and aloof that Catherine didn't know what to make of it. When she spoke again it was with a queasy sympathetic briskness. She was already bustling towards the cupboard.

"Well, Sarah, I suggest that you take this and sweep everything to one side. We will be placing a table up there, so hardly anyone will notice. Then we can see about these bottles."

"Yes, ma'am."

Yes. Definitely. A hint of irony. A pertness unbecoming in a woman of her age. Catherine felt herself begin to blush. She put the broom in Sarah's hand and, as she began to leave, she said, "And ignore my husband, please. I know how distracting he can be."

She couldn't have said this to her face. Even so, she was disappointed at the upwards, ingratiating lilt that she could hear in her own voice. Sarah paused, briefly, in the doorway, but it was hardly noticeable. Then she assumed the correct posture: a donkey's shoulders; a menial's rapid walk.

There was barely an hour and a half before the guests were meant to arrive, and Catherine lost herself in preparation. This girl, the girl who was still pressing her fingers gormlessly into the meat, was easier to supervise. It relaxed her to be able to insist on the right way to shred the lettuce and the way that you had to sprinkle it over the trotters. Small hearts of beef, ripe venison (where *had* Charles found it?), potatoes and vegetables and now the bottles, polished then taken carefully upstairs. Both maids went up and down, and the other one—the difficult one—told her that Charles was supervising them. At one point she stood, flushed, in the doorway.

"String."

"I beg your pardon?"

"The master says that he wants string."

There was something about the word that seemed comical to them both. It was its insufficiency when placed against what felt, with less than an hour to go, to be a Herculean task. Sarah's eyes were twinkling slightly and (she couldn't help it) Catherine's face softened into a look of almost solicitous amusement.

"There are balloons," Sarah said. "A lot of balloons. It's very important, the master says."

"Yes," she said. "Well. It would be."

Sarah's mouth travelled in an arc. She dipped her head.

"Is he always so—"

"Thorough?" Catherine shrugged, a little helplessly. "Yes." She found that she was laughing. It had started, an irresistible ripple, in her shoulders. "Yes. Yes he is."

The woman's smile, her lack of conventional regard, seemed to have loosened something in herself. It was as if someone had come at her with a scrubbing brush and she was pushing her face up to meet it. She had the urge to lay her marriage at this woman's feet. At anyone's really—Beard's, Browne's. It was like living with a flock of starlings. But no one was ever inclined to take her seriously. She had tried, on more than one occasion, to have this conversation with her sister but her sister was unable to envisage a Charles who was anything other than the Charles that he envisaged himself. She had the impression, sometimes, that Mary thought that she was ungrateful. But there were times when, in the midst of her husband's hullabaloo, she wasn't sure if she existed, he looked through her so. This woman's pert regard, the way her gaze met Catherine's so insistently, was an invitation. More: a form of recognition.

"He is a figure," Catherine said apologetically. "A personage. Perhaps you have heard of him?"

"Mr. Dickens, Ma'am? Everyone's heard of Mr. Dickens."

"Quite so. And, you see, there is always so much to do, and he is always so very good at doing it."

Sarah nodded. Again, she smiled. She moved her head, slightly, towards the bottles.

"I'd drink."

Catherine laughed.

"It would feel a little strange, I think, to attempt to drink for two."

Sarah studied her belly. She seemed to be frightened of it.

"Will it happen soon?"

"Yes. Just after Christmas."

"And do you get ..."

Her face had begun to look a little ponderous. Her mouth seemed weighed down by the words she wasn't sure that she could say.

"... sufficient help?"

Catherine laughed again. She shook her head. "No." She wanted to be fair to Charles but she wanted, also, to be able to tell the truth. To just say it: not ameliorate it with the buttermilk of understanding.

"He tries."

Sarah was rubbing at her nose. It looked like she was thumbing it derisively.

"Men," she said.

"Yes."

"All arse over tit." She grabbed Catherine's arm. "Oh God. I'm sorry."

"It's perfectly alright."

Catherine made herself stay where she was. She could feel Sarah's hand, like a burn, on her own. She was intensely aware of the fingers that she was releasing, one by one.

"But it's not even that. He writes. Well, as you know."

She tapped her forehead.

"He lives up here. He is a very practical man, my husband. Practical to a fault. Only it doesn't seem to have any bearing on what's actually in front of him."

Sarah laughed at the ceiling. Catherine thought: perhaps I *am* ungrateful. Now Sarah was looking at the floor.

"But you are ..."

Again, she didn't know how to say it. Perhaps she simply didn't know what to say. Happy, she meant. She was gesturing outwards at the room and the flat around her. Surely, she was saying, you must be happy. Catherine knew why she had asked. This bright domestic space; these friends; the jolly theatrical. But in some ways it was a terrible question. It depended, she supposed, on your criteria. She was still hugging her belly. It was like touching solid ground. But it was also a form of self-definition. She was Charles's wife. They were a family. That was happiness enough. She found that her desire to give an honest answer was waning rapidly. But her desire to reassert her domesticity was making her feel guilty. She smiled as broadly as she was able.

"I'm sorry. I'm being rude. Would you like one? A drink? It's Christmas."

Sarah shook her head.

"I dursn't." She grinned. "I'd show you up."

"Nonsense."

Catherine poured her a sherry. Sarah downed it eagerly, and Catherine watched her in the same way that an explorer would if he were encountering a member of a primitive tribe. Sarah wiped her mouth. She was looking keenly into Catherine's eyes.

"You're kind," she said. She nodded, once, then looked away. "I should have known."

It was as if only her mouth had said it. Her eyes caught up and she became confused. Catherine didn't know what she meant, but it hardly mattered. What was much more apparent was the way she reddened. She seemed angry at herself. Catherine felt that she understood. In her place, she would be clumsy too. All this: the piles of meat; the oven; the dim light burnishing the stairs. And Charles. How intimidating it must be.

"I am an ogre sometimes."

Sarah shook her head. "No," she said. "Not you." She gave Catherine back the glass. As she did so, she lightly patted her hand. "You're a saint."

Neither of them knew what to say. Catherine went searching awkwardly for the string and then presented it as though, obscurely, it was a gift. Sarah turned on her heels and hurried upstairs. It looked like she was running away. She seemed, just for that moment, like a street urchin. Catherine felt the superiority of her own position, and, if she felt guilty too, it was nonetheless warming her insides. The trouble was, Sarah was a woman in a way that Catherine was not. Her eyes were full of something that seemed like hunger. Like dread, but dread that was expressed in such a way that it became a kind of poetry. She looked so fiercely at things that you felt their reality for the first time.

Catherine walked slowly up the stairs. The bottle that she was carrying was her excuse but really she wanted to see what was happening. What would happen, rather, when this unpredictable element was introduced into the determined neatness of her husband's plans. As she approached, she could hear him. He was declaiming. He had broadened his London accent until it seemed to come bowling out at you. It was supposed to be insinuating, but he was too actorly to allow himself to murmur. It was only a sitting room but he must articulate towards the blankness of the back wall.

"What have we here? As the waiter said to the turbot."

"Here" had two syllables. He was balancing on the balls of his feet. He had one hand on his waist and the other was scratching, rather obviously, at his hair line. Mary curtseyed.

"I'm just a poor shepherdess, sir. I've come all the way from—" She looked down at her feet. "Oh dear."

"Kent, Mary. Kent. And you might look a little more surprised to bump into me. I'm supposed to be one of the urban sights."

She grinned. "You are."

"Cruikshank. Where are you?"

"Here." Cruikshank came slowly out from behind the scenery. He had thick mutton chop whiskers and an impressive nose. He was not there; this was what his eyes were telling you. His body was, but he himself was far away. He was blinking and wiping his mouth.

Charles said, "Here, Cruikshank." He pointed to a spot a little to the left of where he was standing. It looked like he was bringing him to heel. "You should have already begun to notice her. Fondle those whiskers a little, if you please."

Mary was looking at the clock. "Charles."

"I know. I know. Five minutes more. So. Kent."

He had relaxed into a more ambivalent posture. Now he drew himself up into the boldness of his previous silhouette. "Kent, is it? Blooming, is it? Like yourself."

"Oh sir!"

"Now don't mind me. It's my London manners what gets me into trouble every time. Cruikshank. Whiskers."

Cruikshank looked at him for a long moment. Slowly, he drew one finger along his chin.

"I was there once," Charles said. "Hop picking. The old lady I was with was a proper article. Sincerely smelly; it was a religion with her. She looked like an apple too. One day she fell out of the tree and we was hard-pressed to tell one from t'other."

Cruikshank eased his way behind them.

"Allow me to introduce myself," he said.

Mary played an introductory chord and Cruikshank began to sing. His voice was a delight: a croak that was positively ingratiating, it was so cheerfully reluctant to hit the notes. The music plonked merrily along, with words by Charles, while Cruikshank edged Mary from one side of the room to the other. Charles, "Sam" rather, looked knowing and superior. Frances was doing rather well. She had created the right atmosphere: a boozy, slightly threatening romp. She kept looking down at her fingers, urging them on. At the end, Browne sashayed out to a place in the middle of the scenery. He really did sashay, too: his legs twinkled together and apart like brightly garnished cut-outs.

"Bernard!" he said. His voice was an octave up but it was still a man's. Of course, that was partly the point.

"Stop!" Charles had his forehead in his hands. He still looked actorly: he was communicating so clearly that, if you were outside, you would easily be able to interpret it. "It doesn't work," he said.

"Oh Charles." Mary had actually stamped her foot. "Really. We have half an hour."

"I know. I know. But it doesn't work. She can't just drag him off. Where is the drama?"

"I could hit him," Browne said eagerly.

"You could not."

Cruikshank was turning as slowly as a dancer on a music box. He had put out his hands for balance.

"Shhh," Charles said.

Cruikshank dangled there for a moment. He was deciding whether to be angry. Meanwhile, Charles had marched over to where the maid was standing by the table. Charles was still acting, it seemed, but it was difficult to know quite what. Once he was standing in front of her, he looked awkward: trapped between the dictates of one role and another. He had taken off his hat and now he looked like he was holding on to his hair. The maid was still winding string around the bottom of a balloon, but she was doing it so slowly and automatically that she was barely doing it at all.

"Tell me your name."

She didn't know what to make of him. She eyed him with a doomed fixity of regard. Catherine noticed that there was a glass beside her. It had a thimbleful of sherry at the bottom of it.

"Sarah."

"Sarah."

Charles had allowed his voice to modulate into something insinuating. Or mock-insinuating. He stood at a careful distance, fondling his hat.

"What do you think?"

"Me, sir?"

"If this was Drury Lane what would you do?"

"God, sir, if this was Drury Lane, I'd probably be asleep by now."

Catherine laughed. Charles was too intent on Sarah to take any notice.

"What does it need?"

"I don't know, sir."

"You do. You've been watching it all afternoon. Tell me. What."

There was a pause. It was almost impossible to tell what either of them was attempting to communicate. In the end,

Sarah looked out of the window. She seemed exasperated. Defeated. She had been preparing herself to say something but she had swiftly looked at Catherine and now she had decided to say something else.

"I'm sorry. I don't."

Charles, clearly, had not been expecting this. He floundered for a moment, but only for a moment.

"Well, I do. It needs conflict. It needs ..."

He examined her. Then he grabbed her arm.

"You. It needs you."

"No sir! It doesn't! *Please* sir!"

Why did she appear to be acting? It was the theatricality of the atmosphere, Catherine supposed; it infected everything. Whatever you saw, it seemed to be for your benefit. She took a step forward.

"Charles."

"It's perfectly alright."

He was dragging Sarah towards the stage. He had a look of demonic self-possession. It was the same look he got when he was acting out a character at his desk: the same lack of propriety; the same weird certainty. He placed the maid at the edge of the stage. She had fought briefly but now she acquiesced. She had looked again at Catherine but it wasn't quite a plea for help; more of an apology. She stood smoothing her dress and staring at Charles. She was angry. Or, at least, aroused to something like full consciousness. She was wary, but also ready.

"There," Charles said. "Stand there. Browne, I'm sorry. You are superfluous. For now."

He raised his hands.

"For now. And Cruikshank you ... Cruikshank!"

Cruikshank edged back around the scenery.

"Stay, Cruikshank, if you please."

"Well, if you're going to rewrite the thing."

"I'm not. This is a tweak. Mary. Look innocent."

"I am!"

She had been eyeing Sarah doubtfully. Charles pointed at Cruikshank. He said to Sarah, "He is your husband."

"Not bleeding likely."

"No. Well. I grant you that it is incongruous. Imagine: he chases women." He smiled, slightly. He glanced at Cruikshank, who appeared silently to be giving his feet instructions. "Not literally. He is a rake. He barely gives you any money. He's out at all hours, carousing."

Sarah raised her eyebrows.

"Yes. I know. You have to suspend your disbelief. What would you do?"

"I agree with 'im." Sarah had jerked a thumb at Browne. "I'd brain him."

"Really? Now? Or would you wait until you got home?"

She appeared to be thinking about it. Mary had crossed her arms. Catherine was rather enjoying her sudden pettishness. But she also sympathised. How disorientating it was to feel the hot glow of Charles's regard and then see it swing to someone else. He was thoroughly enjoying himself, but then so, it appeared, was Sarah, whose accent had also become slightly exaggerated. There was a gap between her normal voice, so very meat and potatoes, and the one with which she responded, now, to Charles.

"I'd take him by the ear."

"Oh no you wouldn't."

"Be *quiet* Cruikshank."

No one could look more furious than Charles. Apart from Charles's father. But now, once again, he was honeying his words.

"And what would you say? Come over here. Belabour him, by all means."

He grinned.

"But lightly."

Sarah stepped slowly towards Cruikshank. She wasn't tentative, exactly. More thoughtful. She had the same look of concentration that Charles had when he wrote. It seemed to partake of both anxiety and confidence. Lightly, she took Cruikshank's ear.

"Bedswerver."

"Yes."

"Besprawler."

Mary said, "I don't know what that means!"

She sounded helplessly lost. It was unedifying, Catherine thought, to watch your own sister become so exceptionally feminine. Sarah looked at her with the same flatness of regard that she had looked at Catherine. But there was also a hint of superiority.

"It means someone who dribbles."

"But he doesn't."

"No. He doesn't." Sarah was exhibiting the same laboured patience that a mother would. "But he might. He's not far off."

She had glanced, quickly, down at his trousers. Cruikshank was attempting to retain his dignity, but it was difficult when someone had a firm hold of your ear like this.

Charles was laughing. "Go on," he said. "Carry on."

Mary shook her head. Sarah was fingering her lip.

"Blimey. I don't know." She looked off into the distance. Then she turned her full attention on Cruikshank's face. "Besprawler. Who do you think you are? 'oo is she? Your sister? You 'aven't got a bleeding sister. I should know."

She looked genuinely angry. With her free hand, she made a fist and waved it in mid-air. "Come 'ere." She started to drag him towards Mary. "If I catch you with your shirt out again I'll jelly your eel for you."

Cruikshank had no choice but to follow her. Charles was delighted. As they got level with Mary, Sarah turned to her.

"And *you*," she said.

That was all she said, but she said it with such malevolence that Mary looked frightened. She took two steps back and bumped against the wall. Sarah stared at her for a moment longer. The animus had not entirely left her face. Then she released Cruickshank and dusted her hands together. She turned to Charles.

"Something like that?"

"Perfect. *Exactly* right. And, then, right at the end—"

But Mary was saying, "Really, Charles."

If she was a bird she would be ruffling her feathers. She had shaken herself so that her dress seemed to be dancing around her. This was unfortunate: it emphasised how silly it was.

"I know I said Sam should find love but this is ridiculous."

This was more than a sally; it was a barb. Charles looked at her like a teacher might.

"Mary. It's perfect."

"It's vulgar."

Catherine was worried that Sarah might spring at her. She felt sure that she would have to intervene. You could see the struggle it took for her to keep her mouth firmly shut. You could almost see the words bumping against her teeth. Lightly, Charles placed his hand on Sarah's arm.

"Yes. But that is the desired effect."

He was beaming in a way that seemed deliberately paternal. He was distancing himself from Mary and, it seemed, aligning himself with Sarah. No, it was with what was effectively the product of his imagination. This is what Catherine saw: that Sarah may as well have leapt, fully formed, from Charles's head. He was also a little drunk. She experienced a brief thrill of concern; it was like being in a boat and having to crest a wave. Mary was flushed. But that was ... well, she didn't want to examine what that was. It was disproportionate.

"And is that all? Are we done? Or would you like me to stand on one leg?"

"Dear Mary."

Catherine knew just how infuriating Charles's smile could be.

"You are done. Please take a break."

"That is most kind of you."

She swept out of the room. Charles said, "Now," and began to push Sarah into position. Catherine knew better than to interfere with him. Instead, she followed Mary. She was in the kitchen, with her back towards her. She was staring out of the window. Catherine put her hand on her shoulder.

"Mary. Dear."

She was rubbing furiously at her eyes. She turned and glared into Catherine's face.

"This is supposed to be for *you*."

"Well, it still is."

"Not with that—"

She made a loud noise of disgust.

"She is a maid. That's all. You know what Charles is like."

"I thought I did."

"Oh Mary. You do. Come now."

Catherine found that she was smiling. What she felt now wasn't anxiety exactly. It was more the knowledge that there were rocks ahead and that they were going, somehow, to have to negotiate them. She was rubbing Mary's shoulder in a rough gesture of commiseration.

"He is exactly the same as he has always been. He is enthusiastic."

Mary snorted. Catherine continued to talk over her.

"He grabs at things and then, of course, they're his. Do you see? He has to bind them to him. Else, where is he? He is constantly at sixes and sevens otherwise. How did you not know this?" She paused. An angrier note had entered her voice. She willed it away. "He has no firm ground. None, Mary. We think we constitute his rock. I know you feel this: that we are the home to which he will always return. That you are."

Mary went to object.

"It's true. And let us hope that this is the case. But, in the meantime, we must allow him his enthusiasms. We must allow him to appear ..." She shook her sister, hard. It was supposed to be affectionate. "To *appear* to have forgotten us. He hasn't. In a moment he will realise what he has done. He will not apologise. But he will make a joke and we will laugh."

Mary looked keenly at her.

"And why are you so certain, all of a sudden?"

Catherine smiled. She lightly touched her belly.

"Ballast," she said.

She nearly meant it.

"Now," she said, "Mary. You must laugh. Because it is Christmas and because you love him and because you love me. And all of this is meant to be for me. The poor feeble-minded invalid."

She was still smiling. Mary had just about decided to do the same when they heard the door of the living room open. Someone was taking the stairs two at a time. Catherine nodded.

"I told you."

But it was Beard. He was obviously bringing them news of the utmost importance. He was, however, dressed in a velveteen waistcoat, an ostentatiously pink shirt and the most ridiculous of moustaches. It was difficult to take him seriously. Or even, really, to give credence to the fact that it was him. He was more like a visitation; an extension of the world that Charles was trying to create above.

"An actress," he said. He was out of breath. "She's an actual actress. Hence. You know."

He was not an actor, Beard. He was a nice man, but he was only here because he was a friend of Charles. Too good a friend, Catherine suspected; the kind of man who would turn a blind eye because he didn't know what to say. Or because he admired Charles so much that whatever he did was, somehow, grist to the mill. He was attempting to communicate the forcefulness of Sarah's personality but it looked, what with the broad busy parenthesis of his arms, like he was pretending to be a gorilla. Mary giggled. Now Beard was shaking his head.

"Astonishing."

He scratched the place where you felt his hair ought to be.

"I don't know where he finds these people. He is some sort of magnet."

He was pretending to be more simple-minded than he was in order to include them in his determinedly sunny view.

"Characters," Mary said. "Not people."

"No," Beard said. "Really. I know that she is somewhat—"

Those arms again.

"—abrasive."

"To put it mildly."

"Mary."

Catherine still had one hand on her shoulder. She had become aware, belatedly, that she was patting it. Beard, meanwhile, was exhibiting what was, it had to be said, a ghastly grin. He was trying his very best to smooth things over. In a moment, Catherine thought, he will begin to dance. And *where* was Charles? Why this amanuensis in his place? Despite what she had said earlier, she was beginning to become a little irritated. Beard didn't know what to do with his hands. It was because he didn't know what he was supposed to say.

"But imagine. Being employed as a maid and then being asked to do the very thing that you most love. It must be like money being dropped in your lap."

"And where, pray, has she been practicing her trade?"

Mary had recovered, or nearly so. She had decided to employ a look that Catherine was sure Charles had never seen. It was demurely supercilious. Beard shuffled there for a moment.

"In penny gaffs," he said.

It sounded more like a question than a statement. He was afraid of their reaction. Neither of them was sure what it should be. Before they could speak, there was what sounded like a growl. There was the briefest of pauses, and then a clattering of shoes on the thin carpet. Something pushed Beard then Charles's father thrust his head between Beard's head and the frame of the door. He was there before Catherine was properly aware of him.

"Repeat that, sir."

It was looking more like a farce by the minute. Beard was stroking his moustache, uncertainly. His face was flushed, but then it had been before he came downstairs. Was everybody drunk? No. Charles's father wasn't. But he was flushed too. There was something beginning in him: something that was already starting to shake his frame.

"Come, sir. What was it that you said? Repeat it please."

"Penny gaffs, was it?"

Charles's father gave the impression of size largely through the way that he communicated with his body. His gestures were large; his speech was overwhelmingly oratorical. In other words, he was slightly ridiculous. It was disorientating, therefore, when you saw something rawly genuine in his face. He made a rush for the stairs, and Beard, after a moment's bewilderment, ran after him. Mary said, "Oh!" and stepped backwards, bumping against a bottle that had been placed under the window. Catherine steadied it then made her way up the stairs. It was slow going. Her belly was an annoyance, and she still had her skirt in her hand when she came through the door. The first thing that she saw was Fred, who was jumping, uselessly, from side to side. Then she saw Charles's father, who was holding Charles by the throat. Neither Beard nor Fred knew what to do: they wavered on the sidelines while Sarah looked indignantly down at her uniform. Catherine saw that it was torn. It was a moment before she caught up with what was being said.

"Dancing."

He had pushed Charles against the wall. Cruikshank and Browne both seemed astonished. They were, yes, cartoonish. Frances, meanwhile, appeared to be embracing the piano.

"Dancing."

"Father. My ..."

Charles's hands were fluttering at his throat. His father let him go, but then he blocked him in. He stared at him for a moment. Stared into him. Charles was brushing briskly downwards at his clothes. His hat had fallen off and Catherine saw that it was troubling him. He wanted to place it on his head.

"It's a play. Father, it's a *play*."

He was tugging at his hair. He couldn't seem to help himself. Catherine felt as though she was balancing on the balls of her feet. She wasn't. How could she be? Nevertheless, she felt like she might be called upon to jump, literally, to Charles's defence. She found that she was reluctant to. There was something. An anomaly. Quite apart from the obvious. Charles's father had stopped talking. His face had swelled with a feeling that he seemed unable to express. With the flat of his hand, he slapped Charles, hard, across the face. He looked at him almost lovingly, then he did it again. There was a terrible pause. It seemed to gather in the room like heat. No one, not even Charles, did anything. Catherine was trying to work out what to do when there was a knock at the door. Still eyeing his father, Charles cocked his head a little to one side.

"Your job, I think."

There was a livid mark on his cheek. Catherine was relieved to hear Mary open the door. It was guests, she was sure, but the tone of voice was wrong. She heard Mary walk up the stairs. It didn't sound like her normal step. Normally, she ascended either as though she was attempting to levitate or as if her feet were clumps of mud. Now she was simply hurrying. She put her head around the door.

"It's something about a necklace."

She came into the room and looked at Charles, who slid slowly out from under his father's stare. He mustered as much dignity as he could but you could still tell what had happened by the mark on his face. And by his walk, which made it look like somebody had kicked his rear. As he began to go down-stairs, she could hear him saying, "Now what's all this nonsense about?"

That was a relief, too: the confident richness of his tone. The whole room seemed stunned, even the furniture, but Charles's voice gave her a certain amount of hope. He would, in some way unknown to her, tidy everything up. She nodded to herself. She touched her hair; slipped back a loosening strand. Attempting a smile, she turned into the room and saw that the maid was climbing out of the window.

CHAPTER THIRTEEN

THERE WERE THREE men at the door. They seemed so much a part of the outer darkness that, as they entered, they appeared to be bringing it in with them.

"Mr. Dickens?"

"Yes."

"We have a bill for you."

The first man, the biggest man, thrust it into Charles's hand. It was difficult to see more than a row of zeros in the dim light of the hall.

"This can't be for me. Whatever is it for?"

"You know what it's for, Mr. Dickens."

"No. Really. I'm afraid I don't."

One of the other men stepped forward. He had a full-bore ferrety nose and a face that seemed to be crowding itself around it. He was briskly rubbing his hands together but this seemed more an excess of animal spirits than a response to the cold outside. He was about to throw his entire body into the act of speech. Charles put up his hand.

"One moment."

He was pleased to note that his voice was still sufficiently actorly to compel assent.

"Maisie?"

There was a pause. Charles was an expert at pauses. He could almost see Maisie step away from the door.

"Yes sir?"

"Could you please go upstairs and see if anybody is wanting anything?"

"Yes sir."

The brisk alacrity with which she answered him would have been amusing under any other circumstances. She had only just disappeared when the man began to talk.

"Mr. Dickens. You know what this is about. Your face is in the newspaper; it's on every omnibus. We only have to step outside the shop and there you are. How could you think that you would get away with it?"

Charles was rubbing at his mouth. He was looking from one man to the other and back again. Eventually he said, "I haven't got the money."

"We didn't think you had."

Nevertheless, the man looked sorrowful.

"We're not unreasonable men."

His eyes were glittering. His hair was unevenly distributed under the rim of his hat. It looked like heather, or gorse. He might have been a Christmas visitation; a tutelary spirit.

"What do I have to do?"

"Pay it. Pay it, Mr. Dickens. That is all. Else we *will* distrain your goods."

And there it was: the spectre that had always haunted him. He could roll naked on a patch of grass; he could stand in the street and laugh after he had committed a crime. He could go to bed, repeatedly, with a woman who might as well have been a sprite for all that he understood her world. But he could not bear disgrace. He nodded.

"Yes. Yes, yes. I will."

"Two weeks."

The man pointed an admonitory finger. They were standing so close together that it nearly touched Charles's nose. The third man, a man whose quietness seemed, also, to be instructive, leant down and murmured something into the other man's ear. He pulled himself slowly erect. All he needs, Charles thought, are a pair of scales and a sword. The man in front of him said, "But we will need something on account."

"I haven't got anything."

"Whatever you have."

Oh, this was hard. To have to go upstairs and tiptoe, virtually, through his wife and father and find the table, hidden behind the scenery, in which he kept his wallet. He felt, walking through his own living room, like he was once again covered in urine. Every step felt more-than-life-size. Every breath felt taken with the permission of those around him. He had had to lift up his hand, like an impresario. He had had to say, "One moment." And he had had to say it in a way that was suitably calm and confident and mellifluous. Safely downstairs, he gave them all the money he had. The little man bowed. He gave Charles one more look of exemplary fierceness and then he softened. He jabbed him with his finger. This was meant to be a familiar gesture.

"What made you do it?"

He really wanted to know.

"Broad daylight. Your face everywhere."

He shuddered. It seemed genuine. Charles searched his memory. He saw it again: that cavern and its treasure, like gold in a fairy tale. He felt the man's assumption that he was, in some way, inferior to the glitter that was dancing in his hands.

He saw Sarah's breasts; her smile. And Grimaldi's face, itself a gauntlet. He shook his head.

"I don't know," he said.

After he had closed the door, he rested his head against it. He counted to ten then made himself walk energetically up the stairs. He went straight to his wife. He took her hands.

"I'm sorry," he said. "Darling, this is really most embarrassing."

He knew enough to *not* act, now. He was lying; it was much easier.

"I. Um. I bought you a necklace."

He allowed himself to look around the room. They were all staring at him. He found that he wanted, at the lowest point in his marriage, to anchor himself in Sarah. If he could just see that she understood. But he couldn't find her anywhere. Even as his eyes were coming back to Catherine's face, he was saying, "It was this."

Her belly. He sketched it, lightly.

"Him. Her."

He laughed. Another sketch. The outline of a laugh; no more.

"I wanted to surprise you. But the jeweller thinks I haven't paid."

He squeezed her hand.

"I have. I promise you I have. The stupid man mislaid a receipt somewhere."

He waved an airy hand.

"It's done."

She looked at him. What was it in her face? He couldn't see it plain.

"Oh Charles."

Useless to try and interpret that. Or to fight against it, whatever it would turn out to be. Later, when they were alone, she would be grateful.

"Your maid has gone," she said.

"What do you mean?"

"She heard the word necklace and left. By the window."

"By the window?"

"By the window."

Charles threw what was meant to be a laugh up at the ceiling. He had never thought so quickly in his life.

"Oh Lor.'"

It was like the moment at the end of a book. Not that he would know yet. He imagined that you must pull all the threads together.

"So this," he said. The necklace, he meant. He drew a line from one shoulder to the other. "It was stolen."

It sounded like what it was: a line from a play. He resisted the temptation to throw his arm in the direction of the window. He looked around at the assembled company.

"Now that *is* funny."

He hoped that his face was poised enough. He felt like he was only just keeping it in the air. Fred's face was trying to agree with him. Beard was looking carefully down at his shoes. His sister had her back to him and he could just see Cruikshank's foot peeping out from behind the scenery. Only Browne was laughing. He did it with such wholeheartedness that Charles wanted to embrace him. He looked, as fiercely as he could, at his father's face.

"Now, sir."

If anyone was an old tragedian, it was John Dickens, and if ever there was a moment for consanguinity to count it was this one. The girl was gone; his wife was getting a necklace. More: the creditors had disappeared. The shadow of debt had lowered around them but had been erased. What would you?

Seriously. What? Was it now for his father to pull everything down around their heads? Charles was trying to communicate all of this in what looked, he hoped, like an indignant glare. He pictured Grimaldi. He tried to glare with his eyes but ask for, yes, succour with his eyebrows and his mouth. His father walked slowly towards him.

"Charles," he said. "My Charles."

He was surely not going to get down on one knee? As it was, he merely dipped it slightly. He was knuckling his forehead and staring into Charles's face. This seemed to go on forever. His eyes, Charles saw, were so very complicated that they might as well have been opaque. He thought: defeat will do that to you.

"I knew!" his father said. "You only had to look at her. A penny gaff!"

He made a gesture that, even for him, was magnificent. He appeared to be trying to hurl his hand away.

"And you. You! You brought her here. To sully. Yes."

Charles wasn't about to interrupt him. He was rather enjoying this. Nevertheless, his father placed a hand in front of his face.

"To sully this lovely home."

He had revolved in a full circle; had seemed to address each wall and everybody in the room. Charles knew what was expected of him. He bowed his head.

"I didn't know."

"A writer!"

His father was also enjoying himself.

"A writer, Charles! And you can't tell the kind of person who will *slash* your throat and murder you in your sleep."

That slash; the cutting motion that he made. He could easily have made his living in a penny gaff.

"Father, I am contrite. I thought that she was poor."

He was rocking both hands in front of him. "Poor," here, was obviously meant to communicate the helplessness of a baby. He looked around the room. Only Beard seemed not to be paying attention.

"I gave her the benefit of the doubt. My apologies to you all."

What could they do? Ruin Christmas? Everyone was gracious. Catherine kissed him, lightly, on the cheek. Mary nodded; she had evidently been vindicated. Cruikshank had missed it. His brother and sister were, in the end, his brother and sister, and Browne looked delighted to be able to give more of his appalling impression of Widow Twankey. The show was a success. The evening was delightful. There was a fusillade of praise.

Three weeks later, back in the oyster bar, Beard looked at him warily. He said, "It was her, wasn't it?" His face looked overfull of blood. He had a glass of porter in his hands. He had been swilling it from side to side and looking down at it, as if he was concerned for it. Now he determinedly held Charles's eye. "Wasn't it?"

"Yes."

"Oh Charles. You bastard."

Charles couldn't help it: he reared backwards slightly. It was worse than being slapped in the face. Over Beard's shoulder, he could still see his business card:

CHARLES DICKENS,

RESURRECTIONIST,

In search of a subject.

Well, he had certainly found one. He had dug up Grimaldi and look what happened. Beard was glaring at him but that, in a sense, was what he had come for: if not exactly for absolution then for penance.

"And stop that, please. It's a little late for the whited sepulchre, don't you think?"

"That isn't—"

"Fair?"

Beard downed his porter. When he spoke, his lips were glimmering with it. It was a distraction; an ironic commentary.

"'Their little hearts.' Dear God. 'And are you seeing her?' 'Good Lord, dear fellow, no.'"

"You impute a simplicity to the human heart that simply isn't there."

"*I* do!"

Beard appeared to be taking stock of Charles. He looked dismissively at his waistcoat, his tie pin and his carefully disordered hair. Then he looked into his eyes. He appeared to be frightened that he might not be able to do it.

"In your own home. Right under Catherine's nose. And Mary's come to that. And what was that little charade about? Dragging her up on stage like that? It was the worst acting I've ever seen you do."

"Oh, so you knew."

"Of course I didn't know! How could I? No one—listen to me, Charles—*no one* has a brain that is remotely as convoluted as your own. I thought *you* knew. That she was an actress. I thought she'd told you and you'd taken pity on her. Had you? Is that what this whole thing is about?"

This is what Beard wanted, still. Milder, roseate colours. The reassuring outline of one of Charles's novels. Charles was tempted. But he couldn't bring himself to say it.

"We'd arranged it. Beforehand. She wasn't meant to be so very reluctant. She was supposed to *think*, you know, for two or three minutes and then come up and show us how it should be done."

Charles sighed. He longed for a glass of wine. He kept staring at his own card. The man who had left it here had had the type of self-confidence that he couldn't imagine ever possessing.

"But she had evidently changed her mind. She didn't want to do it. I thought it was nerves. So I dragged her. She's never complained before."

About being dragged, he meant. He was boasting. He wanted to grin. Extraordinary man.

"And then, of course, there was my father."

"Who knows."

"Who thinks he knows."

"Why, Charles? This is ..."

Beard seemed beset by invisible enemies. It looked like his thoughts were poking him. So many of them. How would you illustrate them all? He was shaking his head as vigorously as if there had been a wasp perched on his nose.

"This is worthy of an asylum."

Charles settled in his seat. He had the vertiginous feeling that you get before a plunge. It wasn't wholly unenjoyable. He touched Beard's hand.

"Listen."

He told him everything. He told him about Sarah and about Grimaldi and Davey, too, and the necklace and the threats. About the nature of the threats: how it was made clear to him that this, their world, was nothing when placed against the right sort of malevolence. There were almost tears. Almost. Then he sat up. He felt briefly purged, but only briefly. He could feel his feelings, ready to crowd in again. Beard's face was no longer so impregnable. He was shaking his head, but much more slowly. He was turning over his thoughts in the same way that a cow might chew the cud. Charles wanted to hurry him.

He had a giddy urge to kick him under the table. At last, Beard said, "Are you going to pay?"

"In actual money? Yes. I have."

"*How*, Charles? Did you just pay for one?"

"No, of course not. What would I say to Catherine? No, I had to find something. Um."

"Expedient."

"Quite."

"How then?"

"Ah. Well. You see."

Charles looked down at his lap. He was still wearing his gloves, he noticed. He took out his right hand and stroked the other. It felt oddly unsoothing. He realised that he had been expecting that, if he lay his finger against the softness of the material, it would function like a pet. Again, he almost grinned.

"I've made an agreement."

"With who?"

"Whom, Beard. Buck up."

Before Beard could reply he said,

"With *Bentley's Miscellany*. It starts next month."

"What does?"

"A serial. Something different."

He hadn't put it into words before.

"Something coherent. Harsh. Slightly lubricious."

"Lubricious."

"Sad."

"Charles, please."

"I'm going to set it in the slums. There are going to be thieves and prostitutes. You wouldn't know they were, of course. The prostitutes, I mean. There's an old Jewish fence, and a poor lost boy."

"You're scaring me."

"Why, pray?"

"You haven't finished Pickwick yet!"

Charles straightened in his chair. He seemed suddenly to want to show that he could bear himself, his own strange wants and needs, with fortitude.

"A flare, Beard. Remember?"

"Or an early grave. Or both. One doesn't necessarily exclude the other. Slow down, man."

Charles was touched. When he said "I can't" he meant it. It was the sort of statement that you make if you have given up on your keys and can't imagine how you're going to get back into the house. Beard did it this time: he touched his hand.

"Dear fellow," he said.

And that was it. He sat back and they were men again. After a long pause, Beard said, "And the girl?"

"I don't know."

Beard considered this. He was the only person who Charles would allow to do so.

"You should."

"I know."

"You escaped by the skin of your teeth."

"I know."

"You have a *child*."

"I do."

Beard seemed to be attempting to tug the skin on his own face. He wanted to grasp something, Charles saw. He wanted something tangible to grab hold of. He put both hands on the table. He squared his shoulders.

"Charles. The Cut is not so very far away."

"I know. We all do, don't we? Experience is there for the taking. Only it isn't, is it? It's just as much a fantasy as everything else. Listen."

He had taken off the other glove without even noticing. He was rubbing his hands together like the debt collector had.

"She is not a '*cocotte*.'"

He said it with as much distaste as if he had found a dead bird lying on the table.

"Nor is she of the slums. In them, yes. But not of them. She—"

"Lives a life apart. Of course. She would."

"She does."

"She'd have to, wouldn't she? For you. Is she an heiress?"

"Be serious."

"I am."

"Please understand. I have to make as much of her as I can."

"Dear Charles. Do you not know that you already have?"

Leaving the oyster bar, he found London both bare and cold. The sky was as sodden as a wet overcoat. The shops seemed almost as barren as the trees. The noise of the coaches and the crowds was like the noise of a great engine, but it seemed to be struggling today. It ground you, London, and it wore itself down in the process. What it was really was a set of jaws. You had to keep an eye out for when it attempted to close upon you.

It was one o'clock on a Tuesday. He had wanted to come in the morning but Beard had insisted; had dragged him out of the newspaper offices and into the oyster bar. Saffron Hill crouched like a dog in the dull light of the afternoon. It seemed rubbed raw. There were still girls here. They were still leaning in what might have been provocation against the wall. But they looked at him as though it was his fault.

"Try your luck, dearie?"

It sounded like an insult. Or, at best, like something entirely without hope. There was some quality that was lacking in him today. He felt this most of all when he got to Sarah's house. It looked deliberately unaccommodating. He walked as boldly as he could to where he thought he could be heard. But he couldn't bring himself to shout. Instead, he walked backwards and forwards between the house and the larger street beyond. He was almost certain that she wasn't there. He didn't know what he was doing. He felt that, if he wished hard enough, he might be able to conjure her. When the front door opened his heart leapt into his throat. He wheeled around to face the woman who, only a couple of months ago, had been trying to sweep the step. She was still holding a broom. She stared at him. Her face was so attenuated that it looked like she was wielding it.

"I'm—"

"I know exactly who you are."

She spat into the space between them.

"Clear off."

Charles couldn't believe that, if he exercised the proper charm, he wouldn't be allowed to stay. He was swaying slightly on his feet. He was like a dancer, readying himself. She all-but-snarled.

"I've said it once. Don't come round here no more."

Her face was so bleak that it was frightening. At first, he thought: I have never been so close to a woman like this before. But, of course, this was what Sarah was. It had always been part of what attracted him. He looked, quickly, up at her window, and the woman took a step towards him.

"She ain't here. And I wouldn't go to the pub, neither, if I was you."

It was almost enjoyable. He had had a surfeit of domesticity and this exchange had perked him up. It was the kind of opposition that he knew that Sarah would put up. A squall, or a bout of shadow-boxing. No more, really, than that. He smiled, lifted his hat and set off for the pub. He made the journey with the pleasant sense that he was sober—that this was not in any way impulsive. It was what he should have done at least a week ago. But, of course, there had been Christmas and the birth of Charley and the necessity for the kind of attention that, over a lengthy period of time, made him feel weak. You couldn't locate yourself in all of that. He felt, out here in all this noise and cold, spectacularly free. He walked as though he owned everything around him. He took in air like it was burgundy.

But the pub was just like Sarah's house. It seemed to have turned its back on him. He looked in at the leaded window but he couldn't work out what the shape was that was moving behind the bar. It seemed to flow in and out of itself. It could be either feminine or masculine. It looked cuboid. Then rhomboid. With his nose pressed firmly against the pane, he felt like a child again. The indeterminacy of the shape was only confirming what he already knew: that he could no more go in than if a spell had been placed upon him.

He decided to sit it out. He found a space just to the rear. It was a side street, suburban enough, with pots of flowers and a pump that seemed somehow apologetic. The sky was lower here, more threatening, but also more contained. It seemed to hide between the chimney pots. There was a bench from which he would see her when she came out. It wouldn't matter how long he had to wait, he told himself, and, indeed, it didn't. It took on the nature of a vigil. The longer he waited the more approving of himself he was. In his imagination, there was something medieval, something almost exemplary, about his profile. This was what fidelity would look like if you should want to draw it.

He became colder and colder but he would not stop. He *would not* give in. Sometimes he paced up and down but that was all that he allowed himself to do. He was there for hours. His thoughts seemed to clang around, uselessly, inside him. All they were, really, were the tail end of his observation of the stones beneath his feet, the small street and the gap at the end, a natural proscenium: the pub on one side and a house at the other and the clouds looming above them both. It was nine o'clock in the evening now. There were, he calculated, hours to go. But he would not move. He was not only proving something but exhibiting it to himself. As a child, in the factory, he had locked hands with the other boys and arm-wrestled over the packing cases. Not often. They had easily defeated him. But this felt like that: the way that all of you was rolled up into one fierce gesture of concentration; the way that the strength of your opponent was something that you were staring down. He would not allow himself to feel the cold. He would not think about how hungry he was feeling. And now he would not even stand. He took on the bench in the same way that he had taken on all of the things he had had to wrestle with since he was a boy.

Then, there she was. It was all wrong. She was not rolling in her usual manner down the street. She wasn't buttoned up. She was in the arms of another man. No, it was more complicated than that: it was like the time she had carried Grimaldi, only it was difficult to tell who, exactly, was carrying whom. As he stood up he realised that it was Davey. He had never noticed the fact that Davey and Sarah were exactly the same height. Nor had he seen how their mouths were vivid in exactly the same way: how they broadcast the same overwhelming hunger. Davey's face was buried in her neck. One hand was on her breast. It was half out of her dress; it looked astonishingly bare. Before he had allowed himself to think, Charles shouted, "Sarah!"

He was scared, of course. Davey came swinging round to meet him. It was like watching an animal in the zoo. The street, you felt, was too small for him. It defined him: made him seem even larger and more ferocious than he was. He had on a battered hat, and his hair was wild in the way that his body was. He had a bruise over one eye. In his imagination, Charles saw the knife. It was tiny, but that made it all the more threatening. It was so prosaic that you never doubted that he would use it. Sarah put the hand that was furthest away from Davey on his arm; she had drawn her arm across him so that it, too, became a cage. She leant and murmured something in his ear. He shook his head, furiously, but she did it again. Her head went up and down, like she was hammering the words into his head. He jerked his head rapidly, once—her words were as constricting as her arm—then stepped away from her. She smiled at him and it was terrible. It had a wild kind of gallantry in it. A recognition of equality. Space seemed to gather between them in the way that smoke jumps in, replacing the flames of a roaring fire. She shouted "Oi!" and threw something across the gap. It jangled. Keys. That was the worst moment of all. Davey brandished them. He waved them in Charles's direction. Charles realised that he had never seem him smile properly before. It was a terrible smile: all teeth.

He lurched away. This, too, appeared exemplary. He was the cut-throat you were most afraid of in your sleep. As Sarah watched him go, she tucked her breast inside her dress. She did it almost thoughtfully. Her hand caressed it like it was at the end of somebody else's arm. She turned to look at Charles, if looking was what she did. Any kind of appraisal might have given him hope. She saw him. That was all. He gestured to the bench.

"I ..."

Waited. But she was still caught in the brute glamour of Davey's arms. She was still in the middle of her triumph, like a flamenco dancer. Charles went to walk towards her but she placed her palm between them. She did it more quietly than he was used to, and that was terrible too. There was no passion in it; no punishment. But there was something. A tremor. Perhaps it was simply the gas above her, but Charles clung to it.

"I wanted to see you."

"Yes. You want. You always do."

"And is that wrong?"

"No." She shook her head. "No. But it's wrong for me."

"You said—"

"What? What did I say?"

What *did* she say? All he remembered, at this moment, was the warmth of her skin. Her room had everything. There was enough, always, for what they needed. It seemed specifically to tend the thing they had; the thing that they carried between them like a bright bolt of cloth. He thought of Catherine's necklace in his pocket: a lump of stones rather than a trail of stars.

"You can't remember, can you? Not one word."

"My mind—"

"Misgives? Too bloody right."

She drew her hand beneath her nose. She wiped it on her dress.

"Three weeks."

"I have a son."

"Beg yours?"

"A son. I have a son."

She nodded. Her profile softened. It was like the shape that had been behind the bar: it had become a little more feminine.

"Since when?"

"Two weeks ago."

She laughed.

"Of course."

She put her hands back on her hips.

"You should have come."

Charles looked down at his feet.

"You should have come to me that night."

"How could I have?"

"You could have found a way. I crawled out of the fucking window. Were you not just a little concerned?"

He went to speak, but she rode roughshod over him. With her legs apart and her hands fixed firmly on her waist, it looked like she was guarding something.

"I wandered the streets. It was fucking freezing, if you want to know. I had on that little maid's outfit and that stupid cap and I had to keep hiding in doorways. Somebody slapped my arse." She shuddered. "It was a nightmare. I was fodder. At least they were honest about it. There you were, up in the royal box with your concubine. A lovely cozy, comfy family Christmas. It was silly of me, I suppose, to have expected something. A visit. A fucking turkey."

"My father slapped my face."

"Your father ripped my dress. What do you think cost most?"

Charles's mind was only now catching up with the situation.

"And yes," he said. "Three weeks."

He shook his head.

"Meaning?"

"Meaning that animal."

"A girl gets tired. Have you not ever worked that out? That wife of yours looks like she's about to drop. And your girlfriend won't be lifting a finger, will she? All she has to do is waggle her curls."

"Sarah, she is—"

"I don't give a monkey's what she is. Although I think you should." She shook her head. Slowly, she gathered herself. "It doesn't matter. It gets so tiring, all of that. Caring. Coming up with the right thing to say. Wondering." She looked off into the middle distance. She looked heroic. Charles, his habits, were her Trafalgar. "Will he? Won't he? With Davey you never wonder. Davey always does what he says he will. We've been at it for years. Not while, you know, we had our little tête-à-tête. But not long before. You say he's an animal? Well, he is. You should see his dog. Bullseye." She laughed. "You can imagine. But he's kind to me. Kinder than you were."

Charles's head seemed to be shaking of its own accord. The whole thing was monstrous. It might have come out of his worst imaginings.

"He is, Charley. He doesn't wish that I was different. See me? I'm that creature that lives among the thieves. I have never, so help me God, known any better life. And there are days when I thank God for it."

"You can do better than that."

"Can I? What will you do for me? Will you leave her? Will you?"

She left a pause.

"No, 'course you won't. You're worse than him. You look at me like … like you're writing me. You're just as much a thief as he is, and at least he doesn't lie about it. He nicks stuff all the time, and then he tells me. He says he 'come upon it' some-where posh. It's a game to him."

She was smiling, but the shadows made it look like the broad gash that you made for a pumpkin's mouth. He hardly knew her, and he found that knowing her, at the last, was all he wanted.

"And you. You waved that necklace like you'd bought it from the proceeds of your house."

"I have bought it."

"You haven't."

"I have. Today. I even have the bloody receipt."

She looked like he had produced something amazing, like a dolphin. Then she threw her head back.

"Oh dear God. Dear God almighty. Charley, Charley, Charley. How *green* are you?"

"Whatever can you mean?"

"Look at him. They wasn't the jeweller's men."

He didn't understand. She put her hands on her knees and yelled it at him.

"They wasn't the jeweller's men."

She jerked a thumb behind her.

"Go in there now. Or, on second thoughts, don't. They'll eat you alive."

"But I—"

"But you."

She had enlivened her vowels with an actorly rotundity. It didn't sound anything like him. Only it did.

"That's Davey for you. He wanted to give you a scare. He wanted to warn me, too."

Charles sank back down onto the bench. He rubbed his eyes. He thought of the new serial that he would have to write. He felt the necklace that was coiled, like a lump of dough, in his right-hand pocket. He felt the fear that he had felt as he was walking down the stairs. He tried to laugh.

"I suppose I was."

He took a breath, then held it. He thought: I am a balloon. A cloud.

"Out of my depth."

He felt his hair, for company.

"Where will you wear it?"

"Wear it? How? It was stolen property. I've given it to Davey. He'll know what to do with it."

Charles groaned. Just for a moment, it was like being on a boat. The houses seemed to dip and swell in front of him. He couldn't talk. He tried, but it wouldn't come.

"It's his reward," Sarah was saying. "Let's face it, we did rub his nose in it."

"Why didn't he—"

"Kick you all the way to Timbuktu? Joe told him not to. Joe likes you, Charley. He says you're a better clown than he is."

They remained apart. They had returned, it seemed, to what and who they were. They were not mingled any more.

"But you love me."

It came from deep within him. He was having to grip on to the bench.

"I do. I do, Charley." She looked at him almost tenderly. "But it makes no difference in the end."

What could you say? The urge to get down on his knees had almost gone. At last she said, "What's his name? Your son."

"Charles. Charley."

"Good," she said. She nodded. "Good."

And she was gone. Charles didn't watch her go. He was trying to stare at something, anything, that wouldn't resist him. He looked at the street, and the walls of the street. He looked at the sky. He tried to listen to the pub. But nothing would tell him what it was. London had washed its hands of him. It turned its back as he stood, brushed himself down and stumbled blindly home.

CHAPTER FOURTEEN

THEY HAD BOUGHT a Georgian townhouse. It was in Doughty Street, too near to the slums for Catherine but with a porter at each end in a gold-laced hat. Charles never failed to be amused by this. And, of course, impressed. It was commensurate with something. He wasn't sure what, but he would grow into it. He owned five floors: room for his wife and baby, his sister-in-law and his brother Fred, who was working, now, as an accounts clerk for John Macrone. It, the house, seemed to suit them all. Catherine had made her peace with baby Charles. She was no longer so heavily laden with his needs. She seemed lighter; freer. The late spring air; the three sash windows in the drawing room; the view of the trees as you looked out—they all represented freedom in their own way.

The three of them were going to the theatre. Charles tended to think in threes. Fred was only his brother, he was not at liberty to tend to Charles in the way to which he had become accustomed. Not that Charles thought of it in this way. He knew that he relied upon the female element but not that he demanded it. He had the sense that, whenever he chose, he could come to rest. This everybody understood.

Tonight, the three of them were going to form a party. He was in the master bedroom, polishing his shoes. Catherine was calling up the stairs.

"Charles! Charley! What are you doing?"

He walked to the door with his shoe still in his hand. This, more than anything else, was what gave him pleasure. An environment as formidable as a safe, as impressive as a hotel, and him in the middle of it, performing some useful task. He also liked to tease his wife; it was a swift and lively note in the great, resounding chord that was his life.

"I am gathering myself."

"Oh Charles. Really. It has been an hour."

"I am a personage. I have had Maisie pour milk into the bath. I made Fred wear a turban while he cut my toenails."

Her voice, when it came, was as playful as she could make it. Charles often felt that, if he took a pencil, he could draw the slightness of the upward curve.

"Did he do a good job?"

"He cut them into little hearts."

"That's lovely, Charles. But please come down. Mary is doing pirouettes. I can't seem to stop her."

He was in his very best regalia: a dark blue jacket, a velvet waistcoat and a cravat that was so irrepressibly gorgeous that it might as well have been a butterfly. He took one more glance in the mirror and saw that his hair looked russet in the light. It, too, was gorgeous: richly faceted and almost playful, as befitted a famous author. Let her look at him now, he thought. Let her see what he had become. It was a half-hearted sort of fantasy. He knew that she would laugh. He dismissed her, physically. He shook his head with as much irritation as Davey had; he closed the door with gusto and leapt downstairs.

Mary and Catherine were standing, self-consciously, side by side. This was the way with women. With *his* women. They spent hours preparing themselves in order to look like trinkets. It was delightful, of course, but then you didn't know where to put your hands. Charles did what was expected of him: he stepped backwards and examined them. Their dresses were pulled in at the waist, but then they blossomed outwards. Catherine's sleeves were long and Mary's short, but the latter were so covered with lace that you could barely see her arms. What you could see were her shoulders. They glittered as brightly as confectionery.

"You look beautiful," he said.

Mary curtseyed. Her eyes were as vividly present as you might expect. She was seventeen. She said, "And especially Catherine."

She clung on to her sister's arm. Her neck, as she placed her head on Catherine's shoulder, made a plangent arabesque. Charles retreated into roguish gallantry.

"You are both exquisite. I shall want you both on my arm this evening at all times."

Catherine pointed at herself.

"*Is* she his wife?"

Her smile was still a little tentative. She had not taken to the child, or, rather, it had not taken to her. A wet nurse had been employed. Catherine was still wont to walk around as though her feet were made of glass.

"It's a stupid title."

"Charles. Tush."

"No. Really. It is. You can say it in several ways, of course. Is *she* his wife? Is she *his* wife? Is she his *wife*? But none of them redeem it."

He had taken Catherine's hands and he was swinging them from side to side. The politeness of marital gestures—the way that they were a version of all the things that they still weren't doing. It wasn't just her feet that seemed to be made of glass.

"But, you see, it's rhetorical."

"Charles. Dear. I know that it's rhetorical."

He kissed her hand.

"My apologies." But he could feel his stomach sinking. He made himself dance around them both.

"Nothing," he was saying, "but enchantment this evening ladies. Nothing but champagne bubbles and fairy cakes. And me. And I, as you can see, am delicious."

Mary was giggling.

"Well, I must say," Catherine said.

It was faux-appreciative. Was it meant to be comic? It was offered in lieu of a smile. Charles felt so many things at once that he wished he had a pen. He decided to be tender. He bent and kissed her forehead.

"Must you? Or will you allow yourself to be transported?"

"Well, it depends, dear, on what kind of transportation you've arranged."

"Touché," Mary said.

She was doing pirouettes again. Her skirt was lifting and revolving around her. Her feet were arched upwards into shoes that could, if you squinted, be Cinderella's.

"The coach!" she shouted.

So then there were muffs and wraps. Delicately, he arranged his wife's shawl around her neck. He helped them both up the steps. Mary squeezed his hand. It was excitement, of course. Enthusiasm. She sat then sat again. Catherine settled herself into the nest of her billowing skirt. Charles closed the door but then he stuck his head out. He had booked the coach beforehand, of course. Nevertheless, he took great pleasure in shouting, "To St. James's Theatre if you please!"

It was still light, but the sky had the look of being dipped in ink. It was like velvet: it seemed to bulge there above the city. He had arranged for a proper coach; not one that displayed an old coat of arms or whose seats were stuffed with straw. The wheels rumbled politely while the streets went swiftly by. The city was legible again. Each building, almost, had its own association. Set him down, and he could have found his way by touch. Set him down and he would gladly become part of the chaos that seemed, always, to express his secret heart. There was a fire eater in Drury Lane. The flame came sprouting out of his mouth. It was better, bigger, than speech. The people were all louder than the people that you were used to. But he would be too. He would blossom. He would be as rooted as the beggars seemed to be. He wasn't lost, of course. He was ascending on a trajectory as vertiginous as the flame had been. But it seemed, sometimes, indistinguishable from being lost.

The theatre was in King Street. There was a four-column Ionic portico and a balustraded balcony. Inside it was all French white. A border of flowers, embossed in gold, ran round the dress circle and the panels of the boxes in the front of the first circle were ornamented in the style of Watteau. The proscenium was painted with loves and graces and there were two slender Corinthian columns, supported on pedestals of imitative marble. Mary couldn't contain herself. She kept thumping Charles's arm.

"Oh dear. Oh dear, oh dear."

Catherine was sitting on Charles's other side. She leant across.

"Whatever is the matter?"

"It's *him*," she said.

Again, she thumped him.

"And this. I can't put the two of them together."

Catherine's smile took in the two of them. It tolerated them. Assimilated them, rather. Into what, Charles couldn't imagine. As the lights went down he found that he was much more aware of Mary than he was of Catherine. It was like having a brazier in the seat beside you. She squeezed his knee, quickly, once. It was permissibly innocent. He made himself stay where he was comfortable: in his head. He was not, he would not be, aware of his own body. He crossed his legs and smiled, a broad, satisfied author's smile.

The stage disclosed itself as just that: a stage. What he had seen in his head was both more and less diaphanous, somehow. It floated more freely when it came to furniture but it was definitely a sitting room. It was the equivalent of a thumb print: his mind had had to negotiate it. This, however, was self-evidently the representation of a sitting room. The thing had popped out of his head and ended up here, on a stage in the West End. It had its own reality but it was only as much reality as a theatre was wont to give. He tried his best to be a member of the audience. There was a table, and a couple eating breakfast. He knew, and the audience didn't, that they were called the Lovetowns. This made him want to crouch down in his seat. Mr. Lovetown yawned.

"Another cup of tea, my dear. Oh Lord!"

He was not what Charles had imagined. He had envisaged someone rather like a pin. This one looked like a swimmer.

"I wish, Alfred, you would endeavour to assume a more cheerful appearance in your wife's society."

She was pushing the words up and outwards. She was using not only her chest but her neck and shoulders too. It was hard work, and it detracted from the person she was supposed to be. She was paying too much attention to what she was saying. She was lobbing the words at the audience like tennis balls.

"If you are perpetually yawning and complaining of ennui a few months after marriage, what am I to suppose you'll become in a few years? It really is very odd of you."

"Not at all odd, my dear."

Lovetown was better. He seemed naturally languid. He was slowly fondling his own foot.

"Not the least in the world; it would be a great deal more odd if I were not. The fact is, my love, I'm tired of the country; green fields, and blooming hedges, and feathered songsters, are fine things to talk about and read about and write about but I candidly confess that I prefer paved streets, area railings and dustman's bells, after all."

And so on. Charles had not attended rehearsals. He had known that the thing was negligible. It was his own fault. He had been asked for something and had gone to the cupboard to get it. He loved the theatre but hearing the way that his words were delivered was distinctly odd. There was a doubling. He wished to disclaim responsibility. He wished for a penny gaff: for the way that everything was so obviously glued together with spit and sawdust. For the way that no one listened like this audience were listening, as though the words were simultaneously the musings of a child and an urgent missive.

Catherine and Mary were laughing in all the right places. There was a series of contrived coincidences and implausible misunderstandings. There were jokes about adultery, and there was an ankle, turned in the light like a vase or a piece of crockery. It was a puff for Boz, that was all, and in the interval he was eager to wash his hands of it. Catherine patted him on the back. She was either being approving or sympathetic. Or forgetting that she wasn't in the nursery. But Mary shook her head.

"I do not see why you should have to be so very modest, Charles. Look around you. Look where your 'little thing' has ended up."

"Dear Mary. I am. And my poor play seems to be cowering in the corner."

But he *was* smug. It was a success. People congratulated him. As brightly caparisoned as a flag, he paraded his family from one side of the room to the other. They looked at Mary. *Was* she his wife? It made him laugh. He made a point of straightening a detail on Catherine's dress and of rubbing gently at her nose.

"Nothing," he said. "A smudge."

She smiled at him so gratefully that he felt perversely cross. She was his wife, damn it. Why could not this be normal? Why must he pat and cosset her like a child? Mary was still holding on to his arm. The gesture was childlike in its insistence, but it did more for his sense of her womanhood than any amount of simpering or careful chitchat. She was drinking with such gusto that it made him want to laugh. When she went wheeling around to replace her glass, the gas at the bar made her into a chain of dancing lights.

What was she? His better angel. If a man's compass should go occasionally awry then that was to be expected. He sat next to her and thought: one's own sister, leaping upon you, can inspire something that is positively horrifying. But then you have to realise that that is what the body is: a horror. A little Moloch, devouring everything.

As they drove home, he could feel the streets seething around him. Within him, too. He had never left them. If his body was a horror then it partook of the city around it. One's dreams, all of their terrors and willing degradations, were part of London. And Sarah? Better not to consider what she had been.

Because now, of course, he was a domestic animal. At home, they sat and drank together. Charles stretched his legs out consciously, like a paterfamilias. Or like a man who had just seen his play performed on the West End stage. Catherine was tired. Her face looked pale. It had puffed up, like dough. Her hands were so carefully arranged that they looked like they were visiting her lap. She had been up to check on Charley, who, of course, had been asleep. It was hard to tell if this had pleased her. Already she seemed more comfortable in the nursery than in the living room. She came down so consciously a mother that Charles felt inclined to prod her in the stomach. One's love for one's child was surprisingly tangible, but so was a jealousy that he had to disguise to himself as husbandly concern. He could see Sarah's face: her frank enjoyment of his discomfort. She would have laughed at him. But she would have laughed at all of it: the chairs so neatly placed around an empty fireplace and the delicate glasses and the smug disposal of the fire tongs and everything else that was there, really, to bespeak the life of hearth and home; to continually chatter about it so that you couldn't hear anything else. Even now, Catherine's head was tilted, slightly. She was listening for something that wasn't strictly audible; some shift in the atmosphere in the house that would tell her that Charley needed her. Charles studied her for a moment. Her body seemed more self-important, but her face was almost constantly apologising for it.

"My mother would have left me there," he said. "I might have been awake and trying to bring the house down but I would have seemed dumb for all the notice she took of me."

"I don't think that that can be so, Charley."

"You don't?"

He was too pleased with himself to make an issue of it. Nevertheless, he must follow where it led. Catherine was attempting to defend her. Her hands were fluttering in her lap.

"She is—"

"Oh, I know what she is. Vivacious. Tell her there's a party in the offing and she lights up like a carousel. But place a child in the vicinity."

"She loves you, Charles."

"She loves me in the way that you might love a doll. Or a familiar suitcase. You are perfectly happy to carry it but you will also be relieved to put it down."

Mary was smiling.

"Charles was brought up by wolves."

She was very slightly drunk, or else extremely sleepy. Her body had a slight ethereality. There in the candlelight, it looked like it was floating. But it kept catching up with itself; kept shifting jerkily back into consciousness. She was more present than he was used to. She had more quiddity. Perhaps he simply meant more certainty. She was a woman tonight; perhaps she always would be now. She smiled.

"But wolves in topcoats. And natty hats."

"No, no." Charles sat up. He rubbed his hands together. "What are they? Not wolves. My father? My father is. Um. A hippopotamus."

"Charles. Come."

"No. He is!"

Mary had pointed with such force that the lace had quivered along her arm. Charles reached across and took Catherine's hand.

"Consider. The waddle. The enormous—"

"Charles."

But Catherine was laughing. She had the sweetest face, he told himself.

"And your mother? Please tell us, Charles."

And there it was: Mary was a child again. It was a relief. She had dipped her finger in her drink and was lifting it to her mouth.

"Oh, she is one of those tiny birds. Egrets? The ones who slip into the hippo's mouth and peck at all the leftovers."

Mary's shoulders shook. Her face was flushed but, whereas, with Catherine, the colour came out almost surreptitiously, with Mary her face appeared to welcome it. Catherine was laughing, too. But it was like her blush: she was reluctant to give it house room.

"Charles," she said. "That is shocking."

"D'you think so? Have you not seen her dart her head? Like this."

And, just for a second, he was his mother. It was a most satisfying sort of revenge.

"She is voracious," he said.

He finished his drink.

"Whereas I am simply thirsty."

He reached for the bottle. Catherine pointedly shook her head. She placed her hand over her glass. She said, "Mary. No more."

Charles tended to agree with her. It was a relief, in any case, to treat Mary so unequivocally as their child.

"I shan't," Mary said. "I am suddenly very tired."

She stood and yawned. Her arms were bright red in the candlelight. They were as finely turned as candlesticks. She gave Catherine an impish look.

"And what is Charles?"

Catherine smiled.

"He is unique. And he is ours."

She was still holding onto his hand. Mary kissed them each, demurely, on their foreheads. She seemed to be carrying her body reluctantly. No more ethereality: each step looked like she was dragging herself through treacle.

The room was quiet. The clock ticked slowly behind Charles's head but he had no consciousness of time. He and his wife were experiencing a long moment that was like the moment between breaths. He was as happy as he ever was: ambition sated for the night, he considered kissing his wife's neck. He had nearly decided to do it when there was a cry from Mary's room; a thump, like the thump of an axe. It was as disturbing as an axe: a loud, incongruous noise in an empty house. Charles was on his feet almost before he realised what he had heard. When he looked back, he had no memory of the time between hearing this and the moment when he was in her bedroom, trying to lift her onto the bed. On the way up, he bumped against the banister but didn't notice it: it felt part of the horror of the journey up—his surging breath and the terrifying silence and the fact that this distance was suddenly an obstacle.

When he got there it was almost as if he couldn't see her. Her body was just that: a body. It wasn't her. It was a new reality. It was as though someone had lifted the house and shaken it until nothing remained but that sense you have when panic and a swift, heedless activity are hopelessly intertwined. She was so light! He had never lifted her before. She had always been conscious. It was that, the absence of reciprocation, that was the real horror in the room. He put his ear against her mouth and found that she was breathing. She was, thank God, still fully clothed; he was still able to think about that, and he was able, when Catherine arrived, to give clear and curt instructions.

He would take charge, just like he always did. It was in the order of things. Catherine brought him the brandy bottle, and he poured some into his hand. He lifted Mary's head and poured in the brandy. It was 1:23 in the morning. A picture had been pushed aside, and he felt an urge to straighten it. He was taking refuge in detail. But what else could he do?

"Catherine," he said. "Get Fred."

Which meant, once again, the relief of something being done but it also meant that he could spend a minute alone with her. He resented his wife's intrusion. He was best placed, he knew, to deal with this. With her. With Mary. What it amounted to, he felt most strongly, was that he could love her in the right way. He could bully her; entreat her; succour her. Although, none of these distinctions mattered. She was unconscious. She didn't look quite asleep. It was more that her body was out of step. Here it was, the world, and she wasn't in it.

Fred fetched the doctor. The doctor came. He could do nothing more than wave his stethoscope as though he was performing an incantation. He was an odd-shaped little man, broad at the bottom and narrow at the top, and it added, somehow, to Charles's fury. He shouted, "Help her!" Shouted as hard as he could, as though his own voice was the fulcrum upon which the world was teetering this way and that. His will, he knew, was prodigious. It could move mountains. But it could not coax one ounce of awareness from the woman—the child; the child/woman—lying on the bed. He thumped one of the bed posts and was ashamed. He overpaid the doctor. It was a propitiatory gesture. And then he waited. He waited and waited and waited. He had a vague notion that she would open her eyes when the sun came up. That she would be encouraged upwards, like a flower. He arranged her hair carefully, so that she looked more like herself. This, too, was supposed to be encouragement. Catherine was in the room, and she said nothing. She didn't appear to be able to produce a sound. There had, earlier, been a whimper and he had listened out for another one; it was a new note in the room. He knew that it wasn't coming from Mary but he attached it to her anyway. Then he was irritated. Catherine must not give way; they must not allow themselves to be defeated. Then he realised that it was coming from him. He placed his hand over his mouth. But that was unfortunate because it was, in its own way, a form of comfort. And what did he need comfort for? What he needed, what the whole house needed, and the world—the air and the sun and God and London—was the determination to see her through. He said it, once, to his wife: "She will fucking live." And she forgave him; he saw her do it.

Three o'clock in the afternoon. The light like butter on the bed. His wife so very stationary that she felt like part of the room. The girl asleep in Charles's arms. Of course asleep. How thin her skin was. How gentle her mouth. What could he promise? Who could he promise to?

"Charles," Catherine said.

"What? What?"

What had she seen? He longed for the slightest movement in the same way that, in another life, he had once longed for sex.

"Charles."

She couldn't bring herself to say it. It was typical of her, this pragmatism. Because he knew what she was going to say. And then he furiously didn't know, because he wouldn't put it into words. He refused to know. He held Mary closer. But it wasn't like holding her. It was like holding a leaf, or a ream of paper.

Catherine stood up. She made her slow way to the bed. She put her hand on Charles's shoulder. He made himself look up at her. Her face was terrible: it had been hidden, partly, in the darkness, but now it seemed to be crumbling in the light. What he thought he saw—what, in a way, he wished to see—was the most awful inability to cope. Even now, he thought: must I be the one to bear this for you? But then her face changed. It hardened. She looked like her mother. She looked like his, but then he realised that this was more a feeling than an observation. He wanted to sob in her arms.

"Charles," she said. "Put her down."

"How can you—"

"Put her down, darling. Please. Don't do this anymore. She's gone."

He was crying. Or, rather, his body was. He couldn't control it. His entire being was given over to what felt as much like fear as the appropriate form of sorrow. His hand was shaking.

"She's *alive*."

Catherine shook her head: no. She was crying too. Of course she was crying. But it was *his* grief. That was the thing. His grief was *his* grief. He needed to be alone with it. With her. But Catherine was still staring at him.

"Leave me," she said.

He tried to look into her eyes. She slapped his arm.

"*Leave* me."

She dragged him to his feet. She stared, for one more moment, into his eyes, and then she pushed him out of the room.

CHAPTER FIFTEEN

HE SAW HER in his dreams. This was in many different places:
pubs and the Houses of Parliament and a river steamer and here
in bed, of course. Sometimes she told him things. Nice things.
Sometimes she merely beckoned. These were the dreams that
he described to Catherine. But sometimes she was naked, or
half-naked. She would be pointing to her breasts. Or else she
would be stroking the place between her legs. Her breasts were
tiny, and this seemed to inflame him all the more. Everything
was perfectly in proportion: her breasts and the slow tilt of
her neck and her stomach, which was like silk. When she said
his name she said it in the way that Sarah used to say it, but in
her, in Mary's, voice. It was humorous and musical and almost
unbearable. He said her name as sensibly as he could. He was
trying to stop her; to warn her. But it didn't work. She would
take him and guide him into her. The first moment was so
exquisite that it felt, when he woke up, like he would have to
put it into words. He would place his face inches above hers
and they would fuck. The word resounded in his head like
cannon fire. It stayed there after he woke. The conjunction of
its awful-seeming bluntness and Mary's body was almost too
much to bear.

He was terribly ashamed. Ashamed, too, of the emissions that stained the sheets. Could he have been feeling this all along? Feeling it so that it underlay whatever else was going on? His mind rejected it, although his mind, these days, seemed terribly unreliable. What he felt most strongly was that, if he had harboured these emotions, then they had in some way killed her. The strength of this theory seemed to reside in, rather than contradict, its irrational nature. Her heart, the doctor said. But Charles felt that he had cast a spell: sex as a vicious, miserly retribution that lay waste to everything.

He refused to believe it. He had always—*always*—treated her with the utmost love and respect. This much was true, but what it left out was whatever it was that he had felt. He chose to believe that, by a kind of syllogism, they were one and the same. He wore her ring. He cut off a lock of her hair and kept it in a special case. Ten days after her death, he wrote to Beard.

"I presume you heard from my father, that on the Saturday Night we had been to the theatre—that we returned home as usual—that poor Mary was in the same health and spirits in which you have so often seen her—that almost immediately after she went upstairs to bed she was taken ill—and that next day she died. Thank God she died in my arms, and the very last words she whispered were of me.

"Of our sufferings at the time, and all through the dreary week that ensued, I will say nothing—no one can imagine what they were. You have seen a good deal of her, and can feel for us, and imagine what a blank she has left behind. The first burst of my grief has passed, and I think I can speak of her calmly and dispassionately. I solemnly believe that so perfect a creature never breathed. I knew her inmost heart, and her real worth and value. She had not a fault.

"Mrs. Hogarth has suffered and still continues to suffer most deep and bitter anguish. Kate, I am glad to say, made such strong efforts to console her that she unconsciously summoned up all her fortitude at the same time, and brought it to her own assistance. She knows that if ever a mortal went to heaven, her sister is there; she has nothing to remember but a long course of affection and attachment, perhaps never exceeded. Not one cross word or angry look on either side, even as children, rises in judgment against her; and she is now so calm and cheerful that I wonder to see her.

"I have been so shaken and unnerved by the loss of one whom I so dearly loved that I have been compelled to lay aside all thoughts of my usual monthly work, for once; and we have come here for quiet and change. We have a cottage of our own, with large gardens, and everything else on a small but comfortable scale. Kate is very anxious indeed to see you and as I can assure you that you will derive anything but pain from seeing her, I hope you will join us in the old way. Name your own time and believe me that there is no one to whom it would give us so much pleasure to welcome as yourself."

Had she? Whispered? By now he was almost convinced she had. He had rented a cottage for him and Catherine, but now they were back in harness. Marital relations had begun again, but it was not the two of them in the bed so much as the couple in the letter: the one whose continuing existence it was necessary to reaffirm. As for the other thing, he no longer thought about it. It had been a year. It had been cauterised by Mary's death.

He had seen her once, around the beginning of September, when he had been wandering, like a disconsolate ghost, round the East End.

It was eight o'clock at night. Rainy, with gusts that were so strong that they made him want to laugh. There it was again: the penny gaff. He hadn't been conscious that he was making in its direction, but now he was here he allowed himself a moment to look at it properly. He thought that he could do that: subtract her from it. He stared for a moment at the patch of grass, almost convinced that there would be something, some mark, that showed what had happened here. He grinned. The famous writer, rolling over and over like a dog fighting for a bone. He couldn't entirely believe in it. Not the act itself: the grass. It was like a piece of scenery. It was so imbued with its significance to him that it didn't seem to belong here, in the London streets, so much as in some personal collection. So there: he was becoming nostalgic. Which was why he bought a ticket. He didn't know what he was hoping for. It was the same: the same crowd; the same languidly caustic boys beside the band; the same laughter and slap-and-tickle in the auditorium.

Then, suddenly, there she was. No Shakespeare. No other actor to take one's eyes away from her. Just her and a piano. It was a different pianist. He was younger, more tentative, and he was clearly terrified of her. How did she look? Up there? Like she was nearly an angel. A lesser spirit, almost beautiful enough, and thumbing its nose at the heavenly host above her. She had put on weight. Once, she turned round—she was doing a bit of business—and you could see her rear pulsing against her dress. But what really mattered was her voice. He had never heard it. It was clean and accurate and, yes, unsullied. She had hidden it from him. It had survived him, and he was pleased. It was a kind of truth. Herself, writ large. He was proud of her, but he didn't wait until the end. He couldn't bear to be any nearer to her. He liked to think that his feelings had become as clear as a glass of water. It didn't do to shake the glass.

And, in any case, Grimaldi was dead. There was a whole world, it seemed, that the two of them no longer shared. He had died only a couple of weeks after Mary. Puffised and rheumatised, presumably. Charles was sadder than he thought he'd be. Grimaldi had saved him from a beating, yes, but it was more than that. He represented something. There was something about him that Charles aspired to, although he couldn't have told you what. Perhaps it was only the act of aspiration; that movement towards a person who shares some of your qualities, but in excelsis. He had forgotten about it when, one morning, he received a note. It came through the door of his house, and it was unsigned. It simply said "Don't fuck it up."

A week later he was summoned to Bentley's office. Did he like Bentley? He wasn't sure. A publisher, he was a more appropriate figure to aspire towards. And yet he didn't. Bentley liked him; he respected him. But he always treated him like an employee. When Charles walked in, there were papers everywhere. Bentley made a hopeless gesture.

"Detritus."

"Thanks very much."

"Not you, dear boy. The *Miscellany* is all that's keeping me afloat."

He put his head in his hands.

"Deadlines," he said. "Deadlines. Deadlines."

But he said it happily enough. He was a talented old ham. His hair was up like a cockatoo's. His face was flushed with self-approval. What he was, really, was a brigand. He flourished a document. If it was possible, that is, to flourish something with both hands.

"This," he said.

"That?"

"This!"

"Being—"

"Being something else apart from *Oliver Twist* and your, ahem, superior editorship."

"Oh, Bentley, no."

"Wait. Wait, dear boy. This is right up your alley."

"What is?"

Grimaldi. He had written an autobiography. It had been butchered by a hack named Wilks and now it had found its way into Bentley's hands. Charles looked at it like you might an unmuzzled bulldog.

"Look," Bentley said. "He's done a terrible job. He seems to have used an old hammer and a hacksaw. But, damn it all, it's Grimaldi. And the man's only just dead."

He looked at Charles shrewdly.

"You," he said, "are fascinated by this stuff."

What he felt, though, wasn't entirely fascination. He vacillated. He was, in actual fact, something of a *cocotte*. But, in the end, he agreed to do it for three hundred pounds. Of course, he needed the money. He would always need the money. And he was intrigued. But it was more than that, just as the note had never felt as though it was a simple threat. There was a bond between them. Something distinctly filial. Not that this was necessarily a matter of one's finer feelings.

It felt appropriate, in this instance, to pay his father. He came over to Doughty Street and diligently wrote while Charles paced up and down with the manuscript in his hand. He found that he could edit the document in his head. It amused him. It made him feel somewhat taller. His father looked sternly down at the page and would sometimes lift a finger. He would question a point of grammar. Occasionally, he would shake his head.

"If only we had known. It makes the cheerfulness of his demeanour rather wonderful."

He nodded at Charles.

"You made his acquaintance."

"When?!"

Charles had gone cold.

"When you were little. You were greatly struck. I had to stop you." His father made a great business out of clapping his hands. "You were a *most* enthusiastic child." He smiled. "In many ways you still are."

They had, in this room, reached something of an understanding. His father hadn't asked him anything, nor had he wanted him to. But what he had managed, in some measure, to communicate was that all was now on an even keel. Which it was, almost entirely. It was time to lay Joey to rest. He stood by the fire with his legs apart. He found that he was declaiming,

"Many readers will ridicule the idea of a clown being a man of great feeling and sensibility: Grimaldi was so notwithstanding and suffered most severely from the affliction which befell him. The loss of his wife, to whom he had been long and devotedly attached, preyed upon his mind to a greater or lesser extent for many years. The reckless career and dreadful death of his only son bowed him down with grief. The young man's notorious conduct had embittered the best portion of his existence: and his sudden death, when a better course seemed opening before him, had well-nigh terminated his father's days."

He was doing it all from his head. It was entirely his, this superior sententiousness. It was giving him the utmost pleasure.

"But although, in the weakened state in which he then was, the sad event, preying alike upon his mind and body, changed

Grimaldi's appearance in a few weeks to that of a shrunken, imbecile old man; and although, when he had in some measure recovered from this heavy blow, he had to mourn the loss of his wife, with whom he lived happily for more than thirty years, he survived the trials to which he had been exposed, and lived to recover his cheerfulness and peace."

His father was nodding approvingly. Charles took a sip of brandy. He had almost laughed. He felt the fire against his legs; the way that it seemed to confirm them—to confirm *him*, in all his health and vigour.

"Deprived of all power of motion, doomed to bear, at a time of life when he might reasonably have looked forward to many years of activity and exertion, the worst bodily evils of the most helpless old age; condemned to drag out the remainder of his days in a solitary chamber, when all those who make up the sum of him were cold in death, his existence would seem to be a weary one indeed; but—"

Charles raised a finger, humorously. He was in capital spirits.

"But. (No: just one of those, father.) He was, um, patient and resigned under all these trials. And in time grew contented, and even happy. This strong endurance of griefs so keen, and reverses so poignant, may perhaps teach more strongly than a hundred homilies that there are no afflictions which time will not soften and fortitude overcome. Let those who smile at the deduction of so trite a moral from the biography of a clown reflect that, the fewer the resources of a man's own mind, the greater his merit in rising superior to fortune. Let them remember, too, that in this case the light and life of a brilliant theatre were exchanged in an instant for the gloom and sadness of a dull sick-room."

He surveyed his glass. He had an impulse to mark the occasion by throwing it into the fire. He thought: I win. He turned to Catherine, who had very slowly and very quietly entered the room. She was bearing a tray of sandwiches.

"It's done."

"You clever man."

She kissed him on the cheek. She also kissed his father.

"You too," she said.

His father made a complicated moue down at the floor. It was humble but it was also not.

He said, "Just a scribe, m'dear. Just a scribe."

Catherine's heart went out to him. He was, she realised, sad that it was done. She must encourage Charles to continue to spend time with him. She said, "And now?"

"And now it is five o'clock in the afternoon. Brandy, I think."

"Go slowly, dear. Beard comes at seven."

"I will."

Gently, he cupped her chin and pecked her on the mouth. She patted him lightly on the head.

"I'll leave you men to do whatever it is you do."

"I'm not sure what it is we do do. Father, what do we do?"

"I don't know, Charley boy. But I'm sure we do it very well."

Such peace and amity. It could have come out of Pickwick. What concerned her was its febrile nature. They would never be entirely at ease, these two. Too similar. If you inflated Charles a little you would get his father. Quite pleased with this, she smiled and eased herself out of the room. They had four servants now, and she would be kept busy until Beard arrived. She had not yet developed the appropriate manner, but she had, at least, learned to think of herself as the mistress of the house. It was never going to be easy, being the wife of a Great Man. People expected more, she thought, than she could give. But she was at least aware of their expectations.

As ever, she resisted the thought that Mary might have done a better job. She had been wrong when she had talked to her about the baby. It was her, her own presence, that was the ballast. By now, the house had begun to embody her. Charles was everywhere, of course—his chair; his wallpaper; the wainscoting; the sideboard that he loved so much—but the house was much, much more than what the house contained. It was an idea: something that she kept having to think into existence. Wherever Charles placed himself, he expected it to be home, but he was as negligent with the concept as if it were a toy. He expected to be able to ignore it until, just when he wanted it, there it was. It was like knitting, the way you had to replenish the wool, and replenish it, moreover, with a certain amount of invisible elegance. It was her constant breath that kept the home alive. Her faith. She had tended it even in those awful days immediately following her sister's death.

And they had been awful. The fact that Mary had been snatched away was bad enough. What did you do with that empty space? Too often, you would turn around and realise that you had thrown yourself into a sort of hole. A thought; even a word. You produced them and there was nowhere for them to go. She missed her so terribly that there were mornings when she lay in bed and wouldn't open her eyes. Because everything, even her own bedroom, seemed emptied of its essence now that her sister was gone.

And Charles? Dear God. She had caught him once, going through her sister's clothes. He had her dress in his hands, the one that she had worn when they had watched his play. It was as though she had caught him *in flagrante*. Surely he couldn't have been whispering to it? How could one grieve when one's partner's grief was so very much more intense than yours?

Strength was something that she had been given by default. Her mother she had expected. The night after Mary died, she had come round but had then been prostrate for the entire evening. Catherine had left her there—had partly, to be honest, taken refuge in Mary's bedroom. Whenever she comforted her mother after that, she felt very strongly that she was acting, and acting as badly as Charles had on the night of the theatrical. There were gestures, both physical and verbal, that her mother was expecting, and you just had to get on with it: you had to be the older sister and, now more than ever, her mother's mother.

Two maids were in the kitchen and, abstractedly, she told them what to do. She was courteous, and kind. She was always, or nearly always, kind. But kindness was an abstraction too; it was an attribute that suited her but too often it was like being forced to wear something that you didn't like. Mary was everything else. She was cleverer; she was more vivacious; she was prettier, and, what's more, she knew that she was prettier. When one's younger sister takes what is yours as though by right then one can either fight or accept it graciously. Once, when she herself was seventeen, she had made a watercolour. It was nothing: it was so insipid that she couldn't think about it now without wanting to laugh. What was it? Ducks? Not ships, surely. Whatever it was, it glowed, feebly, in her room until it caught Mary's eye. Mary was thirteen, and already the thing your eye would go to in a crowded room. She became humorously servile. It was all "dear sweet Catherine" and "my darling sister" until she had to give it to her. It was only two or three days later that Mary had dragged their father into her room.

"Look, Father, look!"

She didn't say that she had painted it, but she didn't say she hadn't. Catherine knew that she was relying on her quiescence.

Everybody always did. The something bovine that she culti-
vated because ... Oh, because she was lazy, she supposed. And
shy. And distrustful of outward emotion. Her father always
laughed as though he expected the entire room to be grateful
that he was so very happy. It was a fault. Each sister seemed to
have taken sides: one had her father's garrulous but cunning
charm and the other the slowness of her mother. Emotions
seemed to visit their mother. She was brightened by them but
that was all. And she was, all the girls were, terribly sensitive.
That night, Catherine had said, as casually as she could, "I see
that Mary showed you my watercolour, father."

Mary had rushed, sobbing, from the table. Catherine had
never done it again. She had known that what Mary possessed
was an artist's sensibility. But she wasn't an artist. Catherine
gave up painting shortly afterwards; it seemed unfair to wave
it under Mary's nose. Charles, when he plunged into their lives,
didn't seem sure, at first, which sister he was going to choose.
She thought, perhaps wrongly, that he had chosen her partly
because she was the appropriate age. He had been very definite
about what he wanted, and she had been very careful to give it
to him.

But now he was mourning her sister just as though she was his
wife. How did she feel? She stood in the kitchen while the maids
worked carefully around her. She was aware of them in the same
way that you were aware, out on the edges of consciousness,
of your own child. She was thinking that, partly, Charles was
expressing what they both felt. He had taken it upon himself
to grieve for both of them. But, no, it wouldn't wash. It was
too much his own, this outpouring. Mary was everything that
Catherine wasn't; she was everything that Charles's fierce need
for security wouldn't allow her to be. She had never learned

to be flirtatious, but she had wanted to be. She had waited for Charles to treat her body as something more than a charming aspect of her personality. She had watched him nearly do so, and she had understood that, in many ways, he would prefer not to. This, she understood, was not her function.

She had seen him with her sister, and with that actress, behaving in a way that she supposed all men behaved when they were alone. It was not that he propositioned them: it was that he treated them as co-conspirators. They were much more his *age*, somehow. She had seen him with her sister, on that bed, and she had seen what he wasn't able to: that even then, when she was stretched out nearly dead, he had desired her.

So. She was glad that she had died. But, of course, she wasn't. She missed her terribly. She had loved her all her life. She was like daylight, dancing across the carpet. Sometimes, what with Charles, it had seemed like there were two children in the house. Then, briefly, three. Who knew what sort of woman she would have become? And now she was a ghost. She had become a work of fiction. She would never share his bed.

She was still looking out of the window. Would she have? Her breasts used to speak, almost. She seemed entirely unaware of it. They would nod at you; would press eagerly against you. She had a smile that seemed so unaware of how beguiling it could be that Catherine had wanted to pummel her with both fists. Perhaps that—her seeming ignorance of her own charms— was what used to annoy her most. Well, no more of that. They would make love, her husband and her, as though there was nobody else in the house. She would learn, she was sure she could learn, to be abandoned.

And the actress? The minute she had climbed out of the window, she had known exactly who had bought that necklace.

But she had also known that it was over. It had finished the moment that Sarah had patted her hand. It was at least a kind of power to know what he had done. He was beginning to refer to himself as The Inimitable. As The Sparkler, too. But she would never, now, have to take him at his own estimation. Her necklace was cheap, of course it was, but she knew her own worth and it had nothing to do with necklaces. She was his hearth. She was his peace. She knew how his heart could tremble like a bird at the slightest noise. She knew his dreams. And she knew that, if she could only keep him away from actresses, she would never lose him again.

ACKNOWLEDGEMENTS

The two main sources (and sources of inspiration) for this book were *The Pantomime Life of Joseph Grimaldi* by Andrew McConnell Stott and *Becoming Dickens* by Robert Douglas-Fairhurst. I'd particularly like to thank Mr. Douglas-Fairhurst, who was kind enough, when I emailed him (the modern equivalent of cold calling), to read the first two chapters. I don't think I would have completed it without his encouragement. I'd also like to thank Vine Leaves Press, for taking a chance on this, and Melanie Faith, whose thoughtful and insightful edit was the equivalent of making sure that it went out of the house with its clothes straightened and its shoes properly polished. Love and thanks also, and always, to my unfailingly supportive partner, Naomi.

VINE LEAVES PRESS

Enjoyed this book?
Go to *vineleavespress.com* to find more.
Subscribe to our newsletter: